Critical Praise
The Fall of Rome

"In this powerful book, [the hero] achieves a tragic grandeur as he inches painfully close to real human connection . . . only to fall back on his delusions and emotional inaccessibility."
— Elizabeth Judd, *The New York Times Book Review*

"A powerfully moral and human work . . . a tour de force of what might be called post-Movement race realities in the United States."
— Michael Pakenham, *The Baltimore Sun*

"The teacher [and] the student . . . come to life through Ms. Southgate's clear, penetrating examination of the story's real conflict, which is between ambition and self-knowledge. To her credit, she does not let it be easily resolved."
— Janet Maslin, *The New York Times*

"A bracingly honest look at race, class, and self-acceptance."
— *Essence*

"*The Fall of Rome* is a brave, harrowing, and beautifully written tale about the perils of integration and the consequences of desire. Martha Southgate writes with control, compassion, and clarity about the very muddled state of race relations at the turn of this new century."
— Danzy Senna, author of *Caucasia*

"Southgate [is] a figure to be reckoned with, a voice we had best get to know."
— Jesse Green, author of *The Velveteen Father*

"A quietly accomplished novel about race, identity, and holding fast to one's integrity."
— *The Oprah Magazine*

"A wonderful, thought-provoking read."
— Benilde Little, author of *Good Hair*

THE FALL
OF
ROME

a novel

Martha Southgate

Scribner

New York   London   Toronto   Sydney

SCRIBNER
1230 Avenue of the Americas
New York, NY 10020

First Scribner trade paperback edition 2004

SCRIBNER and design are trademarks of Macmillan Library Reference USA, Inc., used under license by Simon & Schuster, the publisher of this work.

For information about special discounts for bulk purchases, please contact Simon & Schuster Special Sales: 1-800-456-6798 or business@simonandschuster.com

Designed by Kyoko Watanabe
Text set in Aldine

Manufactured in the United States of America

5 7 9 10 8 6 4

The Library of Congress has cataloged the Scribner edition as follows:
Southgate, Martha.
The fall of Rome : a novel / Martha Southgate.
p. cm.
1. Teacher-student relationships—Fiction. 2. African American teachers—Fiction.
3. African American students—Fiction. 4. Boarding schools—Fiction.
5. Classicists—Fiction. 6. Boys—Fiction. I. Title.
PS3569.O82 F35 2002
813'.54—dc21   2001034225

ISBN-13: 978-0-684-86500-3
ISBN-10:   0-684-86500-9
ISBN-13: 978-0-7432-2721-6 (Pbk)
ISBN-10:   0-7432-2721-2 (Pbk)

This book is for Joe Wood Jr.
(1964–1999)

You don't miss your water
'til your well runs dry.

—William Bell
"You Don't Miss Your Water"

Their outbreaks were terrible; civil wars such as our world has not seen again; dealings with conquered enemies which are a fearful page in history. Nevertheless, the outstanding fact about Rome is her unwavering adherence to the idea of a controlled life, subject not to this or that individual, but to a system embodying the principles of justice and fair dealing.

—Edith Hamilton,
The Roman Way

But as we've seen, black America isn't just as fissured as white America; it is more so. And the mounting intraracial disparities mean that the realities of race no longer affect all blacks in the same way.

—Henry Louis Gates, Jr.,
The Future of the Race

1

The Roman Way

THE CHELSEA SCHOOL is in the middle of a field so lush and vivid as to make the eyes water and shine with its light. There's grass everywhere, acres and acres of it, green and falling away, rolling. Up on the hill, a grand red barn sits, incongruous, bright, the biggest in three counties. Black cows dot the hillside. Sometimes you can see boys in orange down jackets walking among them, slapping the rumps of the cows to get them to shift and calling to each other in raucous, sarcastic voices. But the barn serves no real purpose here. It was built by the school's founder in the belief that manual labor in the open air would make stalwart men out of callow boys. The boys can take a class called Animal Husbandry, playing at being the farmers they will never be. The small amount of milk that the cows produce is donated to a nearby bottler and sold in greenish glass bottles for more than three times its value.

I have served this school since 1974. For most of that time, I have been the only Negro on the faculty. (A note: I am fully aware that *Negro* is no longer the fashionable term. It is, however, the term I prefer to use.) I have always been, and remain, the only Negro in the Classics Department. Given the waning interest in the classics manifested by today's young men, the fathers of the school have seen fit to render me the only classics teacher. It could be worse, I suppose. When I first arrived here, there was some serious talk of eliminating the entire department in the name of "relevance." Only an impassioned plea by the then–department head and some grumbling from our more conservative alumni preserved the few classes that are left. Fortunately, I have enough students to fill them, but there is not much demand for my knowledge of Greco-Roman culture outside of those classes. The vigorous and lengthy discussions that I imagine used to take place regarding matters of the classical mind are all in the past now.

When I was hired, John Hays, who was headmaster at the time, said that I was exactly the person they were looking for. I remember his words from my hiring interview quite distinctly. "It's time that the Chelsea School took note of the advances your people have made," he said, rearing back on the legs of his wooden chair. "Our boys will benefit from your fine example." He paused. "I know you'll take this in the spirit in which it's intended—you're truly a credit to your race." I smiled briefly. I did take Hays's comment as the compliment he meant it to be— though I suppose many would not have.

So it is that in more than twenty years of faculty pictures here, you see me—or rather, you don't see me, a quiet, dark space among all the bright, pale faces, my heavy-rimmed glasses catching the light. There was a time when I was not alone. I was hired to teach here along with two other Negro men. Dexter Johnson was one. The other was Hugh Davenport. They had stellar credentials—Amherst and Yale—as did I, with my degree from Harvard. We spent time in one another's cramped apartments, discussing this or that student or, more often, the issues of the day. However, a few months into our acquaintance, I began to feel a rift growing between us. More and more, I had become convinced that the way to effect the greatest good was to toil within the system that Chelsea had long had in place. I believed our very presence could begin to create change as long as we behaved honorably. My colleagues did not. While they started out full of hope, as soon as one or two of their proposals were dismissed out of hand—such as the one about having every Chelsea student take one course of Negro history—they began to complain about "the Man" and about how "a black man would never get a break" at this school. One day, after yet another litany of unhappiness, I said to them, "Some would say that we got a break by being invited to teach here. It is up to us to make of the opportunity what we will."

My colleagues stared at me, then looked quickly at each other. "So it's like that, huh?" said one. "I thought you were slipping over to their side."

We completed our meal but never spoke again about anything but class schedules. Within a year, they had both left the faculty. I have no idea what became of them.

The conviction that I began to form in those earliest days has only strengthened and taken root with the passage of years—it is up to us to make of opportunities what we will. I believe that I can affect the hearts and minds of boys who might never have seen an educated Negro before—boys who knew only the women who cleaned their floors and the men who trimmed their lawns and, maybe later, Bill Cosby from the flickering television screen—simply by my presence and skill as a teacher. More important, my presence stands as a testament to the notion that we are not all cut from the same cloth, that individual effort and rigor will ultimately win out over all.

I have seen some of my charges go on to run large companies. One is a United States senator, one a popular and well-respected writer. All of my most successful students have been white. But that doesn't trouble me a great deal. I know that I have opened their minds somewhat; that they see that there are some Negroes who value the things a Chelsea man values: order, decorum, rectitude. I have given my life over to passing on these ideals at Chelsea. I would gladly do it again.

The other thing I love about teaching here is the constant promise of renewal. Every fall, one gets the chance to begin again. Perhaps that is why the school is at its best in the fall. The grass has not yet lost its startling greenness, but the leaves are aflame with color, brilliant orange and deep red. The young men who are our students greet each other with loud shouts of pleasure. The faculty is full of resolve. It is a lovely time. It is unfortunate that it is so brief.

The moments before the first class of the year hum with a particular tension, one I have never entirely gotten used to. I start by standing quietly in front of the class, my back to them, writing out my name and some simple cases and conjugations. Behind me, the freshmen enter, some boisterously, as if to show that they are not intimidated, some so shyly that I hear only the clatter of their shoes and the shifting of desks and chairs as they find seats. I do not turn around until they begin to quiet and look at me, expectant and nervous. Even then, I let the silence linger a fraction of a minute longer. I wait until every eye is upon me.

"My name is Mr. Washington, and this is Latin One," I say, my voice pitched slightly louder to carry to the back of the room. "Latin is considered by many to be a dead language. In this room, it is not. While here, we can revel in the clarity of thought that produced it and the glory of the civilization that once used it.

Much of the world we know rests on the foundation created by the Romans. It is a language to be treasured and respected. I assume that your presence here means that you feel as I do."

Those students who were pretending not to be intimidated before are generally stunned into silence by this speech. I know perfectly well that most of them are there because their fathers insisted or because fewer years of Latin are necessary to fulfill the language requirement than of French or Spanish. But I want them to understand the seriousness with which I regard what they are about to undertake. I know they have never seen anyone like me before.

They, on the other hand, tend to have a very similar look. I have grown used to it over my years of teaching. The well-cut blond or brown hair, the smooth boyish skin, the perfect teeth (or teeth on their way to being made perfect by means of expensively glittering orthodontia). They look lush, if I may use such a term, as though great effort has rarely been required of them, as though they are used to getting what they want. I suppose they have been.

This year, as I looked over the rows of students, I saw a young Negro boy who was new to the school. Looking down the class enrollment list, I saw that he had one of those rather absurd African-inspired names. Rashid. That was it. Rashid Bryson.

He wore his hair in dreadlocks, the unattractive mass of ropy knots favored by many young Negro men these days. It is a style that looks angry to me—I see why the word *dread* is used. He was neatly dressed, but there was a slightly insolent air in the way his legs were spread, feet planted, on the floor. I was quite surprised to see him in my classroom.

As the only Negro member of the faculty, I have historically been called on to provide support to the Negro students here, of whom there are admittedly very few. My feelings about this are mixed. I want, always, to do what is best for the school. I am well aware of the pressures attendant on our current headmaster, Ted

Fox, to create a diverse student body—one with more Negro students in particular. I am well aware that I am a beneficiary of the kinds of programs—or at least the kinds of outreach—that lead students like young Mr. Bryson to the doors of the Chelsea School. But I do not feel that it is incumbent upon me to help every young man with skin the color of mine who comes through the doors of this school. Let all be accepted on their merits, let them rise or fall as they may. That is something else I have learned from my long study of Rome. There are those who believe otherwise, but I share the view of those scholars who have argued that ancient Rome was a place of racial egalitarianism. I believe that they accepted each man on his individual merits, with little regard for the color of his skin. I am not so naive as to believe that this country's long history of racial prejudice has been eradicated. But I do believe that those of us whom Du Bois called "the darker brothers" could profit from accepting the values that Chelsea at its best espouses. And while I see this school's standards softening under the relentless onslaught of preferential treatment, I want to continue to uphold the values that the school's founders held dear.

I have come to my unwillingness to be lumped together with others of my race over many years of watching young Negro men come into Chelsea. All too often they have been given some sort of dispensation or aid to come to the school, and all too often they spend their brief time here huddled together, looking out at the other students and the faculty with a cynical gaze that condemns us all and offers little appreciation for the gift they have been given. These students are being presented with a chance to study the greatest works of the greatest minds of Western civilization, and they would rather spend their time listening to so-called music with no perceptible melody performed by young thugs and reading, if they read at all, works by vastly inferior contemporary writers who happen to be the same race as they. I feared young

Mr. Bryson might be such a one. His quiet, measuring gaze on me as I spoke did nothing to dispel that impression.

The first class of the year, I do most of the talking. I offer a brief history of Greek civilization as it affected the Roman and talk a bit about the Latin roots of our own language as well as that of the Romance languages. I make little attempt to be jocular or engaging. I want them to be engaged by the journey we are embarked on, by our efforts to learn this elegant, controlled, and graceful language. I don't require that we have fun. I require only that they give it their best effort and their full attention. They generally look slightly shell-shocked after the first class. Inevitably, a few have dropped out by the end of the second week.

"Well then, gentlemen," I concluded, "the period is nearing an end and you have your assignment for the first week. It should keep you fairly occupied after you settle into your dorms this evening. Are there any questions?"

To my surprise, Mr. Bryson raised his hand. "Is there any extra credit work?" His voice was unusually low pitched for someone only thirteen or fourteen years old and his gaze an odd combination of frank and fearful. His eyes were the same unfathomable dark brown that my brother's had been, the challenge in his look similar.

"Oh-ho, an eager beaver here," I replied. I must admit that I was impressed by such a show of initiative so early in the year, especially from such an unexpected source. "Why don't you see how you do with tonight's assignment and allow me to prepare something for those who are interested for next week? Fair enough?" The boy nodded, his eyes never leaving mine. To the class as a whole, I said, "All right, you gentlemen are dismissed. Don't make too much noise as you depart."

Their faces were blank and relieved as they left. Despite my warning, their noise level began slowly but rose to a tidal wave as soon as they hit the hallway. Young Mr. Bryson was one of the last to leave. He glanced toward me as he left the room, and a fleeting expression—anger? kinship? appraisal?—crossed his face. He looked as though he wanted to ask me another question but then decided not to linger. I finished organizing my papers with a peculiar feeling of unease. His eyes seemed to be on me long after he had left the room.

2

There Goes the Neighborhood

THE DAY THAT Kofi Bryson got the letter admitting him to Mt. Herndon, their mother met him and his brother, Rashid, after school, something she rarely did—she usually trusted Kofi to walk Rashid safely home. As long as either boy could remember, they had been told they were in this world to do their best and to protect each other. She stood in the middle of the sidewalk, clutching the heavy, cream-colored envelope to her chest. When she spotted the boys, she began waving it wildly, like a banner. They ran to her quickly. "Dag, Ma, what is it?" said Kofi, already developing a thirteen-year-old's fatigue with his parents. "You out here waving that thing around like a crazy woman."

"It's your letter from Mt. Herndon. I couldn't stand waiting. It's thick. Feels like it got some other papers in it. That's good, isn't it?" Her words came out in a rush.

Kofi nodded slowly, a young man in a dream. Rashid could

still remember his dark fingers sliding under the edge of the envelope, all three of them shifting from foot to foot, then Kofi reading the first sentence, "We are pleased to inform you of your acceptance . . ."

His voice trailed off as their mother's rose in a shout: "Kofi, Kofi, I knew you could do it!"

Kofi stood stock still, reading the page over and over, his hands tightening on the edges of the paper until it began to wrinkle. "They gave me money, too," he said after a long time. He didn't seem to know what to do after saying this.

"Give your brother a hug," Rashid was instructed. "He just got into one of the best schools in the country. He's on his way."

Rashid didn't really need the instruction. He might have been only eleven then, but he knew how important this was. It was his victory, too. Other kids leaving the school looked at them standing together, their mother weeping joyously, and walked warily around them. Their mother kept her arms around both of them the whole way home, humming some old song and pausing to kiss the tops of both of their heads at corners, the kind of affection she never displayed. The boys were too excited to be embarrassed.

When their father got home and got the news, something even more unexpected happened. His eyes filled with tears. He stood clutching his son's acceptance letter, reading it over and over. Then he stopped reading, hugged their mother, then the boys, and he said, "Well, we've sure got something to say when they ask about blessings at church on Sunday this week."

The night before Kofi's departure, the two boys lay in the small room they shared, their heads buzzing from the talk and congratulations of Kofi's going-away party and from the fizzy remains of a couple of illicit half-drunk beers sneaked off the table. ("Mama's gonna whup your ass, she sees you sneaking those, Kofi." "Who's gonna tell her?" Then the thrill of the slightly warm beer—it tasted nasty at first, but then you kind of got used to it—going down their gullets. They smiled at each other like men.) Kofi's packed bags, one of them already starting to split at the seam, sat in the corner. The room smelled warm, of boy's sweat and humid city air. Rashid spoke first. "You nervous, Kofi?"

"Nervous? Naw. . . . Well, maybe a little. The work's gonna be hard up there. Harder than old chump-ass Banneker."

"You can do it, though, right? I mean, they wouldn't even have let you in if you couldn't, right?"

"Right." Silence. "It's gonna be different, though. A lot of white people. A lot of work," Kofi continued. "I'ma miss you, you little punk."

Rashid was silent for a moment. "I'ma miss you, too."

Barbara and Henry Bryson had scraped together enough cash for a rental car to drive Kofi to school (Henry praying silently through the whole transaction that they wouldn't actually put a charge on his severely overextended Visa card), and each member of the family struggled downstairs with a piece of Kofi's luggage when it was time for him to go. There was no one to see them off or wish them well—just the group of corner boys fixing them with the same contemptuous stare with which they greeted everything. Once they were all in the car, Henry took a deep breath and said briefly, "Lord, bless us this day as we take our oldest boy on to his next stage of life. We ask for your protection and care."

"Amen," said the boys and Barbara. They all smiled nervously at each other. Then Henry turned on the radio and pulled away from the curb. All you could hear was the sweet voice of Al Green on the Sunday oldies show.

When Kofi came back from Mt. Herndon for the summer, he seemed frightened, uneasy. His hair was a little too long ("I can't find nobody . . . anybody . . . to cut it around school. There ain't . . . aren't any black people in Stonington, Mama"), and he had lost his taste for sitting outside on the stoop, watching life go by. Both boys had been regarded as oddities at Banneker anyway because of their ambition, but now words Rashid didn't know the meaning of appeared regularly in Kofi's speech. Rashid caught Kofi staring out the window for long periods, a lost look on his face. And then on Kofi's second or third Sunday home, the usual shuffle and run to the apartment's single bathroom began early and Kofi didn't join it. "You better get goin', man," said Rashid. "You know Mama don't like us to be late."

Kofi sat on the edge of the bed. "You know, I don't know how I feel about Jesus anymore."

"What?"

"I said, I don't know how I feel about Jesus anymore. Up at school, we take this course in comparative religions, and there are so many different things a person can believe. I mean, are all Jews going to hell? Are all the Muslims? I don't know. It makes it hard to sit up there and say this is the only thing I believe."

Rashid looked at Kofi like he'd just started speaking in tongues. "You better not let Mama or Daddy hear you talk like that. They'll snatch you out that school in one hot minute."

Kofi sighed. Rashid noticed for the first time how much older he looked. "Yeah, yeah. And hard as it is, I'm not ready to give up. You don't know, R. You don't know what it's like at Herndon. I feel like . . . like they have everything and I end up feeling like I got nothing. Like I am nothing—just got in there on some kind of fluke. Don't know nothing." He stood up and pulled a tie from the cheap bureau, his voice ragged. "It's no joke, going to this school, man. It's no joke."

Rashid was silent for a few moments. Then, confused, he said, "Well, I won't tell what you said. About Jesus and all."

Kofi shook his head and smiled, his eyes still focused elsewhere. "Thanks, little R. Thanks a lot."

They went to church that day. Kofi sang beautifully as always, his eyes focused on some far-off place, confusing Rashid even more. Three weeks later, Kofi was dead, killed in a holdup as he

left a local bodega with a lukewarm Coke in his hand. Rashid sang
at his funeral. After that, he stopped going to church.

The Sunday after Kofi's funeral, Rashid just didn't get up, didn't
wash up, didn't make his face shine, to shine unto the face of the
Lord. There wasn't any big raging-at-God sort of feeling. He just
could not get out of bed. His mother stuck her head into the room
that he had shared with his brother until four days ago—there was
nowhere else for him to sleep, the apartment was too small—and
said, "Boy, ain't you ready yet?" And Rashid said, "I'm not going."
She stood, silent. Then sighed. Then said, "All right," and walked
out, shutting the door. Rashid sat bolt upright after she left, gazing
at the blank wood, terrified. No yelling? No threats? No "Boy,
you goin' and that's that"? He could hear his heart pounding in
his ears. He had a wild impulse to throw on some clothes—
anything—and run out the door after them. But he didn't. He just
lay back down in his bed, his eyes dry, staring at the ceiling. They
went a few more Sundays after that, and then, without discussion,
they stopped going, too. For the first few weeks, the phone rang
with brothers and sisters from the church inquiring after them,
and then it stopped and the three of them were left alone.

Rashid's parents started eating nonstop, sitting in front of the
television, watching whatever crawled across the screen in front
of them. They both made it to work, but that was about it. Gradually, Rashid took over most of the household chores except
cooking. That his mother kept doing. Too much food was
required to smother their grief. She brought out plate after plate
laden with spaghetti, fried chicken, broiled chicken, rice and
beans, day after day. They shoveled the food in wordlessly against
the television's chatter, expanding before Rashid's eyes like balloons filled with water. Every couple of months, Rashid's mother
went shopping and came home with new, larger clothes for both

of them, dresses with hectic, frightening patterns for her, blousy shirts and pants with hidden elastic waistbands for him in easy-care, slightly shiny fabric. Rashid ate little and stayed in his room, not wanting to be near them.

It was on one of those nights that Rashid discovered the Chelsea School. He found the brochure among some old things of Kofi's. "No way am I going to an all-boys school," he said at the time, laughing and throwing the brochure aside. "Got to have some honeys around." Laughing boys, serious boys, studious boys, only boys adorned the textured cover of the booklet. Rashid opened it, not thinking. "Here is a place that can shape a young man's life," he read. "At the Chelsea School, the only criterion is excellence. We expect it. We demand it. We create it. And our boys grow into men who will change the world." He flipped the pages a bit more intently, feeling the heavy, nubbly paper stock underneath his fingers. Change the world. Change the world. He could hear tinny laughter from the television set, the shouts of boys outside on the street. There was a sudden high buzzing in his head as he carefully copied down the address of the school into the back of one of his notebooks. Maybe if he left. Maybe if he went someplace pure and single-minded. No girls to distract him. Nobody who knew about Kofi, about how alone he was now. Someplace where he had no history, just the day in front of him. Maybe then his mind would clear. Maybe then he could breathe again.

That night, he went hesitantly out into the living room before going to bed. His parents sat in their usual chairs, in their usual positions. The room had a faint, unpleasant smell of recent cooking and sweat. Their plates sat in front of them, grease congealing with brown gravy. Urgent dialogue stuttered out of the television, but their faces were sorrowful and blank. "Mama, Dad, I . . . I decided something tonight."

They didn't even look up at first. Finally Rashid spoke again. "I decided to apply to private school. A boys' school in Connecticut. This one called Chelsea." Until he spoke, he hadn't felt convinced. But as he gazed at his parents' faces, he had never felt more sure of anything in his life.

They turned to him as if under water. After a long pause, his father spoke. "Private school. Well, if you can get in and get the money, you go 'head on. Might as well have one of you try to do something with your life. Now that Kofi's gone. You the last chance we got."

His mother's eyes filled with tears again. Since Kofi's death, they'd rarely been clear. More than once, Rashid had found her moving swiftly about the kitchen, cooking as she always did, her face wet with tears she made no attempt to wipe off. "You do what you need to do, Rashid. Your father's right. You got to be a man about this now." She turned away, closing her eyes as she did so.

So that was it. No offers of help, no encouragement or applause, neither of them sitting beside him as he worked on his admission essay and got all the paperwork together. They didn't stop him—but they didn't help him. His homeroom teacher, Ms. Havens, looked over his application essay and corrected some things and told him that he was going to go far and he'd do well at Chelsea—but his parents never did. Not once. They used to say that kind of thing all the time, but now . . . Rashid told himself he didn't mind—although he found the image of his mother sitting quietly by Kofi as he worked on his applications floating unbidden through his mind at times, her presence a quiet expression of belief. His stomach hurt a lot of the time as he did what was necessary to get in. He told his mother when to call, he filled out the financial aid forms himself, rummaging through boxes of papers and getting distracted answers to his questions. He slid the papers under his parents' hands for signatures and, when the time came, made sure that they both remembered to take the day off work for the interview. But they pulled themselves together for the trip to the school, looking downright presentable and focused, the way they used to be. They even found some clothes that fit fairly well and weren't too hideous. They waited quietly in the hall during his interview and listened attentively during the tour of the campus. They nodded approvingly at its vast acreage and looked pleased as the admissions director told them of the school's one hundred percent college admissions rate. His dad even rested his hand on his shoulder at one point and told the man, with a slight smile, how proud they were of Rashid. Rashid felt tears start to his eyes at this, but, thank God, no one noticed. He started to think that maybe this was it, that maybe things would get better now and they would see him again. But then his mother cried softly in the car all the way home, remembering when they took Kofi to visit Mt. Herndon. His father stared at the road as if daring it to jump up and challenge him to a fight. He did not speak a single word once they left the school.

When Rashid got in, there was no party, no tears, and if there was an announcement at church, he wasn't there to hear it. The kids who had always hissed at Kofi, "Think you white, huh?" now hissed it at Rashid, if they spoke to him at all. Ms. Havens was happy—she had always been on his side. She gave him a big hug when he showed her the letter and said nothing about Kofi. The look they shared said it all. But she was the only one. When the time came to go, Rashid's primary emotion was relief. Scared as he was to go, it had to be better than home.

Chelsea was a foreign country—and even though Rashid had signed up for the trip, it was a shock. The grass everywhere. The barn—a barn! With cows! At his interview, when he'd asked about it, they'd explained that they had this class in Animal Husbandry, but when he arrived for the first day of school, he still couldn't believe it. He had never even thought of cows as real before. Just images on a carton of milk or something he saw at the children's zoo.

At first Rashid was a little nervous, having so much space around him, so green and open and quiet. He thought of how the kids from his junior high used to ride on the subway, loud and defiant, taking up as much room as they could. As if being loud enough would allow them to take what the world didn't want to give them. But these boys didn't need that. The world was just waiting to give them whatever they wanted. They didn't have to struggle or yell for it. It would be presented soon enough. So they weren't quiet, exactly. But their raucousness didn't have the same fear in it. Nothing to be scared of, really.

They were, of course, almost all white. White people were everywhere, hair flopping in their eyes, that faint wet-dog smell. At the first assembly, Rashid found himself scanning the crowd for faces like his own. He found only a few—twenty, maybe—out of the whole school. This wasn't a surprise, really, but now that it was his life, he found himself uneasy. There was one black teacher on the stage with the rest of them, welcoming the incoming freshmen. He looked almost as uncomfortable as Rashid felt. He was older—maybe fifty or so—with dark African-looking skin, black horn-rimmed glasses, and very short, neatly cut hair—what was left of it. His skin looked polished. He wore a tweed jacket and a bow tie. Rashid leaned over to the guy next to him and whispered, "Who's the black guy up there? The teacher?" He felt a little funny putting it that bluntly, but his race was what made the man stand out.

The boy whispered back, "That's Mr. Washington. Teaches Latin. He's never been known to smile."

Latin. Rashid sat back in his seat to consider this information. Latin. Latin? He thought that's what they used to talk in Greek or Rome times, but he wasn't positive. You did only have to take two years of it, though—he noticed that in the papers they gave him when he was registering. All the other languages, you had to take three. And they said it helped with other languages he wanted to learn, like Spanish. Taking a class with a black man would be cool. So when the time came, he signed up.

He'd thought that by asking for extra work in class today, he'd make it clear to Mr. Washington that he wasn't here to play. Washington had seemed impressed—but then when Rashid got back to his room and took a look at what awaited him in the dun-colored Latin textbook, he felt sick. He was going to be up half the night fooling around with this stuff as it was—and he hadn't even gotten homework from any of his other classes yet. He fell back on the bed with a groan.

His roommate, Gerald Davis, looked up from where he was leafing through a new-looking copy of *A Farewell to Arms*. "Damn, cuz, what's up? Somebody call you nigger already?" His tone was surprisingly mild, as though he expected this insult to be delivered to either or both of them at any second.

Rashid replied without sitting up. "I just got out of Latin. I'm trying to impress the teacher by asking for extra credit. Now I take a look at it and I'm like, Oh shit, I can't even do what I'm supposed to do. Tryin' to be slick." He pulled his pillow over his face and groaned again, inhaling the slight smell of his own sweat from the night before.

"What the hell were you doing asking for extra credit on the first day? You must be out your damn mind," Gerald said, laughing.

Rashid threw the pillow at him. "I know that now. I don't know. He's a brother. And . . ." Here his voice changed, grew low and intense. "I've got to stay here. I've got to."

Gerald gave him a funny look. "It's just the first week of classes, my man. I don't think they're gonna throw your butt out of here yet."

"Mmm." Rashid had turned his attention back to his book and was chewing hard on the edge of his thumb. The words swam in front of him. *Amo, amas, amat.* Transitive, intransitive, present perfect. What? He jumped a little when he heard Gerald's voice, hoping that his roommate hadn't noticed. "You better not get too comfortable, cuz. It's almost time for our next class. What do you got?" Gerald shouldered his backpack easily.

"I got English next. Miss Hansen."

"Me too. Come on, bro." Gerald paused, then grinned. "Washington is such a Poindexter-looking dude anyway. Latin will do that to you. I don't get why you're taking it."

"I don't know. I thought it would be cool. And you don't have to take as much."

"I guess. You coming?"

"Yeah, yeah. Hold up."

Rashid and Gerald were the only black boys on the floor of their dorm, their room the last one at the back of the hall. They'd been quick to dub it "the ghetto," but in fact, this was as close to a real ghetto as Gerald had ever been. Both boys realized this early on, but they couldn't find a way to talk about it. The knowledge was just there, sometimes uncomfortable, sometimes not. The first day of school, the two boys came out of the shower at the same time, Gerald barefoot, Rashid wearing the flip-flops he always wore. He never went barefoot because his mother told him it was nasty. Besides, where was it safe to walk? There was always glass and junk on the ground. "Yo, man, aren't you worried about catching something?" said Rashid, gesturing toward Gerald's feet.

Gerald looked baffled. "How?"

"Going barefoot. You do that all the time?"

Gerald looked even more confused and said, "Yeah. I'm usually naked in the shower, man." He smiled a bit. Rashid shook his head. "I mean, they clean it, right?" Gerald added.

"Yeah, I guess," said Rashid. An awkward silence persisted. What Rashid didn't know was that at Gerald's home, a cheerful Jamaican woman came once a week to clean. The lawns in Maryland's Prince Georges County, where he lived, were meticulously groomed and trimmed. His house had wall-to-wall carpet. Why shouldn't he go barefoot? What was the big deal?

Anyone looking at them as they walked across campus to their English class would not have been able to imagine that scene. They would see only two handsome black boys, walking with a group of handsome white boys across a beautiful campus toward a distinguished, low classroom building. The sons of former slaves and the sons of former slave owners sitting together at the table of brotherhood. The picture of a dream come true.

Just outside the main classroom building, they ran into the proctor of their dorm, an avuncular sort named Rich Stephenson. The dorm proctors were chosen from the more responsible members of the senior class. They tended to seem older than seventeen and be a bit overweight. "How's it going, you guys?" Rich asked as he fell into step with them.

"Okay," replied Gerald. "We're on our way to freshman English. Rashid here just had his first taste of Latin with Mr. Washington."

"Yikes," said Rich. "Wooden Washington. How'd it go?"

Rashid and Gerald both laughed. "That's what y'all call him?" said Rashid.

"Well, I think it fits. Don't you?"

"Yeah, I guess it does," said Rashid. "He's a pretty tough dude, huh?"

"Listen, I had him freshman year, and I did all right, but I practically got sick before every exam. It's like he thinks if he lets up for one minute, they're gonna run him out of here on a rail. Just keep your head down and you'll get through it. Too bad you didn't have anybody to warn you to take French. I sure as shit could have used the advice." Rich grinned. "This here's my stop. See you gentlemen later."

The boys watched him go and continued to their English class, still laughing a little over Mr. Washington's nickname. *Old*

Wooden Washington ain't gonna wear me out, thought Rashid as he took his place next to Gerald in the airy room and turned his attention to the woman writing on the board. *I'm out here by myself. I gotta take this shot.*

The thing was, Rashid realized as he stared at the mountain of books before him in his dorm's basement study area that evening, that he didn't even know where to start. The room was quiet—no one else had come down to start homework before lights out yet—but Rashid's throat was tight with panic, his breath short. He'd never be able to finish all this. They'd just find him here a week from now, staring at these books. Frozen. He swallowed, once, twice, three times. The lump was still there. So he picked up his Latin book and looked at the assignment. Okay. Okay. He forced himself to focus on the words swimming on the page.

After he'd been working for about half an hour and completed maybe an eighth of the translating he was supposed to do, Gerald came into the study room with another guy from their floor, Scott Hayward. Scott was big, blond, broad-shouldered, a freshman like Rashid and Gerald. He looked as though he would smell of hay. They exchanged brief *heys* and flopped down to study in the stuffing-sprung armchairs around the room. All remained quiet for a few minutes, and then Scott spoke. "You know, this is kind of crazy."

"What is, man?" Gerald said without looking up.

"Killing ourselves studying on the first day of classes. We've got all weekend. Let's go catch some tube or go do something before lights out." He closed his just-opened text with an authoritative snap.

Rashid looked at Gerald, his eyes widening. He didn't dare stop working or he'd never, ever be able to stay at Chelsea. Scott and Gerald looked relaxed, at ease. "Jesus, Hayward," said Gerald, "we just got down here. What'd you think we were gonna do, jerk off? They call it the *study* room."

"I know, I know, but hey. We're young. We should be farting around, watching TV, staying up all night cramming the night before tests, not the week classes start."

"Well, call me geek. I'm staying," replied Gerald.

Scott turned to Rashid. "And you? You a geek, too, man?"

"No . . . I mean yeah, I guess I am. I gotta finish this stuff."

Hayward made a great show of mock exasperation and pulled his stuff up under his arm. "Well, I guess I'll see ya later, then." He left the room. Rashid's head was pounding. At his old school, that definitely would have ended up with a fight. But Gerald had turned back to his book calmly. Rashid stared at him for a while. The ghetto. You didn't learn how to talk to a guy like Scott Hayward in the ghetto. Not in any ghetto he'd ever been in, anyway.

Gerald looked up. "What are you looking at?" he said, one eyebrow raised.

"Nothing. Just thinking."

"You need to be thinking about that Latin. Washington's gonna kick your ass. You know it."

"Yeah, yeah." He turned his eyes back to his book, and the words formed themselves in front of him, a little more sensible this time. But that lump was still in his throat. He wondered if it was ever going to go away.

3

They Say That It's a Man's World (But You Can't Prove That by Me)

WHEN I WAS teaching back in Cleveland, I was always the only white woman in the room. So Chelsea was weird right from the start. The room seemed too bright. I was comforted by the sight of two black boys near the back. One was dark and rather handsome, with a head full of short dreads; his leg jiggled nervously and continuously. The other boy was caramel colored and considerably more relaxed, studying me with the same calm gaze as those of the rest of his classmates. Funny, how when I was their age, I never would have noticed if a room was mostly full of white people. But fifteen years in the Cleveland public schools had cured me of that. Now it felt odd to be in the majority, but curiously restful as well. Truth be told, that's how I ended up here. I was hoping that a little of the neatness and prosperity and calm of the place would rub off on me.

"So, gentlemen," I started, after writing my name on the board in the same blocky letters I always used. That felt the same, which was nice. "My name is Jana Hansen—Ms. Hansen to you—and I'm new here. My goal in this class is primarily to get you reading. Really reading, with a critical eye." I paused. The boys' expressions had not changed. "Don't get me wrong. There will still be tests and papers. But mostly I want to know that you're reading, and I want to know what you think about what you're reading. Fair enough?"

A few muttered *yeah*s. I could see that they were trying to make sense of me—and not entirely succeeding. Best to press on. "Let's start here," I said. "It's the first day. We don't have an assignment yet—although don't worry, you're going to get one—but what I'd like to do right now is just read you one of my favorite stories." I dug out my battered copy of *The Complete Stories of Flannery O'Connor* and flipped through it until I reached "A Good Man Is Hard to Find." "The grandmother did not want to go to Florida," I read. By the end of the first page, I had them. I allowed myself a small smile. Nothing like a little gothic southern violence to draw in the young folks. When I finished, I looked up expectantly. "Well? Any thoughts? And tell me your names before you speak. It'll help me learn them."

The first hand to go up belonged to one of the smoother-looking boys in the class. "My name's Max Harrison," he said. "And I don't really get what the story was about. I mean . . . they all seemed like stupid hicks to me."

He sat back in his chair, satisfied. A few of the other boys nodded. Oh boy. I wanted to slap him. One wise-ass like this could shut a whole class down. That's another thing I knew from fifteen years of teaching. Instead I spoke carefully.

"Well, you're entitled to that opinion, Max, but that doesn't really help us see why this story has lasted so long. What it is that people love so much about it. Anybody else?"

The room was silent, and I felt the slow sinking of a failed teaching gambit. I was about to speak myself when the boy with the dreadlocks raised his hand, a bit tentatively. "Um . . . my name's Rashid Bryson. Yeah, they was . . . I mean *were* hicks in that story, but that didn't mean they deserved to die. Nobody deserves that. To get shot like that. Just out of someone else's meanness. I thought that was good, the way the author showed that. . . ." He trailed off and scooted back in his seat as though he had said too much.

"That's a good point, Rashid," I said. Turning to the rest of the class, I said, "What does the story say to us about violence?" Another boy raised his hand, and the discussion began in earnest.

I was flushed and pleased with myself by the time class ended. It turned out that not all of the students were arrogant preps with nothing of interest to say—I was going to have to keep my eye on that Max, though. But most of them, as it turned out, were just boys—naive, thoughtful, goofy, insightful—just boys like the hundreds I had known. Rashid didn't speak again after his first comment, but I could see him soaking up the content of the discussion avidly, looking around the room as though these boys held the key to a building he needed to get into but couldn't without their help. He took a lot of notes—too many, I thought, seeming to attempt to write down everything everyone said. I bet he came from a struggling public school, a school like the ones I had left.

After the class left, I stood alone for a few moments in the empty room. The fall light spilled in with an unearthly purity, warming the backs of my legs. There was a lot of chalk in the chalk tray—five or six full pieces, in fact. All I'd had to carry with me to class was the book I was going to read from and the class list. Everything else was neatly stowed in my tastefully appointed office. It smelled clean. There was a recently vacuumed carpet under my feet. I heard a truck drive by, and in the momentary silence following, a bird sang. Cleveland seemed very far away. I supposed I should feel guilty. But I didn't.

You can't exactly call the cafeteria here a cafeteria in the usual sense of the word. It's—how can I say this—it's a mansion, for crying out loud. Well, the building it's in used to be a mansion. It belonged to Henry Townsend, the millionaire who owned all the land that the school is on. It stands on a little rise, imposing itself on the land around it, the way those millionaires loved to build. When the light is right, it almost seems to glow. I was initially a bit stunned to contemplate that this was where I'd be eating every day, but I was beginning to get used to the idea. I pulled open one of the leaded glass doors and walked in.

When you eat in a cafeteria each day, lunch hour is always a replay of that moment that is so crystallized in high school: Where should I sit? Where are the cool kids? It's peculiar to have it again as an adult, but there you are. I stood, irresolute, looking around, when I spotted Helen Johnston. There's someone like Helen at every high school in America—or there should be. Someone who's seen it all and been fazed by none of it. I didn't know her well, but I sensed it right away. You can always tell those types. They have a perpetual air of faint amusement. They always have the best gossip and often make the best friends. When I left my school in Cleveland, I fancied myself the teacher who was like that. Now I was starting over, and I needed someone to show me the ropes. I walked up to Helen's table and asked if I could join her. She looked up with a quick smile that had a gentle air of appraisal about it and waved her hand to indicate I should sit. While she was probably only about eight to ten years older than me, I felt quite adolescent as I sat down next to her. "Welcome, welcome. Come have a seat and enjoy this fabulous repast. Meat loaf today. My favorite." It was difficult to tell if she was serious about the food or not. "How'd your morning go? Jana? Is that right?"

"Almost. It's pronounced JAY-na. And yes, the morning was good. I've got a good group for freshman English, I think. I read them 'A Good Man Is Hard to Find,' and they really responded."

"You read to them?"

I suddenly felt sheepish in the face of her direct gaze. "Yes. I've done it before. It often works quite well."

Helen turned to a serious attack on her meat loaf. "Think you're going to like it here?" she said after a few moments' silence.

"Yes. Yes, I do."

"Good. We can use all the estrogen we can get." She looked at me searchingly for a moment, then seemed to decide that I had passed some sort of test. "So, folks starting out here are usually a bit younger than you, if you don't mind my saying so. What brings you to our fair campus?"

"Well . . ." I paused but then thought, *What the hell.* "I used to teach public school in Cleveland, but I'm from around here. I came back here because I needed a change."

"Well, you certainly got it, coming here, I would guess."

I laughed. "I did. But it's good." I paused again. "It was time to move anyway. I got divorced a few years ago, my daughter was off to college, and my students were struggling more and more, and . . . well, that's it. I have a friend whose son graduated from here. She told me about the opening. I needed to see some hills again. The light is so flat in the Midwest. I missed being able to get to the ocean sometimes, to get to New York. I wanted to come back."

She kept eating, not speaking, but the look she gave me was understanding, generous even. I had the feeling that people confessed things to her all the time, just came up to her and spilled their guts. "Well. It's nice here. Pleasant, I should think, after the hard labor in a public school," she said.

"Everything is so . . . plentiful."

She laughed. "That's the word for it all right. Plentiful. This is a school with a great abundance of all manner of things. As I imagine you'll find out soon enough." She laid down her fork. "Listen, a group of the women on the faculty get together once a month for brunch. We talk about what's going on, hold each other up, dish various students, that sort of thing. Would that appeal to you at all? We're meeting next Sunday at my house."

"I'd love that. Really. I hardly know anyone in town and . . . that would be really terrific."

"All right, then." She busied herself rummaging in her bag for a piece of paper on which to note her address. I looked idly around the room while she did this, and my eye fell on a black man eating alone. The only one in the room. I'd seen him around in the couple of days before classes had started, but we hadn't met. I couldn't remember his name.

"What's his name over there? The teacher who's eating alone?" I asked.

Helen smiled thinly. "Him? That's Jerome Washington. You haven't met him yet?"

"No."

"Oh, he's been here since the 1970s. He's a bit of an eccentric. Knows everything about Roman civilization. I think he prefers it to ours. Doesn't speak to anyone. Eats alone every day. I don't wonder. I sometimes think he must feel himself a bit on display here. There hasn't been another black faculty member since the guys he was hired with left years ago."

"Not any?" I said.

"Not a one," countered Helen. "They claim to have tried, but nobody wants the long hours and low pay. Plus a school like this one—so old-fashioned, all boys—think about it. What *is* the appeal, anyway?" She gave me a wry look and tucked into her food again. I laughed a little and found my gaze drawn back to Washington's solitary figure.

He ate with a series of precise movements, occasionally turning the pages of a thick book he was reading. His hands were large and curiously elegant; they smoothed the paper as though it were velvet. He looked self-contained and sure, except for the nervous jiggling of one foot under the table. His hair was graying at the temples: it stood out against the warm dark brown of his skin. Helen was still talking, so I pulled my gaze away politely.

She slid a piece of paper with her address on it toward me. I took it, smiling, and said, "Thanks, I look forward to getting together with you all."

"Us too. Well, got to shove off, get ready for my next class. See you around?"

"Definitely."

I finished my lunch—the meat loaf wasn't actually that bad—and noticed as I got ready to leave that Jerome Washington was still sitting there and that I had to walk right by his table to get to the cart where we deposited our trays. I stopped as I passed his table and lowered my tray onto it. "Excuse me?"

He looked up, startled and a bit wary. "Yes?"

I stuck my hand out and he took it, a little tentatively, letting go quickly. I continued, feeling suddenly awkward. "I'm Jana Hansen. Just started here this year. I've seen you around, but we haven't had a chance to speak. I wanted to introduce myself."

"Oh, of course. I'm Jerome Washington. You're settling in well, I trust?"

"Pretty well, yes."

"Well, I'm sure I'll see you at staff meetings and the like. It's nice to meet you."

He kept looking at me until I nodded and walked away. I felt thoroughly awkward, uncertain why it was that I'd needed to introduce myself, to make myself known to him. I just had. I'd wanted him to see me, even though he didn't know who I was. To show him that I was on his side. A gesture, perhaps. That seems about all I can manage these days.

There was something I didn't tell Helen. About why I left teaching. There was this boy, Jason. He was sixteen. So handsome and charming once he dropped his guard. And so smart. He tried to hide it at first, but it started to bleed out after just a few weeks of class. He was one of the few kids who actually did his homework, bringing in papers every week that were littered with misspellings but filled with genuine insight. He got in the habit of hanging around after school, at first on a series of pretexts—I forgot my hat; Did you say page fifty or page sixty?—but then it became clear that he just wanted to hang around. He liked being in school. And he liked me. Teachers aren't supposed to confess this kind of thing, but I felt girlish around him. Nothing happened, nothing inappropriate, but I liked talking to him, watching him use his hands as he told stories—Cal was gone anyway, I had no one at home waiting for me. There was no rush. You would think, with all those years of teaching, that I would have noticed that not everything was right. But I wanted it to be.

The last time I spoke to him, I gave him my copy of *Song of Solomon*. I thought he could handle the difficult imagery and that he'd like the Milkman Dead character. He smiled and said thanks, gazing at the cover. I had the distinct impression that no one had ever given him a book before. He turned it over and over in his hands. Then he said, "I hope I get to read this."

I thought that was an odd thing to say. I said, "Well, that's up to you, isn't it? You can do anything that you want to do. Just find your way around the potholes. I'll help you. You know that, don't you?" He gave me a tight, small smile. I had the oddest feeling, as if he was going to embrace me, but instead he gathered up his things and left. I never saw him again.

The first day he was out, I didn't give it much thought—there had been a flu going around. But the day after that and the day after that passed, and then I finally asked someone. "Didn't you hear?" replied the other woman, shocked.

"Hear what?"

"Jason got arrested. They caught him in a holdup at one of those little stores on his block. The owner was shot, and Jason was an accessory. He won't be tried as an adult, but he's going to do some time. I can't believe you didn't hear about it."

I couldn't believe it, either. How could I not have known about Jason's other life? Not his other life. His life. And how close he was to throwing it away even as I thought I was doing him some good. What good was I doing if I couldn't save a kid, a kid who wanted to be saved? Something about Jason—that smile he gave me the last time I saw him, the way he worked so hard to understand what he was reading—made losing him worse, a punch when I wasn't expecting it. I handed in my resignation a couple of weeks after I got the news. I got one postcard from Jason. All it said was, "Im Sorry." I didn't write back. What was I going to say?

I moved back east. My parents would have been thrilled, had they lived to see it. They never understood why Cal and I moved to Cleveland anyway. "They have that orchestra. But really, dear, is it a place that could possibly interest you?" my father would say. I'd counter with tales of the pleasures of Lake Erie and how nice the museum was (and it is beautiful—the lagoon in front of it rivals any city park I've ever seen) and how inexpensive it was. And I did love it once. I could never make them understand that what I loved about it was how emphatically it wasn't the East Coast. The land was different, the ethnic mix was different (all those Slovenian names); the way the whole place felt based on something that was real, a real industry that made real things, not something that was about status or producing money—I loved all that. It was so different from the way I grew up. But after I asked

Cal to move out and then I lost Jason, I found that I began to miss the green plenty of Connecticut myself.

I didn't give up every dream I'd ever had, though. I didn't give up the one about getting to kids through teaching. I hoped I could stand in front of these prosperous boys and force them to think about why they had what they had and lived the way they lived. But I'd be lying if I said that it doesn't matter to me to have enough chalk, to be teaching kids whose parents read to them. It does. I'm tired of fighting the tide. It washed Jason under. Before I left Cleveland it was perilously close to taking me, too.

Truth be told, I was raised to teach someplace like Chelsea. But only until I got married to someone who graduated from a school like Chelsea. After meeting this well-bred Mr. Right, I was supposed to stay home with my two or three children and keep a meticulously clean, well-appointed house. Oddly, Smith, the place my parents sent me to get me started on that path, was the place that led to my departing from it. And of course, like almost always when you're eighteen or nineteen or twenty, the whole thing started with wanting to sleep with someone.

Part of being a proper lady even in the early 1970s, when I went to college, was doing volunteer work. I took up tutoring, primarily because it had a fixed schedule—every Tuesday at three—and the community center where we tutored wasn't too far from the campus. But I guess I should say that going to college in 1971 had a slightly day-after-the-fair quality—Kent State had happened, and everyone was getting tired, tired of fighting. The slogans were beginning to sound just a little bit hollow. I hoped that going out and getting involved with "the people" of Northampton would help me feel less like all the good stuff had already happened.

Cal was the director of the tutoring program at the center, although, at twenty-one, he was only four years older than me.

He had graduated from the University of Massachusetts just the previous summer, where, he later told me, he'd majored in "making trouble for the Man." He actually talked like that. What's worse, I suppose, was that it impressed me. His hair was dark shiny black, almost Asian looking, but he had fair skin and the bluest eyes I'd ever seen. He had grown up dirt-poor Irish in the south of Boston, I found out later. He had six brothers and two sisters and they all had precisely the same lovely coloring and tough way of talking. He was the only one of the lot of them to go to college, the only one of the lot of them to disown the racism he'd been taught since he was a child. I found this all terribly romantic. He made it clear he was interested in me from the start. He had this little sort of appraising half-smile on his face the whole time we talked. And he did this thing, this thing of holding my hand for just a few seconds longer than necessary. I don't remember exactly what he said, but I can still remember how that sent a shudder through me, right between my legs. He was always able to get to me that way, almost up until the end.

So that was part of it. The other part, the part that's stayed, was how it felt to teach, like I was opening a door. My first student was a little Puerto Rican girl named Concepción. She was seven, but she really couldn't read at all. I spent two frustrating weeks with her, weeks where either she or I ended up in tears when we were done before I finally talked to Cal about it. I went to his office after our third meeting. "Cal, I think I need another student. Concepción and I just aren't getting anywhere, and I don't know what to do."

He leaned back in his chair, appraising me. "So you're giving up already?"

"I'm not giving up, but she's trying so hard and I'm really confused. She's just a little kid and I can't help her." Furious, I felt my own eyes fill with tears.

"Hey, oh, hey . . ." Cal's voice softened and he got out of his chair and came around the desk to sit on the front edge, closer to me. "I've been watching you with her, and I think you're a really good teacher. You're so patient. Why don't we meet a few times and work on some things that might help her a little." He paused, then said softly, "I've been watching you anyway."

I looked up, wiping at my eyes. "You have?"

"I have." He reached out and moved some stray hair behind my ear. His hand rested on my cheek for a moment. Does it sound ridiculous to say that that moment sealed all the rest? I suppose it does. But it did. He was right. I became a better teacher, a good teacher, and I loved it so much. And I loved him so much. When he said we should get married and move to Cleveland, of all places, and teach in the public schools, I followed without another thought. Everything was all tied together in my mind anyway, loving him and loving my students. The years went by, and I kept loving my students. But he didn't let me keep loving him. Sometimes I still wonder what went wrong. You'd think I'd be more at peace with it by now. And I am, in part. But not altogether. I can still remember what his hair felt like under my hands.

The day of the brunch at Helen's dawned bright and sunny. I felt absurdly cheered by the prospect of leaving my house with somewhere social to go. When I lived in Cleveland, every Sunday I would have breakfast with Jane and Hannah, two of the other teachers from John Addams, where I taught. We went to Tommy's on Coventry and had whimsically named eggs and toast and bacon dishes. We talked about the week and our students and our husbands, and they held me together as my marriage fell apart. No matter what had happened that week, I always had the breakfast club. We talk on the phone now, but it's not the same. After Smith, I never thought I would do such a thing, find myself without the company of women. But life sweeps us along. You get married, you chase your ideals, you teach child after child after child, then—boom—you're forty-eight and your daughter is a LUG (lesbian until graduation—or maybe beyond) at your alma mater and you have only one or two female friends and you're teaching at this boys' school. I thought about all this as I showered, the water warm and smooth on my body, sluicing gently down my legs. I had a brief sudden memory of Washington's elegant hands turning the pages of his book. What would those hands look like resting on top of mine as I soaped my thighs? I shook my head and finished my shower briskly. Thoughts like that were a fast train to total despair.

Helen lived alone in a substantial Cape Cod on a quiet, leafy street. Of course, all the streets around here are quiet and leafy, so that wasn't particularly remarkable. She had never married and had, in the way of these things, three cats. Her house, impressively, did not smell. She must have changed the litter box daily, if not more than once a day. Her home was filled with beautiful things, mostly from Africa and South Asia. Fabrics, sculptures, photographs. I was the first to arrive, and I found myself wandering around like a child in a museum, wanting to touch everything. Helen sensed my wonderment and smiled. "I like to spend my summers in places as different from here as I can manage. Good for the soul."

"Helen, I can't believe it. You've been everywhere."

"Not really. Well. Most places in Africa and quite a few in India. Been to Australia only a couple of times. I really love Ghana. Have you ever been?"

"No. I wish."

"Well. Perhaps we'll go sometime—I like to go with a friend. Look, here come the others."

The others were four women on the faculty, all over forty,

clear-eyed and sensibly dressed. The leaves all over Helen's lawn and sidewalk crackled and scuffed loudly as they made their way to the door. They came in with much exclaiming and hugs, and each shook my hand heartily, with warm, steady looks into my eyes. I found myself oddly moved. Their names were Nancy, Laura, Judith, and Joanna. "Between the five of us we've logged about a hundred teaching years," said Helen.

"I beg to differ, Helen," said Nancy, laughing as she shrugged out of her dun-colored barn jacket. "It's more like a hundred and fifty." Everyone laughed, and we walked into the living room together.

There was a beautiful spread on the table—shrimp and cheese sticks and all sorts of tasty snacky things and a bright fire in the fireplace. We settled ourselves onto the sofa and started right in.

"So, Jana, Helen tells me that you used to live in Cleveland. Are you from there?" said Judith, her mouth full of shrimp.

"No. I moved out there after college. Actually, I grew up not far from here. Just a couple of towns over, in Darien."

Judith raised her eyebrows slightly. "Mmm. And did you go to school near here, too?"

"I went to Smith. Class of '74."

Laura shrieked a bit at this. "Hey. I was class of '69." We grinned briefly, but as is usual after these kinds of conversations, there wasn't much more to say. But we didn't need an alma mater in common to feel comfortable. Sitting around eating with a bunch of liberal-minded women about my age, who'd lived on the East Coast most of their lives: we just fit together. Laughed at the same jokes; remembered the same things; valued the same things. I sat, a glass of wine in my hand, looking at my new friends. They filled me in on every little detail they could think of about the school. Who was sleeping with whom, who was infatuated with whom; teachers to avoid; students who were stupid (Max, the boy who'd made the snide remark about "A Good Man

Is Hard to Find," was, as I suspected, an alumni legacy liked only by some equally cocky boys and a few of the dimmer girls from neighboring campuses); students who were smart. I didn't say much, letting the talk wash pleasurably over me. But as the afternoon wound down, I did venture this: "What's the deal with Jerome Washington? Is he attached?"

The four of them exchanged quick looks, then laughed. "Why do you ask?" said Helen.

"Just curious." I had my first moment of defensiveness, which I tried to cover with a joke. "You know how us aging divorcees are."

Helen gave me another of her penetrating looks. "Very funny. You're not the only one who's ever had a marriage end, you know." She paused. "Anyway. He's not attached, but it's my distinct impression that he likes it that way. I'd steer clear if I were you. He seems . . . I don't know . . . murky. Like you could get sucked right in and pulled under if you weren't careful."

"Just trying to learn about my fellow faculty, that's all."

Helen took a long, deliberate sip of her wine. "Uh-huh," she said.

I leaned back on the sofa, trying to recapture the ease I had felt a minute ago and trying to forget this morning's brief fantasy about him. I wasn't really interested. Not that way. Not really at all. The late afternoon light cast gathering shadows across the room, and the fire died down. It would be nice to stay here, bathed in these soft women's voices. Nice to stay here for a while and just not have to move.

4

The Past Is Prologue

I SOMETIMES WONDER what my father would think if he could see me now. It is surprising to me how often I think of him, especially when I consider that I have not seen his face in forty years. I chose not to attend his funeral ten years ago. My mother indicated that it didn't matter to her one way or the other if I went, so I didn't go. He was a hard man. A sharecropper. He would laugh until he cried if he saw these boys here playing at farming, treating cows like household pets. He knew nothing but the hardest work there was, for the least reward imaginable, from sunup to sundown, until the day he died.

When I was young, I would get up with him, walk out on those sticky Georgia mornings to milk the cows and feed and rake and plow and till—all for a red-faced white man whom we saw but once a month and who took every dime we earned. I wanted to love my father, but he didn't allow it. Eventually, I came to accept this.

My mother never did. My father won her when he was young, before the sharecropper's life had eaten the sweetness out of his heart. I have a photograph of them from those days. He is standing with his foot on the running board of a gleaming car that probably belonged to a friend, his trousers creased sharply enough to slice through paper, a fedora set just so on his head. He is smiling the smile of a man with possibilities. My mother is wearing a dress that I imagine is violet, splashed with oversize flowers. She is fifteen, although she looks older. Her efforts at sophistication have paid off everywhere except in the soft, girlish way she regards my father. There she reveals herself all too clearly to be a teenage girl with a crush. Perhaps that's why my father punished her so—he couldn't stand that light in her eyes.

When I was ten, she took the money she had been saving in a coffee can buried underneath the porch and came into the room I shared with my brother, Isaiah. She must have been saving—odds and ends, pennies from cakes she sold, money she filched from my father when he was drunk—for at least eight years. When she came to us, it was the dark middle of the night and the air was cool and filled with the sound of crickets. She whispered to us, "We're leaving. Get your shoes on."

We rode all night on the bus to Chicago, the road grinding away beneath the wheels, the air growing colder. She fed us pieces of fried chicken from a bag she kept on her lap and looked out the window with a fixed expression. I was too astonished to ask a single question. Isaiah, three years younger and more prone to talk, asked a few, but her answers were so monosyllabic that he too stopped talking and sat tensely next to me, his leg pressed into mine. I could not understand our sudden departure. Of course, I had heard my parents fighting bitterly on many nights. But I thought that was what marriage was—a series of barely moderated battles broken by the creaking sighs of bedsprings and soft sobs.

We arrived in Chicago at noon. I had never seen so much

pavement in my life. I finally found my voice. "Mama, where we going now?" I asked. I have worked so hard to lose the accent I had then. But I remember what I sounded like, my voice echoing in the grand spaces of the bus station. I could hear how different it was from the voices all around us, and I began to feel ashamed. Already. The minute we arrived.

"Don't worry, baby. We'll be all right. I got a place for us to go." My mother sounded as foreign and frightened as I did. We had no choice but to follow her. Before we left, I looked at the purposeful commuters all around us, smelled the cold, industrial Chicago air. I looked down at my hands, at the fingernails that were always encrusted with dirt. I curled my hands into loose fists so no one would see.

My mother took us to a small, neatly kept house on the South Side. She introduced us to her sister, my aunt Vivian, whom I had never met. I found out later that she did not approve of my mother's marriage. Because of that, and because of some other long-ago falling out that my mother never saw fit to divulge, we had only minimal contact with her the whole time we lived in Chicago, even though we lived a few miles apart. We spent just a few nights with her, nights I remember vividly—the smell of lavender sachet in every room, the paper flowers and doilies that sprouted from every available surface, Aunt Vivian's eyes that never squarely met Isaiah's or mine.

I remember waking one night to the sound of their voices, first Aunt Vivian's: "I knew you'd end up like this, you married that man. He talked a good game, but now look at you. Up here with two kids and no job. Well, you can stay here another night or two. I'll help you find someplace to go. But you can't stay longer than that. You made your bed. Now you best to settle on down in it."

And my mother's quiet, defeated reply: "I know you right, Vivian. And I thank you for helping us. Don't think I don't appreciate it."

It was only years later that the deference slipped out of her voice when she spoke of her sister, to be replaced by the anger she felt that night and ever after. "Yeah, Viv helped me when I was up against it," my mother said to me once I was an adult. "But I wouldn't trust her for long no fu'ther than I could throw her fat ass. And that's with God as my witness."

With Aunt Vivian's help, she found an inexpensive, ugly apartment and a job cleaning floors in an office building. That done, she began her great work of helping me eradicate every trace of Georgia country soil from not only my manner, but my very spirit. If I said "ain't," she was on me with a hairbrush. If I slipped and let my vowels come out at too leisurely a pace, she was there in an instant, with a single tight look that reminded me to speak more crisply. Her voice and manners drip with the honey and molasses of my childhood until this very day, but she had come to believe, in part correctly, that that was what held her back. She was determined that I would not suffer the same fate. A hundred—no, a thousand times a day she ordered me not to end up like my father. She called him "a no-'count hood with no hope and no sense. Be croppin' for pennies until the day he dies. I wish I'd known how he was gonna end up before we got married. I sure wouldn't have stayed with his butt as long as I did." But sometimes, when I had to get up late at night to use the toilet, I'd see her sitting in the pool of yellow light cast by the one light bulb in our kitchen, gazing at the old photo she later gave me, her gaze gentle and regretful. Those were the only moments I ever saw her betray any softness—moments when she thought I couldn't see her.

We had come to Chicago at a propitious time, the late 1950s, when the Negro communities were just beginning to shift under the weight of the poverty and ignorance that flattened them. It is worse now, I know, but then there was a glimmering, a faint belief that if we just held on and educated ourselves for the days to come, there would be a change. My mother had decided that I would be ready when the change came.

She had found a willing student. Not once did I buck her efforts at changing the way I spoke, cleaning up my language, making sure I did well in school. If anything, I redoubled them. I knew almost from the moment of our arrival that it was incumbent upon me to change. The torment that had made my mother run made me desperate to learn, desperate to wash myself clean of the red clay that I had been born to. Education seemed the surest way to eradicate it. So I gave myself over to learning in every respect that I could.

Isaiah tried, but he had not been chosen. Isaiah was fed and cared for, but always roughly. My mother frequently asked him if he didn't have the sense God gave him. He was slight for his age, with skin the color of milk chocolate and teeth that stayed perfect until he was about fifteen and lost one in a fight. One time, she asked him to take out the trash in her abrupt way, and twenty minutes later, when he still hadn't returned from out front where we took our garbage, she sent me out to look for him. I found him intently watching a crow that had somehow blundered into a vacant lot next door and was hopping from pile of trash to pile of trash. His face was shining when he turned to me. "Jerome, look. Remember the crows back home, how they'd caw so loud? You could hear 'em for miles." He sighed. "It's beautiful, ain't it?"

I grabbed his arm. "Your butt's gonna be beautiful when Mama gets finished with it. What you doing standing out here so long?"

"I dunno. I saw that bird, and then I just couldn't move. It reminded me of all the birds back home. I don't miss Daddy, but I sure do miss it there," he said thoughtfully. My mother gave us both a couple of hard whacks with a hairbrush when we came back in for having taken so long. Isaiah's eyes remained fixed in the middle distance as she hit him. He never cried.

By the time I was twelve, most of my evenings were spent

reading and doing homework. My mother would sit literally at my elbow, her breath soft and rasping through the ill-lit room. I was already well into a kind of reading and study she could not fully comprehend with her fourth-grade education, but she sat near me as though her mere presence would spur me to greater achievement. I could feel the weight of her desire with every page I turned. One such evening, Isaiah came into the room clutching a math text, a hopeful look on his face. He approached us as though from a great distance. "Jerome, you did fractions last year, right?" he asked, his voice hesitant and shy.

I looked up to reply, reached out for the book to offer some help. My mother slapped my hand so sharply that tears came to my eyes as I jerked it back, then she turned to Isaiah, her voice like sprayed acid. "Boy, don't you be bothering me or your brother with your dumb-ass questions. He's got important work to do. He cain't be studyin' your little homework that he already did. And probably better than you'll ever do it anyway." She turned back to my book as though no one else was in the room. The only sound was our mingled inhalations and exhalations, Isaiah and I each trying not to cry. After a few minutes, Isaiah walked out of the room, tears running down his face. He did not ask for help again.

It was after that incident that he began to slip away. I do not think that my mother ever understood it. He stopped paying attention in class. By the time he was fourteen he had stopped going to school, except to see friends and hang out on the corner harassing girls as they entered. He came home late, when he came home at all, stinking of smoke and cheap wine. When we were little we shared a bed, and he always smelled like home to me—Dixie Peach pomade and the ashy scent of red clay. But now I barely spoke to him, tried to avoid him in the bathroom. Stayed out of his way as I scuttled from school to my after-school job to home, where he rarely was anymore. For a little while, my mother yelled at him about his behavior, her voice a shrill bullet to the brain. Then she just stopped. She watched his comings and goings with dull eyes and no longer asked him any questions. He was arrested my sophomore year of college for holding up a candy store. He got $35 and a Snickers bar for his trouble. He also got two years in jail. He was killed just a year after his release while participating in a similarly stupid crime—another robbery. There was nothing I could do.

I suppose it seems strange that I did not defy my mother. I suppose it seems strange that I made no effort to save my gentle brother. I suppose it might even seem strange that she would be so cruel to her own flesh and blood. But who had ever been kind to her? Not her husband. Not her sister. Not even her children, really. She never taught us that skill. She had no idea of kindness. If she had ever craved it, she had to put that craving aside in order to do what was necessary to get away from my father and pilot us through our difficult lives. One time, many years later, after it had become clear she could no longer live alone and she had been moved into a Chicago nursing home, I asked her if she remembered Isaiah asking for help with his homework that time. At first she denied it, but then her eyes focused and became clear. "Sure I remember. I remember now. You were busy. You were always so busy, and you didn't need him botherin' you. He was just a little boy, come peckin' 'round botherin' you all the time. He needed to learn to make his own way. Like you did."

She paused for so long that I thought she had drifted away and was going to stop speaking altogether, as she sometimes did. "Like I did," she finally said. "Didn't nobody ever help me. Ain't nobody you can count on for long. Boy just needed to learn that." She looked out the tiny window of her room into the gray sky. She said nothing more. For a moment, I felt the same grief and indecision that I had felt all those years ago. But the moment passed. She was done with me, I could see, so I left.

Cicero said, "Our character is not so much the product of race and heredity as of those circumstances by which nature forms our habits, by which we are nourished and live." Circumstance and nature had formed my mother as surely as it has formed me. If it has not formed great kindness or openness within us—well, those are not the only virtues. And they are, after all, the ones that cost us the most.

When I was in college, I became involved with a Radcliffe student named Jennifer Hargraves. She had skin the color of milk and strawberries and long, curly blond hair that always made me think of honey. Her hand on my arm could make me lose my ability to think, a smile rob me of breath. We met through our mutual involvement with a campus organization called the Association of African and Afro-American Students. It was colloquially known as "Afro," and its primary purpose was the creation of an Afro-American Studies Department at Harvard. Jennifer was one of very few white students and one of very few women active in the group—after 1968, the group basically cast out any white members, but in 1967 things had not yet become so divided. It is incredible to me now that I should have spent my time in such a manner. But I was younger then. What is youth, if not a time to try out other identities to see how they suit one? In any event, we were alone in the office one evening engaged in the endless task of mimeographing flyers to be posted around and passed out on the campus. I turned the handle as she fed the paper in over and over again. After a quiet half hour of this, she suddenly reached out and covered my hand with hers. I looked up, startled. No words came immediately to mind. But she spoke after a few seconds. "I've been wanting to do that since I met you." Then she leaned in and kissed me quickly. "I've been wanting to do that, too." I was dumbstruck, both by her boldness and by joy. I had entertained similar thoughts but had no notion of acting on them—she seemed as far off and unattainable as one of the planets. I was a child of the South, after all, even though I'd been in Chicago for some time. A white woman didn't even seem safe to dream about. So I was struck speechless.

"Well, aren't you going to say anything?" she said after I remained silent for another short time.

I stepped forward and kissed her deeply. "No," I said.

We were inseparable after that. We spent a lot of time in my dorm room or hers when our roommates were off studying or in class. Despite the liberality of the Harvard campus, it was still a time when interracial couples were rare. We didn't mind staying in. I came to know her body better than I knew my own, better than I have ever known another's flesh. When one is young, every inch of the loved one's skin is a new joy, a new source of pleasure or a pain so sweet that it becomes pleasurable. I could not keep my hands out of her hair. I'd never felt anything like it, elastic yet soft and slightly silken—I spent hours brushing it, wrapping it around my fingers when we were hiding out in her room, supposedly studying but really just trying to touch each other as much as possible.

The first time we made love, I remember we were both very shy, easing out of our clothes without looking at each other, as though we were readying for a shower alone in our rooms. I remember that the first thing I touched was her hair, then her hip-bones, delicately ridged under freckled skin. I remember how warm it was, the feel of her hand on the back of my neck, and that it was over very quickly. I remember knowing that I had crossed some bridge. That I could be killed for what I was doing in some states, my hands all over this white woman. That made it all the sweeter, more intense. When we were done, she looked at me steadily for a long time, then leaned her head down and licked my arm. I laughed, a little uncomfortable. "What are you doing?" I said.

She turned her face to me. "I just wanted to know if you taste as sweet as you look. Like chocolate." She smiled. I smiled back. She could say anything to me then. Nothing she could do would offend me. I absorbed it all. I was utterly hers, devoted, in the way of young men. In the moments we were together, I silently made my pledge. She, however, did not.

A few weeks after we made love for the first time, and four months after our first kiss, I met her, as we had arranged, at a small dark local café, one we frequented. But this time, when I arrived, she was still wearing her coat, hunched tensely over the table. "Jerome," she said, "there's something I've got to tell you. I . . . I mean, we can't . . . It's best if we don't see each other anymore. There's . . ." She trailed off, sweeping her hand fiercely over her eyes.

"There's what?" I said. My voice sounded tinny and loud to me.

"Look, I just think we have to stop seeing each other. I . . . you're taking this a lot more seriously than I am. I can see it when you look at me. I just can't." She got up and walked away.

She never came to another meeting of Afro, and when I saw her on campus, she would not meet my gaze. My friend Vaughn counseled me, "Man, what'd you expect? She was just looking for a little dark meat. I don't think she cares about what we're trying to do one way or the other." So that was that. There was no one else I could turn to.

I was alone after Jennifer left me. Not long afterward, I wrote in a journal I kept at the time, "She's killing me. Why is she killing me?" Occasionally I spotted her on campus and I would begin to shake as though palsied at the sight of her. I do not think she had any idea of the effect she had on me. Vaughn was probably right. I was simply an experiment for her, a walk on the wild side, as the slang of the time would have it. Imagine me, a walk on the wild side.

I threw myself into my studies with a dizzying intensity. I did not dare return to Afro. In fact, I turned as far away from it as I could. It was after Jennifer that I began my study of Roman civilization. It started as these things often do—thoughtlessly. I had seen photographs of some statuary that I liked, had some idle notion that studying the classics would somehow make me less vulnerable both academically and personally. Serious study of the classics was viewed as an oddity by most at this time, particularly by a Negro. But perhaps that's what I liked about it—it fed my newfound need for solitude. And it wasn't long before it became a passion with me—the clarity and the force of the thought. The organization and rigor of the civilization. Rome at her best seemed to me to be everything that America hoped to be at her best. And wasn't that what we had been working toward, after all? When I tried to make this analogy to my classmates, I was met with derision. But I didn't care. I was already growing used to being alone, even as it pained me. And then one day, doing some reading for class, I found these words: "In fact, the whole passion ordinarily termed love (and heaven help me if I can think of any other term to apply to it) is of such exceeding triviality that I see nothing that I think comparable with it." Cicero said that. That settled it for me. I longed to be so untouched. To possess the clarity that lay within those words. Sometimes I would recite them in my head as if they would save me.

I never talk about those days, the late 1960s. I know the young men here could not begin to understand what it was like, the belief that every action had some larger significance. The knowledge that being in college wasn't some kind of birthright, but it was saving you from death in some far off-jungle. Or in my case, additionally, from being run down in some southern street like a dog. That was the other reason I took my studies seriously. They were, literally, saving my life. And I found, as I went further into my studies of Latin, that the clarity there was restful. These were men who knew what they wanted. Who were never afraid. They had standards that protected them.

Unlike everyone else, it seemed. First there was my brother, throwing away what little remaining potential he had for change and a candy bar. Then a year later Dr. King was killed, and then

Bobby Kennedy, and then I knew. I knew that the work of protesting and leafleting and picketing was pointless. That while much had been accomplished, no more would be accomplished this way. I cut my full, aggressive Afro to a modest length and girded my loins with knowledge. I began to read more widely in the classics. I posted on my bulletin board the words of Cicero that I write on the blackboard at the beginning of each year: "To be ignorant of what occurred before you were born is to remain always a child. For what is the worth of human life, unless it is woven into the life of our ancestors by the records of history?" I didn't date anyone. My hands were the only ones to touch me the rest of my college career. And on graduation day, as my mother sat weeping tears of joy in the audience, Isaiah already in jail, I made a quiet vow to myself that I would make change through my own superiority. That was how I would overcome.

I must admit, though, that I've become less absolute about some things as I've grown older. After Jennifer left me, I vowed never to become involved with a woman again. Well, that hasn't proved possible or even practical. A man is but a man, after all. I've not been celibate from that day to this. There are those at Chelsea who think I have been. There are those at Chelsea who think that women aren't my cup of tea at all—that my interest in Rome extends to that predilection as well. Neither belief is true. I don't concern myself with petty whispering, but I have been discreet. I keep my encounters off campus and away from the school. When I was younger there were some women at teachers conferences I attended alone. There were even a couple of occasions where a deeper connection began to form—a woman I met at the library in town, a Negro like me, who was also interested in classical literature. But she was more interested in our marriage. And that I would not do. I remembered the look on my mother's face when she spoke of my father. In the last few years, it has become easier simply to purchase sexual companionship when the need (or is it only a desire?) became too great. This is not as difficult to manage as you might think, even in a small town like this one. While I was initially uncomfortable with the idea, I came to prefer the simplicity of it—the illegality part of the excitement. There was no danger of entanglement. Just clean, clear, simple flesh upon flesh. And my own cool, empty bed in the morning. I honestly thought that I had put it all behind me, the noise and sorrow of desire, the wish to talk to a woman who might take a genuine interest in what I had to say. My life, my flesh, my blood, were in my boys. Nowhere else. It was simpler that way.

So I was quite surprised when I found myself replaying my encounter with Ms. Hansen over and over again in my mind. Her direct gaze. The shock of having someone come up to me and speak in the cafeteria. No one ever does that. I am left alone. But I wasn't angry. Her hand was extended to me, her gray green eyes gazing at me directly. She smelled faintly of some grass-scented perfume, and her long dark hair was shot through with gray. She was probably about my age, perhaps a bit younger. As she extended her hand, I saw that she wore several silver-and-stone rings, which caught the light.

A few days after she introduced herself, she came up to me in the faculty lounge and said, "I noticed that you usually eat lunch alone. I wonder if I could join you sometime. Today, maybe?"

"Why?" It was only after I spoke that I realized how impolite and peculiar that must have sounded. But she laughed—a surprising, musical sound. "Because I want to ask you a bit about how you think Chelsea works. Because I want to hear a bit of the history of the place from someone who knows it from . . . from an unusual perspective." She paused, then grinned. "Because maybe you'll share your pudding with me." I don't think she meant this last to be flirtatious, only humorous. But I felt a slight swoop in my stomach, a dangerous tightening I hadn't felt in years.

"Maybe I will," I said.

We were both silent after that. I was stunned by my own boldness. I couldn't begin to guess what she might be thinking. She just studied me briefly, a thoughtful look on her face. "Let's go, then," she said. We walked out of the lounge together.

"I've been a teacher for fifteen years, but never anyplace like this," she said, her voice frank and a little loud. "I lived in Cleveland for all that time, teaching in the public schools. It was . . . it was fulfilling in some ways, but it was tough, too. Always having to scratch. And the kids needed so much. I got divorced about four years ago—I have a daughter who's eighteen. She's finding herself, I guess." She laughed a bit, thinly. "She goes to my alma mater. Smith. But it's so different from when I was there. There are almost no black students. And a lesbian affair is practically a requirement of graduation." She laughed. "I have no idea why I'm telling you all this." But she didn't look particularly embarrassed. I was startled but charmed. I guess I should say. "Anyway," she concluded, " so that's me. What's your story? As much of it as you care to tell, anyway."

We had talked, as she asked to, of the school's history, the pros and cons of an all-male education, our views of the headmaster and various students. She was bright and full of sharply stated opinions. She used her hands constantly, pushing her hair back, cutting her food with quick, deft motions, pausing to brush something away from the corner of her mouth. I found that I was slightly discomfited by the more personal tone the conversation had taken but didn't want to appear too flustered. "Oh, there's not much to tell. I've taught here for . . . oh, more than twenty years. I enjoy the boys, the rigorousness of it. I help with what I can— the debate team, assistant coaching on the cross-country team. But I lead a quiet life. Never married. No children. I run a bit— don't compete, though."

"Long-distance or short?"

"Long, I suppose. I do about six or seven miles a day, more on Saturdays. I take Sundays off."

"Slacker." A slight smile. I busied myself with my food, feeling awkward. She looked at her watch, then spoke again. "It's nearly time to get back to class. But I want to ask you one more thing. Are you a Motown fan?"

"What?"

"I know it's an odd thing to ask, but we're about the same age, and I'd swear I heard you whistling 'Just My Imagination' when you were looking at the bulletin board before I spoke to you." She laughed. "I'm being silly, I guess."

"No, actually, you're not." Heat suffused my face. "I happen to have an . . . an extensive—you might even say exhaustive—collection of Motown records. The vinyl, not the CDs."

"Of course." She was smiling.

"I'm a bit shocked you picked up on it, though. It's not something I talk about. It . . . it doesn't really go with the way I'm perceived."

"Yes, well, things aren't always what they seem, are they?"

"No, I don't imagine that they are." She brushed some stray hair behind her ear. A sweet, unconscious gesture. I suppose it was then that I began to lose my way.

The air had that fresh crispness that is peculiar to fall in Connecticut as I made my way out to the athletic fields beyond the school where the cross-country team practiced that afternoon. My encounter with Ms. Hansen still flitted through my mind periodically, but with some effort, I could swat it away. So I did. I drew great breaths of the air and turned my mind to the coaching ahead. What I love about running is the same thing I love about Latin—its clarity and solitude. The slow ache of muscles, the sound of one's own breath in one's ears, the sweet moment when there is nothing on one's mind but the rhythm of one's feet against the ground. That moment when you are only running, nothing else, not flesh or thought or body; only speed. I got into coaching under duress—the head coach, Jonathan Sasser, found out about my running and drafted me. But I have come to genuinely enjoy it. Today was our first practice of the year—I was anxious to see who had come out for the team.

The boys skipped and shifted in nervous clusters, jogging their knees high and occasionally dashing out of the group. I could hear someone's laugh carried on the wind as I approached them. Jonathan was already there, rummaging around in his gym bag, probably for his roster and a stopwatch, but really waiting for me. He was the closest thing I had to a friend on the faculty, though he was a good ten years younger and led a very different life. He had three young children and a cheerful, harried air. He was never cautious around me. So many of the other faculty members treated me as if I were some sort of dangerous explosive. Walk wide here. We don't know what's going to happen. I had adjusted to that sort of reaction and saw little reason to change my habits on account of it, but I have to admit, I enjoyed Jonathan's easy jocularity to a degree that surprised me.

"Hey, Jerome," he said as he stood up, "good to see you. We got a nice crop of boys out here this year." His hand, as he shook mine, was rough and dry, but warm.

Some of last year's stars—Rob Hanrahan, Ben Gould, Max Harrison—were all there and greeted me with distracted waves and "How ya doin', Mr. Washington." A number of freshmen were there as well, among them the Bryson boy. He eyed me warily as he stretched his quadriceps muscles. Jonathan called the boys to attention.

"Okay, guys. I'm Mr. Sasser, and this is Mr. Washington, the assistant coach. It's a new season. We're going to start with a clean slate, just go for a half mile to warm up, see where you guys are. We're even gonna jog it with you—though that's not gonna happen every practice." He laughed. "Okay, then. Let's go." We broke into an easy lope down past the football field.

One thing that became clear to me after I had taught at Chelsea for a while is that for the most part my students were likely to grow up and lead lives as successful but also as mundane as those of their parents. That made it all the more thrilling when I saw something extraordinary in a boy. Watching the Bryson boy run was such a moment. He was possessed of a fluidity and easy grace that, frankly, I'd never seen in a high school runner. His breathing was ragged, but he was out of condition and had not been coached before—that would be easily rectified. He pulled smoothly to the front of the pack, ahead even of Hanrahan, who was at least two years his senior. He looked as though he could go on forever. Jonathan and I shot each other a look, and a big grin spread across his face. I could not help smiling myself. I admire excellence, even when it shows up in the most unlikely of places. We were running a loop, and Bryson was the first to arrive back where we had begun. He bent over, gasping for air. Jonathan and I ran up to him and Jonathan spoke first.

"Rashid, have you ever run cross-country before?"

Gasp. Gasp. "No, I just . . . I thought it would be fun."

Jonathan clapped him on the back. "Well, you got a stride like nobody's business, son. I'm mighty pleased to have you. Mighty pleased."

I said nothing but smiled and touched his thin back as well. He looked up and smiled uncertainly. "Welcome aboard," I said. He nodded and bent back over, attempting once more to catch his breath. My hand rested on his back, which was damp with a boy's sweat. His breath was ragged. My throat felt oddly tight. Neither of us spoke.

5

School Days

IT DIDN'T TAKE long for Rashid to become familiar with the routines of life at the Chelsea school but he sometimes thought that he would never become entirely comfortable with them. Up at 7:00, breakfast en masse at 7:30, morning chapel at 8:15. That lasted forty-five minutes, although it more often felt like ninety. First Mr. Fox would talk, usually about how great Chelsea was. Even when that wasn't his exact subject, it was the subtext. He stood at the podium, his iron gray hair cropped closely to his head, wearing khakis, a rumpled jacket, and, usually, a tie with a pattern on it that looked dignified from a distance but when you got closer turned out to be Kermit the Frog or Tweety and Sylvester or something like that. He talked about being a man among men, or what some guy a hundred years ago did, or he asked them to think about some head-crushing subject like the meaning of love or truth or honesty. He used his hands a lot and spoke in sentences so short and quick that his speeches resembled machine-gun fire in their rapidity and monotony. He was so different from the only other speakers Rashid knew well: the preachers from when he was still going to church, with their rolling cadences and the way they ran—literally ran, sweat flying off them—back and forth in front of the congregation, trying to get them on their feet, to get them singing, to get them to feel the spirit. Rashid never got the ghost the way some of the old ladies did, crying and falling out, but he used to love the singing and the music and the joy. But that was before.

Sometimes Rashid had to fight off sleep during chapel, but he never had the nerve to be as openly bored as Gerald. More often than not, he could see that Gerald had sneaked a *Spawn* or *Batman* comic book into his notebook or a textbook and was reading it quietly as Mr. Fox rattled on.

"Ain't you worried about getting busted?" Rashid said to him once.

Gerald looked surprised. "Not really. So I'll get the big talking-to if I do. It's not something they'll throw me out over."

Gerald had told Rashid repeatedly to lighten up, but to little result. The schoolwork at Chelsea was so much more dense and intricate than anything he'd ever done before. He felt that eyes were on him every second, here, back home, everywhere. Everything was weighing on him.

He couldn't believe how much he didn't know. At Banneker, he'd done all right—had good enough grades to get on the honor roll and won the praise of his teachers. But now—it seemed as though he'd learned almost nothing. In history class the other day, there was this huge discussion of the discovery of America—did Christopher Columbus find it or not, and what changes did that bring about—and he didn't know one single name of any of the other explorers. Vasco da something. Magellan. He'd just been taught about Columbus from the old, falling-apart history books they had at school. It was like that with everything. Jokes he didn't get because he didn't know who some snowboarder was. Seeing a picture of this bearded German guy, Freud, and being the only one who didn't recognize him. It was all making him so tired. It seemed he would never get enough sleep again.

After Mr. Fox's speech, a student had to give a chapel talk. Rashid generally perked up for these, mostly because next semester he was going to have to do one. All of the freshmen would. What you had to do was pick a topic that you found interesting and do research and then get up and talk about whatever it was for ten minutes in front of the whole school. Rashid supposed it had to do with that "man among men" stuff they were always talking about.

At 9:00, after chapel, classes started. The movement of these boys through the hallways was very different from what Rashid was used to. Back when he was at Banneker, class-changing time was a study in barely controlled chaos. Security guards watched closely as the kids walked, tumbled, and ran through the halls. Sometimes a phalanx of them surrounded two fighting students, but more often they just stood stern watch, making sure nothing happened. The assumption was that the kids couldn't be trusted. Some lived up to that assumption; others tried to duck it, act like they didn't know it was there; some, like Rashid, spent an inordinate amount of time pushing against it, trying to show that they were different and not get beat up or teased or ranked on for it. In any event, it always seemed as though a disaster had been narrowly avoided by the time everybody got to class.

But here it was like everybody was running on invisible tracks. They laughed and horsed around but the air didn't crackle, there was no sense of imminent trouble. No one shouted, and the word *nigger* was never heard. It was very quiet. If he'd thought about it a little longer, he might have realized that at least some of the relative calm came from not having any girls to scuffle for and impress, but their absence was a subject Rashid found difficult to contemplate. He thought about girls all the time whether they were there or not. Perhaps not having them around focused the mind, as Mr. Fox seemed always to imply, but Rashid found that it primarily focused the mind on not having them around. Back home, a lot of guys had already slept with one or two girls by ninth grade. Some of the girls his age in his neighborhood were already swelling with their first pregnancies, their faces round and grimly accepting. He didn't want to end up like that—with some girl and her baby on his conscience. And before Kofi died, his mother really wasn't having it—always telling both of them to stay away from those fast little girls who would trap them. None of that kept him from thinking about thighs the color of raw honey and soft whispers in his ear. Sometimes he woke up startled in the middle of the night, feeling as though he'd just been kissing someone whose face was already fading even as his eyes opened, his hands already between his legs. His years of sharing a room with Kofi were paying off in this department: he was good at getting it over with quickly and quietly. And Gerald had pictures of all kinds of girls over his bed. Not a day went by that he didn't make some joke about it. So Rashid figured he knew the score.

Still and all, he hadn't anticipated what it would be like to actually live with so many people. Waiting for the shower in the morning. Watching Gerald cut his toenails at night. Having to talk all the time, with people he not only didn't know, but who didn't even know the likes of him. One time, he was in the bathroom after a shower, twisting his dreads up one at a time with oil, and another freshman, Tony Hoge, just stared at him.

"I always wondered how black people got their hair to do that," said Tony.

"Well, now you know," Rashid said evenly.

"You just leave them like that, huh? What is that, gel?"

"No, it's a kind of oil. Helps your hair lock." Rashid felt his stomach contracting into a ball.

Tony looked in the mirror at his fine straight brown hair. "Wild. Well, see you around."

"Yeah." After that Rashid did his hair in his room. He didn't tell Gerald about the incident. He probably wouldn't have been fazed.

That was the thing about Gerald. He wasn't scared. He knew who Freud was. He was at ease at the dinner table. He liked Rashid, but he wasn't like him. Like the other day. Gerald, Rashid, and Nate, another black guy who, like Gerald, had grown up in relative affluence, were all sitting together at dinner, groaning over how much homework they had to do; Gerald and Nate with the good-natured confidence that characterized most of their conversations; Rashid with some genuine panic that he tried his best to hide. Anyway, they were just talking, and Gary Duggan and Dave Steele, two white football jocks, came up and sat down with them. Without listening at all to the conversation that had been going on, Dave leaned over to Gerald and said, "Yo, my man, what is *up* with the Knicks this year? They suck."

"I don't know, *my man*," replied Gerald, a slight edge in his voice. "Soccer's really my game. Listen, did you start any of the reading for European history yet?"

And thus the conversation segued smoothly back to what they'd been talking about in the first place. Rashid sat through the rest of the meal silent. Nate headed to the library after dinner, and Rashid finally spoke as he and Gerald walked through the approaching darkness to their dorm. "Gerald, man, don't you feel like the brother from another planet around here sometimes? I mean, what was that guy doing? Trying to talk to you about basketball when we weren't even on that. Does he think basketball is all we think about?"

Gerald laughed shortly. "Him? He's just a jarhead. Thinks it gives him some kind of street cred to talk like that to an actual black person. You can't let a guy like that get to you. Some of 'em's cool. Some of 'em's ain't. Got to deal with all of 'em. You know?"

"I guess," said Rashid.

Most of the time with Gerald, he was more open, more himself, but there were things he didn't say. School had already been in session a month, and they'd had the requisite "Do you have brothers and sisters?" conversation, but when Gerald had asked him if he had siblings, Rashid had simply said, "No," and busied himself straightening out a drawer.

"You're lucky, man," said Gerald. "My sister drives me just about out of my mind."

At that comment, Rashid almost told Gerald about Kofi, but the burning in his throat made it impossible to speak. So he still hadn't said anything. He thought a lot about that conversation he'd had with Kofi—when Kofi told him that he didn't believe in Jesus anymore and how school was making him question everything. He hadn't understood it at the time; it made more sense to him now. It was like standing in quicksand but not being able to call out— everyone had to think that the ground beneath his feet was solid.

His parents rarely called. Rashid called them every other week or so, collect. He usually spoke to his mother, who quietly conveyed *hellos* from his father. It would have been less expensive for them to call him, but every time his mother would comment on the cost and promise to call the next time, and every time she didn't. In the old days, his mother never would have kept doing that— she used to watch every dime like it was going to be her last. Rashid felt that he had to keep talking to her, to them, or they would disappear altogether. The conversations were filled with long pauses even when he tried to tell her stuff that he was excited about:

"Ma, I'm running cross-country. I've got one of the best times on the team."

"Is that right?"

"Yeah."

"Well, don't let it keep you from your schoolwork. What's the weather like up there?"

"Cold."

"Well, make sure you button up that coat. Work going okay?"

"It's a lot of it, but yeah, I'm getting it."

"Good. Your daddy and I, we knew you could. You a smart boy. Just like Kofi was . . ." Her voice trailed off. She made some reference to Kofi every time they spoke, and every time, it seemed to render her mute with sorrow.

Sometimes Rashid wanted to say, "Well, I'm the one who's doing it, Mama. I'm alive, goddammit, and I'm fucking doing it. It's kicking my ass, but I'm doing it." Sometimes he just wished he was a little boy again and could go crying to her and she'd hug him. Sometimes he felt numb. But all he said was, "Yeah, Ma. I know."

They didn't send him anything. He didn't ask for anything. But he would have liked to go to his mailbox one day and find the slip that meant he had a package to pick up. One with chocolate and clean socks, like the ones that Gerald got periodically. Or with a brand-new sweater that cost $250 if it cost a dime. Jonah Adams got that. They all seemed to accept it as a matter of course, that your parents might drive you crazy but you would get stuff from them, talk to them once a week, feel a part of the family, even though you weren't living at home anymore. Just like they all seemed to take it for granted that they deserved to be there, that Chelsea had, in fact, bestowed on them some special characteristic that was theirs and theirs alone. That it wasn't all just luck.

He was loaded down with these thoughts as he walked out of the dorm one morning. Gerald had just gotten yet another care package (what an expression, "care package"; where was his package of care?), and while he'd generously shared some of his Milky Ways, it didn't brighten Rashid's mood any. It was mid-October, and the air had that insistent coolness that tells you winter is not far off, not yet uncomfortable but undeniable. The grass had a dull, brownish cast dimming its lushness, and the trees were bare and angular. A few kids sat on the wall that ringed the main academic building, their puffy coats open, trying not to look cold. The sun was hard on their faces, their bright hair. Rashid felt himself to be some sort of small, dark foreigner, a cabbie, perhaps, an absence in their midst. He wished he had English class before Latin. He liked Ms. Hansen.

It was funny with Mr. Washington. The ease that he had assumed would quickly grow up between them simply hadn't appeared. Between cross-country and Latin, he saw the man all the time, too. But he didn't feel close to him—talking to him was like dancing to music that was a little bit off the beat. You could keep going, but it didn't feel quite right. It was odd, too, because Rashid was used to teachers wanting to help him. Like Ms. Havens back at Banneker. If it wasn't for them, neither he nor Kofi would have ever even heard of the schools that they ended up attending. But Mr. Washington—there wasn't any of that "We're brothers alone here" feeling that he'd hoped he'd have. Especially in Latin.

Cross-country was a little better—mostly because he was really good at it. He relished the speed of it, the few moments when he wasn't thinking, only using his body—but he wished he wasn't laboring so under the weight of what Mr. Sasser and Mr. Washington wanted. He had always liked to run—the wind against his face, the pound pound pound of his feet. But back home there was always a stoplight or a missing manhole cover or nowhere to go. Banneker sure didn't have a team. So he never thought of running as a thing you could do. When he first went out for the team here, he thought he was going to fall out on that first day. He could hardly breathe after the first half mile. But they kept telling him he was good. And he started passing people in practice all the time. The first meet was in a couple of days. He was nervous. Everyone would be watching him.

He worked hard on his Latin assignments, and sometimes he had moments where he actually found himself enjoying the effort of translating, turning one set of words into another; but his papers always came back covered with a sea of red marks and comments like "Try harder, Mr. Bryson" and "Are you sure about this?" Of course he wasn't sure—he didn't know Latin. But it seemed to him that a supposed brother could have made more of an effort to help him out. He was trying. And Washington wasn't helping him a damn bit. He started to sit in class with his feet planted apart, ready for a fight, the way some of the guys back at Banneker always sat.

The other thing that was getting to him was that Washington was very slow to call on him in class. At first Rashid thought he might be imagining it, but after a while he decided to truly put it to the test. He raised his hand every time a question was asked, whether he knew the answer or not. But Washington did not call on Rashid one time. He'd even call on known dummies like Jack Carlson and Todd Rich, who received brisk corrections after their inevitable wrong answers. Rashid would have been wrong on one thing, but he knew some of that other stuff. He knew it. But Washington seemed determined to call only on white boys. What was up with that?

He went up to Washington's desk after class. The man was standing there whistling through his teeth as he gathered up his papers. It sounded as though it might be that old Temptations song, "My Girl." Rashid's heart was pounding, but the fury he carried with him now made his voice even and calm.

"Mr. Washington, can I talk to you for a minute?" he said. He was tall enough to look straight into the older man's eyes.

"Certainly, Mr. Bryson. What's on your mind?" His eyes were guileless as he looked up. He seemed to think nothing was amiss.

"Well, I was just wondering. I was just wondering if you can see me all right from where I sit."

Washington furrowed his brow. "Obviously, Mr. Bryson, I wear glasses, but they correct any problems I have with my vision. I can see you. What would make you ask something like that?"

Rashid took a deep breath. He felt his hands curl lightly into fists. "Sir, it seems as though you never see me to call on me. I raise my hand to give the answer, and you don't seem to see me." He struggled to keep the rage from making his voice ragged, his hands from rising to sweep the papers off the desk.

Washington spoke evenly. "I assure you, Mr. Bryson, that you register quite well in my sight. I'm sorry if I've given you another impression."

"I just wanted to make sure. I want to participate in this class."

"That's good to know, Mr. Bryson. Thank you for bringing this to my attention."

Rashid walked out, a roaring in his ears. He went into the bathroom, his breath starting to rasp. Miraculously, the room was empty. Rashid went quickly to a stall, and after double-checking to make sure no one else was around, started slamming his fist into the door. *Fuck. Fuck. Fuck. Fuck you, motherfucker.* He didn't know how long he was in there, only that his breath was ragged and his hand sore before he was done. It was almost time for cross-country practice. Washington didn't have any trouble seeing him there. Was he visible only when he was running?

Rashid was usually nervous before practice, but not today. His confrontation with Washington had left him both drained and focused. He stretched, and, with no particular feeling at all, strode around the edge of the soccer field where the cross-country team warmed up. He did not, however, speak to Washington, only to Mr. Sasser. They had to do wind sprints first—ten of them. Rashid won every time, enjoying it, not having to think: the moment of tension before the start, the suddenness of beginning, feeling that his heart was going to pop out of his chest before he was finished, his legs about to burst, and then one final push—he'd won again. Washington and Mr. Sasser always told them that they weren't racing during the sprints, but the boys knew different. Max Harrison, who was in Rashid's English class and had been the undisputed king of the cross-country team before Rashid's arrival, looked more annoyed after each sprint. Rashid pretended that he didn't notice. Once they were finished with sprints and the coaches sent them on the day's long run, each boy was too preoccupied with just getting through it.

But in the locker room after practice, as Rashid took off his running stuff, he heard Harrison at the lockers on the other side from him, talking to one of the guys he hung around with—Ben Gould, it sounded like. "You know, the way Bryson runs, it's just natural with him," he said. "I mean, he's fast, yeah, but aren't they all like that? You know, running from the cops and guns and all that shit."

They both laughed, stupid har-de-har-har sounds. Rashid's breath turned to glass in his throat. There was a moment when he could see himself going around the lockers, slamming his fist into those stupid faces, roaring obscenities that began with their names. But if he got into a fight, he'd be out of this place in about a second, just another ghetto mistake. He rested his head against the cool metal of the locker door, grinding until the pain blocked out all other feeling. His eyes were hot. He swallowed past the lump in his throat. He wasn't going to get kicked out. Not for them. And not for Washington. After a while, all he could hear was the sound of his own breath. Maybe that was enough.

6

Revelations

I WAS A LITTLE surprised when Jerome told me he was a runner. He seemed as though the life of the body wouldn't interest him very much. But after he told me, I began to notice a certain kind of muscular grace in his walk. I found that my eyes would follow him a bit when I saw him around the campus. Nothing heavy. My eyes were just drawn in his direction.

It was odd, feeling this. The thing about looking at men, once you're divorced, is the ever-present thought *Could this lead to something?* When you're married, if you're faithful, you might look, but you know you can't touch. You just stop at a certain point—maybe you go home and make love to your husband with a little extra gusto for a while, but then you open your eyes and it's still him and his hair is the same and his breath is the same and his skin is the same and your fantasy softens and fades away like an old drawing. I don't know what it would be like to have been unfaithful—Cal did, which was part of the problem.

Caitlin. Can you believe that was her name? It's like some kind of younger other-woman joke. In second-rate novels, they always have those girlish names like Tiffany or Anique or Caitlin. She was from a big Irish-Catholic family, like him. They didn't seem to feel too much of that famous Catholic guilt once they began their affair, though—not enough to stop them, anyway. He met her in a pottery class he was taking—I used to love that he was always learning something new, usually something with his hands. He was a skilled potter, and he tried his hand at painting, though he didn't like it much. Who knew he'd meet a twenty-eight-year-old earth mother in this second-level class and use those hands on her? At first I thought we could work it out—things had been rocky between us as Sarah grew up and became more independent, but we still laughed sometimes. We still made love. Sometimes it felt as though there was a wide, cold river between us, but I could still see him. It felt like one we could ford. And then he came home one night some weeks after his first confession and my tears and angry questions and his guilty, evasive replies. His hands were shaking, and his eyes were red-rimmed. He told me that he'd tried to stop, but Caitlin was the woman he was meant to be with, and he was sorry, but there was nothing he could do. She was everything he'd ever wanted.

"Didn't that used to be me?" I asked.

"There's always been this thing missing between us," he said. "I couldn't name it until now."

"I can name it," I said. "It's called being a dumb kid with a great body who thinks you're a god."

"Don't be like that," he said. "You don't even know her."

But I was right. He packed his bags and moved out that night as I sat in front of a cold cup of coffee, not moving.

You can imagine what followed. In some ways the worst thing about it was living such a cliché. Well. Not really. The worst thing was how painful it was. But it *was* a cliché, one that left me alone in a big house in Cleveland Heights with a fourteen-year-old to finish raising. By sheer force of will I never even thought about a man, hands on me, a mouth kissing mine, someone to love, for the next four years. No time for that. No room for it.

But now, Sarah's almost grown. And I am alone. Free, I guess, though it doesn't often feel it. To look at a man and know that it could mean something if I wanted it to was a new feeling—one I wasn't sure what to do with. For the moment, I decided not to deal with it. It seemed safest that way. The look in Helen's eyes when I expressed the slightest interest in Jerome was a bit chilling, to say the least.

Still, I liked to watch him—that combination of awkwardness and grace. That's what got me out to the cross-country fields on a fall day that was so cool—but not yet cold—that the air was electric, vivid. So many things about this school's campus are clichés brought to life. The beautiful, lush grounds; the handsome, well-raised boys everywhere, their voices literally ringing through the air.

I stood with a small group of faculty and other students, watching the boys warm up—the high-kneed jogs, the quick sprinting bursts of speed. The head coach, Jon Sasser, and Jerome were completely engrossed in preparations for the meet, talking earnestly to the boys, checking watches, rubbing an anxious shoulder here and there. Jerome seemed more at ease than I had ever seen him, though I noticed that the boys went first to Jon with any questions. After a while, they all assembled at the starting line. Rashid Bryson stood near the back of the pack, his dreads bobbing a bit as he warmed up, the only brown face among the boys. The gun was fired and they took off—Jerome and Jon each checked their stopwatches anxiously as the boys left. Then they consulted quickly, and Jon took off at a quick jog toward his car. Jerome checked his stopwatch again, looked up with a slightly lost expression, and, when he caught sight of me, walked over.

"Miss Hansen, what brings you out here on this fine day?"

I laughed, surprised at his formality, and said, "Call me Jana, please. You don't have to talk to me like the kids do."

He looked abashed and then said, "Well, what brings you out here . . . Jana?" His voice softened slightly.

I looked away, embarrassed. "I like to watch the kids run. And it seems like a good idea to get to know as much of the school as I can just starting out. You can learn a lot from the extracurriculars. How's the team this year?"

"Oh, very promising. Very promising." He paused, seeming to consider something. "The Bryson boy is quite a talented runner."

"He is?"

"Very. It's rather exciting. You probably couldn't see because they all left in a pack, but you'll see when they return. Jon's gone out to check their times and cheer them along on the course."

We stood in silence for a moment. Then I spoke. "I have him in my English class. He seems bright. A little overwhelmed, but bright."

"Yes. Well. He'll have to find his feet quickly if he wants to succeed here. He's struggling a bit in my Latin One as well."

There was a peculiar edge to his voice. I didn't know what to make of it, so I fell silent again. Just as I began to feel uncomfortable, Jon came running over. "Jerry, Jerry, you're not gonna believe this kid's time, it's amazing. His first meet, he's running six-, six-and-a-half minute miles. It's unbelievable."

"Six minutes?"

"I'm telling you, six minutes or so. He'll probably slow down a little, but he's gonna be back here soon. You won't believe it." He stopped and suddenly noticed me standing there. "Oh, hi. Jana, right? English Department?"

"Yes."

"Sorry to interrupt, but we got ourselves this amazing kid. Wait'll you see."

We all turned toward the finish line, where a cheer was starting. Rashid came in, yards ahead of his nearest competitor, arms pumping, breath even, his feet seeming barely to touch the ground. His face betrayed his strain, but his body didn't in any way. He looked like he was floating. All of a sudden, an older, bigger boy from the other school put on a great burst of speed, one that looked like it cost him his last ounce of strength, and passed a surprised Rashid at the tape. But that didn't diminish Jerome's or Jon's excitement. "19:30. Oh, my God. Can you believe this, Jerry? Let's get over to that kid. Holy cow."

They moved off quickly and, curious, not even sure why I was doing it, I followed them. Rashid was finishing a cool-down lap by the time they reached him. He looked at both men, his eyes sad and a little fearful. "I'm sorry, I don't know where that guy came from. I really thought I had it. I'm really sorry, Mr. Sasser."

Jon laughed. "Don't even worry about it. We can work on your finish. Do you know the time you just ran?"

"No. Was it okay?"

"Okay? Tell him, Jerry. Tell him."

Jerome smiled slightly. "It was the best time I've ever seen for a boy's first race, Mr. Bryson. Nice work."

Rashid looked from one man to the other, then at me, a little surprised, but he gave me a big smile. The look he gave Jerome was odd—a little angry, I thought, although I suppose I could have imagined it. Then he smiled again and said, "Well, I'm glad. I feel all right."

"You should," said Jon. "Come on. Get your sweats on."

The three of us watched him go. Jerome spoke first. "I hope that he can live up to his potential. Often it's quite difficult."

The way he said it, I somehow had the feeling he wasn't talking only about running. I looked at him closely, but his expression was careful, opaque. We watched Rashid join his teammates, who immediately surrounded him with much head rubbing and back-slapping. We said nothing more.

"So what's it like teaching those preps, Mom?"

Sarah's voice on the phone was cheerful, distant, and slightly amused, the way it always is when she talks to me. I think she adopted this tone shortly after her father and I separated so she wouldn't have to let us know how angry she was. Not a typical girl way of dealing—no anorexia or carving herself up—but she's not typical. I'd love to take credit for that, but I don't really think I can. She's always been her own person.

I laughed at her question. "These preps, as you so nicely put it, are pretty good kids for the most part. Some of them will probably end up at Amherst or UMass." She made a gagging sound. "Oh, come on, that place is huge. There's no decent people at UMass?"

"'Zoo Mass,' you mean."

"Your father went there."

"But that was a long time ago." She paused. "And look how he treated you." My Sarah. Always defending me. I don't think Cal realized what it would cost him with her when he chose Caitlin over us. "Seriously, Mom. How are you?"

"I'm all right. I've met a few people that I like. It's beautiful here. It's good."

She paused. "I talked to Daddy."

"Oh?"

"He's good. He says he and Caitlin like San Francisco."

"Well, I'm sure it's very nice for them." Oh. Damn. There's that edge. That edge I swore I would never have in my voice when I talked to Sarah about her father, no matter what she might say about him. Damn. I could imagine her face, the twist of sympathetic pain fluttering across. But she decided not to say anything. "How are you?" I said, trying to paper the moment over.

"I'm good. Beth and I have got a nice place this year. Not too far from campus. It's nice to be out of the houses for this last year."

"I'm glad. I always loved the houses, but you have to do what's right for you."

"Right. Well, I've gotta go. Class in a little while. Talk to you soon?"

"Always, sugar bear."

"Mo-o-o-om. Bye."

I stood, holding the phone for a long minute. I've always called her sugar bear, and she has objected since she was twelve. The apartment seemed very quiet. My daughter a woman, loving other women, leading a life without me. When does a parent get used to that?

When Sarah was sixteen, she got the lead in the class production of *Bye Bye Birdie*. If you know show business, you know that while this show is not without its charms, it's not exactly a masterpiece of the musical theater. But I couldn't have been more proud of Sarah. She worked so hard, night after night after night. The rare times she was home, I'd find her sleeping in odd positions, odd places—draped over her desk or dozing with her hand on the phone like she'd just been about to call a friend and hadn't quite made it. I loved to look at her while she was sleeping: the soft darkness of her hair, touched with light, so like Cal's; the smooth slightly freckled skin; the mouth that carried the suggestion of the baby she used to be. Whenever she woke up and caught me staring at her like that, she was wary and out of sorts, her eyes narrowed: "What are you looking at, Mom?" But I stole looks when I could.

When the show finally went up, Sarah was a wreck. She threw up three times before we left the house, as I held her hair back the way I had when she was a little girl. She stared out the window the whole way to school, humming "We Love You, Conrad" over and over under her breath. Cal was meeting us there and, in a surprising show of consideration, was not bringing Caitlin. "You're going to be great, honey," I said. "Daddy and I will both be so proud."

She looked at me for a minute, her eyes clouded with fear, then managed a smile. "Thanks, Mom."

She insisted that I drop her off near the auditorium but not walk in the back way with her so I went straight to the front and found a seat. The auditorium filled quickly, and Cal was, of course, late. By the time he got there, the only seat available was next to me. I moved my coat, my stomach roiling with a combination of nervousness and anger. He didn't look at me, just said, "Thanks," and sat down. The skin on the side of my body nearest him felt electrified.

Well, I cried, of course. As soon as those sweet, silly kids started warbling "Goin' Steady," tears began rolling down my cheeks. And when Sarah came out, capris and sweater clad, her hair in a bouncing ponytail, and sang "How Lovely to Be a Woman," I had to start rummaging around in my bag for a tissue. I couldn't find one, and without a word, Cal handed me his handkerchief. "Here. It doesn't mean anything deep," he whispered.

"Thanks," I whispered back, wiping at my eyes. "She's just so beautiful. I can't believe it."

"I know." He took my hand, looked at me to see if it was all right. And somehow, for those few minutes, it was. I didn't take my hand away. We hugged and kissed Sarah madly after the show. She went off to the cast party, breathless, and left us to our awkward good-byes. He went back to his girlfriend. I went back to my house. Sarah never saw us holding hands. Thank God. They were so glorious, those kids. There was so much life bursting out of them. I suppose that's how you know you've left adolescence behind, when it looks that good to you. You'd think I'd know better by now. But I don't know a lot of what I thought I did. That's one thing that the last few years have taught me thoroughly.

I sighed and returned to my desk to start going over the essays for tomorrow's class. The assignment was for the students to write about things they'd lost. I let them define that however they liked. I wanted to get a sense of what they'd do left to their own devices. As I had expected, I got a lot of silly pieces about keys and socks and the like. There was one rather touching one from Rob Bowen about the day his older brother went to college, and a very nicely written piece about his grandmother's death by Tom Hendrickson, one of the more thoughtful boys in the class. I decided to read that one aloud. I was stacking up the papers and getting ready for bed when I realized that there was no essay from Rashid. I looked through the papers again to make sure—they had just left them on my desk in a pile, and I hadn't counted them up right away: I forget what distracted me. Anyway, nothing from Rashid and no plea from him for an extension or anything like that. It was like he was hoping I wouldn't notice. Damn.

I liked Rashid but I was starting to worry about him. This just added to it. He seemed so . . . well, terrified all the time. His hand never stopped moving across the paper in class—he wrote down everything. And whenever he got up the nerve to speak, though his ideas were usually good, he offered them in a tone of foot-shifting diffidence that made it both hard to hear him and to take him seriously. I'd seen boys like him before, and I knew how his nervousness must look to the other boys and to the teachers. This cross-country thing might help—he was clearly a very gifted athlete—but perhaps it would just add more pressure. That didn't seem like such a hot idea. I wondered if I could find out what had happened with the essay in a way that wouldn't send him into a panic.

As it turned out, I didn't have to do much to bring the whole thing up. Class proceeded the next day without incident until I read Tom's piece as I had planned. It was received in respectful silence—for a moment. Then Rashid snorted. "That's not what it's like," he said.

Every head snapped to look at him. I couldn't believe it. He had never even come close to speaking out of turn in class and now he makes a comment like that? What the devil was going on with him?

"Rashid, what do you mean?" I said.

"I mean that's not what it's like . . . when somebody dies. It's not all pretty and soft."

I felt trapped. I needed to protect Tom, who was looking stricken, but I couldn't let this lie. "Well, I think that one of the first things you have to learn as a reader of good writing is that even if you don't feel the same as the writer, if he's been true to his or her experience, the piece probably has something to say," I said. "I think Tom tried hard to write about what it felt like to him to lose his grandmother. Maybe that's not what it would feel like to you, Rashid."

He looked out the window, sucking his teeth contemptuously. I taught through the end of the class with one eye on him and sent Tom off with a pat on the shoulder.

"Rashid, I'd like to talk to you for a minute," I said as he passed my desk without speaking. He turned to me with eyes the color of coal. "What's going on, Rashid? Is something in class upsetting you? You didn't even give me your assignment," I said. "It's the first one you haven't handed in."

I was startled to see tears come to his eyes but allowed him to look away from me without saying anything about it. "That's just not what it's like, all right? I just wanted the boy to say what it's really like . . . when somebody dies."

"Sounds like this has happened to you."

"Yeah."

"Well, maybe you should write about it. Tell us your version of what it feels like." He didn't speak. "Do you think you'd like to try?" He still didn't speak, but he lowered his chin a little, which made him look heartbreakingly vulnerable, the little boy he was. "Why don't you try? If it's too hard, you can just show it to me. You don't have to read it aloud." He nodded, just the tiniest bit. I watched him go, feeling like I might cry myself.

The next day, this was left in my mailbox:

I had a brother. His name was Kofi DuBois Bryson. He was 15 years old. On a night in July, a hot night, he went out to get a Coke and somebody shot him. The next time I saw him, he was dead at the funeral parlor, his face the color of a plum, wearing a suit he always hated. My mother cried so much that she broke a blood vessel in her eye. My father had to hold her up. She looked like a sack of potatoes. After that, they stopped loving me. I think it is too dangerous. What if I get shot too? When I stood in front of the coffin, all I could think was that I wanted to lift up the edge of that jacket he was wearing and see the hole and stick my hand into it until it was covered with his blood. Maybe then I would understand. But I didn't. So I don't understand. I never will.

I sat in the teachers lounge holding the essay, my hands shaking slightly. I hadn't had a cigarette in ten years, but I'd have killed for one in that moment. His brother had been gunned down in the street? How could no one have told me? I thought of the postcard I got from Jason and the despair that had made me unable to answer. How he must have felt when I never replied. I couldn't fail again. But what was I going to say? What did he want me to say? I sat there for a long time, imagining the calming taste of smoke in my lungs. Finally I thought, *Maybe I should talk to Jerome about this.* Perhaps Rashid had spoken to him about it, too. I felt a little funny deciding this, because their both being black was no reason to assume they were buddies. On the other hand, Jerome spent a lot of time with the boy, between cross-country and Latin, and he clearly had some feelings about him. I needed to talk to somebody. I didn't know what else to do. I gulped. Once. Stood up and left the faculty lounge to go to Jerome's office. My heart was loud in my ears.

As I arrived at the door to the office, I could see Jerome sitting neatly erect in the pristine, small room, one quiz paper right-angled on the desk before him. I knocked and then entered when he gestured for me to come in.

"Jana. How nice to see you. What brings you by?"

I was rattled, but not so much that I missed the warmth in his voice. But I pressed on with what I'd come for. "I just received something rather troubling from Rashid Bryson. I wanted to talk it over with you. I thought perhaps he'd confided in you."

He gazed at me, curiosity and something else—was it disappointment?—playing across his face. "Surely, Jana, you know by now that students are not in the habit of confiding in teachers. Not in my experience, anyway. And certainly not someone like Bryson."

"What do you mean by that?"

"Simply that . . ." He paused, evidently exasperated. "The boy's fourteen and struggling in my class. Why would he come to me?"

"He sees a lot of you, and . . . Well, here. Read this. He gave this to me in response to an assignment I'd given them about loss." I handed him the paper, just stepping in from the doorway and not sitting down. I didn't know what else to say.

He took the paper and read it quietly. He seemed to keep his head lowered longer than was absolutely necessary to read the entire thing. When he looked up, his face had undergone the most extraordinary change. Any exasperation or confusion had vanished. Instead, he looked as though someone had punched him in the stomach and he didn't want to give any sign of it. "Well. This is quite a piece. What a tragedy." He paused. "Why *did* you come to me?"

"I thought maybe he'd told you. I assume by your reaction that he hasn't. Fox must know, but I guess he decided not to tell people. I guess. This isn't answering your question."

I stood there, still wishing for a cigarette.

"Jana, come in and sit down. You seem very distressed."

I sat, my hands pressed between my knees like a schoolgirl. "I am. I mean, aren't you? I'm worried about how this will affect the rest of his year. He's trying hard in my class, but his work is already slipping a little. How's he doing with you?"

"Fair. I really thought . . ." He trailed off. "Well, that doesn't matter. Why did you think he'd told me?"

"Frankly, there aren't any other black adults here he might confide in. I thought he might have formed some sort of bond with you. You're together a lot, after all." He scowled slightly, a slight line appearing between his brows. "I mean, I don't think he'd tell you just because you're black, but I thought he might feel more comfortable. . . ." Now I was trailing off, feeling as though I'd said something horrible when it had seemed so logical to speak to him just a little while ago.

"Ah," he said. And that was all.

"Is there something you want to say?" I said finally into the charged silence.

"No . . . no . . . well, just that that assumption doesn't seem worthy of you, Jana."

I stood up so abruptly that I felt the chair tilt briefly behind me. "Worthy of me? Worthy of me? Why is it so horrible to assume that he might look to you as someone he could trust around here? Why is it so horrible that I might turn to you for advice when I'm trying to help a student who's obviously in great pain? Jesus, Jerome, I came to you because I respect you. If you think it's some kind of weird lumping-you-all-together thing . . . well, that's your problem, not mine. Forget I came in. I'll just go speak to Ted Fox about this. Sorry to disturb you."

"Jana, I didn't mean . . ."

"What, what didn't you mean?" I was having trouble breathing, my voice a fierce whisper. He had risen to his feet right after I had. We were very close together—he smelled warm, slightly of soap. The office suddenly seemed very small.

"Jana . . ." and suddenly, unexpectedly, he took my hand. "Speak to Fox if you feel it is the right thing to do. I . . . I'll do what I can to help you."

"I'm not the one who needs help."

I took my hand back, awkwardly. A long silence passed between us. I spoke first. "I'd better go speak to Fox. I'll see you later."

My face hot, I left the office. I hadn't even said anything to him about the intimacy of his gesture, the surprising gentleness with which he took my hand. I just felt confused, angry, embarrassed. I sneaked a look through his office window before I walked away. His face remained impassive, his head lowered to read the paper he had been grading. His hands rested on the desk, still and elegant.

7

Men Among Men

THERE ARE ONLY a few faculty residences on the campus of the Chelsea School. Most of the faculty live in town either in rustic old farmhouses dusted with children's toys and vibrating with the noise of family life or in smooth, clean condominiums, some with a pool in a center courtyard. There is rarely much competition for on-campus housing among the new faculty. They seem to want to get away from the school in the evening and on the weekends. I have never felt this desire and so have lived in a small, neat, inexpensive house nestled well away from the dorms for many years. Early in the morning, I can sometimes hear the cows lowing distantly as they start their days, a sound I find oddly soothing.

My home would appear rather Spartan to most, I suppose. There is little on the walls save a photograph of my mother, some prints of Roman statuary, and a few pictures of the great Ethiopian marathoner Abebe Bikila, who ran the 1960 Olympic marathon barefoot and won in record time. I have a few hooked rugs and a rocker in the Shaker style. My primary indulgence is books, which line every available wall space. My other indulgence, as Jana discerned, is a rather extensive collection of the music produced by Motown in the mid- to late 1960s. I suppose this seems rather contradictory, but let me explain. Who, after all, is immune to the charms of the music of his youth? Simply to put on a record is to recall a time of infinite possibility, a time when life seemed to stretch out before one as a golden road. But that is only part of the reason for my enthusiasm for this music. Motown is, I think, a testament to the possibilities the Negro people hold within. Have you ever been to the Motown museum? I have—once, after a dreary winter teachers conference in Detroit. I suppose they chose Detroit because it was so undesirable, particularly at that time of year; I assume that it was therefore inexpensive. The wide, wide streets, made for cars that no longer line them. Hundreds of walled-up businesses. The general air of fatigue and decay. Idle one afternoon, I went to the museum, which is Berry Gordy's old home, the place where that glorious music was made. I was astonished. A house, just like all the other houses on that street. But here the basement was soundproofed with cheap tile from a hardware store, the wood floor scuffed from the feet that had shuffled and marked out time there—Marvin Gaye, Smokey Robinson, David Ruffin—making such sounds. Upstairs, an orange Naugahyde sofa with old forty-fives scattered around it. Where Berry Gordy once sat, mailing out records himself, with his wife's help. Here was a man who made his own way, who asked for no handouts. Instead, he took his circumstances and made an empire. Standing in that small house, looking at all the worn memorabilia, the inexpensively made sequined dresses and jackets, I was proud. Here was a man who'd taken all the doors life had slammed in his face and turned it into the sound of joy. That's something to be proud of.

The somewhat monastic aspect of my home helps focus my

mind, I find. It suits me and that is, after all, the only person it need suit. I generally start off my days early with a six- or seven-mile run, then black coffee and a piece of toast before walking over to the campus. This day was no different. The predawn air was cold and clean, and at first I thought of nothing but the slap of my feet against the asphalt of the road and the thrum of my leg muscles as I covered the distance. But before long I found the usual pleasant mental blankness that accompanies a run, that feeling of being only a body, swept away by thoughts of the visit Jana paid me yesterday and by her earnest pleas for my assistance. And, of course, my own ill-advised behavior. To tell the truth, no one could have been more surprised than I was. I will admit that I had become constantly aware of her physical presence—the way she had of touching her hair or the way she sat, girlish, with her hands pressed between her knees—but no clear thought of acting on my feelings ever came to me. Or rather, when it did, I quickly set it aside. We were colleagues, after all. Still, when I saw that I had angered her, perhaps endangered our friendship, I acted without thinking. I could still feel her hand in mine, the firmness of bone beneath her skin, the warm metal and stone of her rings; my only thought an unclear desire not to lose her. So. She looked both alarmed and confused. There was nothing I could say to her in that moment. Maybe later. But I don't know. I was beginning to sweat now, despite the cold, and impatiently wiped my face and pulled off my gloves, my feet still moving, the only sound in the world.

I was somewhat more preoccupied with my behavior toward Jana than with her request—in part because I have dealt with young men like Bryson before, though never one with such a tragedy in his past. I had been inclined to think that Bryson was unlikely to do well here at Chelsea, precisely because of his background. When I first began teaching, I felt as Jana did, that I could make a difference for these boys. I like to think I was less naive than she, but in my own way, I did believe. I even taught in the

Boston public schools for a few years after my graduation from Harvard. But it was so wearing. So wearing. I was never confident that my presence was having any effect at all on the boys. And then Isaiah.

The night I learned of Isaiah's death, I was twenty-four. I was at home in my minute studio apartment, grading a batch of my students' frustratingly illiterate papers. The phone rang, my mother's voice across the wires. I was instantly on alert. My mother had an aging southerner's caution about the phone and was far more likely to send short cards and packages of food—even though writing was difficult for her and she didn't particularly enjoy cooking. "Phone costs too much," she'd say with an air of certainty. "Besides, I don't like all that talking without being able to see you. You know I'm thinking about you anyway, boy."

"Isaiah done got hisself killed. You better come on home."

Those were the first words she said. I said, "What?" in a tone so mild that it sounded as though I was asking her to repeat some local gossip.

"Didn't you hear me, boy? I said, your brother is dead. Broke his parole, got mixed up in another robbery. Got shot dead. I've seen the body. Your brother is dead."

Your brother is dead. My head seemed to float off from my body at those words. I suppose I must have asked a few more questions, made arrangements to go home. But the only thing I remember is those words. *Your brother is dead.* I had a sudden memory of his face the last time he had asked me for help all those years ago—the help he never got. The help he ultimately stopped asking for. I left the Boston schools a few months after his death. I had lost my taste for teaching boys like these, like Isaiah, so rarely like me. I longed to be somewhere clean and uncomplicated, hewing to a higher standard. In this way, I discovered Chelsea. When I visited my mother and told her about it, she asked me only one question: "Is the boys there mostly rich white boys?"

"Yes, Mama. You put it kind of bluntly, but yes. I can do what I like there. Teach boys who are going to make something of themselves."

She was silent for a moment. "Like you did."

"Yes, Mama."

"Well. You done learned enough to hold your own up with them boys. I guess that's what I was always hoping. Now that you're doing it . . ."

"What?"

"I don't know. I'm proud of you. I did what I could." She looked at a picture of me and Isaiah as boys that she kept on the coffee table. She twisted her hands and suddenly looked very old. "I did what I could." She said nothing more. After I returned east and took up my duties at Chelsea, I put Isaiah's death out of my mind. I never think about it anymore.

That is as my mother would have it. That is, I've come to believe, how it should be. I can't bring him back. I couldn't save him. Neither could she. Why he couldn't fight harder to save himself, I will never know. That was why I feared that Jana's faith in young Mr. Bryson might be misplaced, save for his talent as a runner. As the season wore on, it was becoming more and more apparent that he was the kind of athlete a coach might see once in a lifetime. He had almost no awareness of his gift, which made it even more impressive. While I was not wholly in agreement with Jana about his chances, I thought we should work to save him if only to encourage that ability. It would only wither and die at some squalid city school. And if, by some happy chance, Jana was right about the rest, that his work could be brought along . . . well, so much the better.

I guess I should say, too, that though I thought it unwise to indicate so, I was somewhat impressed by the way he confronted me about calling on him in class. I *had* been overlooking him, simply out of my belief that he would not be with us long. I also felt it particularly important that our Negro students realize that the world would give them no quarter. Why should I? In any event, he seemed to possess a clarity that could perhaps be fostered. I was undecided as to what course of action to take, but I thought perhaps I should make some gesture. I ducked my head, barely avoiding a low-hanging branch as I quickened my pace for a brief final sprint to my driveway. Finally, my thoughts slowed as my feet sped forward, gravel crunching beneath them. I stopped and jogged in a few brief circles, waiting for my breathing to slow. Normally, I feel more at ease after a run than at any other point in the day, but today my legs hummed with effort as I finished and there was a peculiar tightness in my chest.

I was forced to rush through the rest of my morning routine as my ruminations had served to slow my run. I headed toward campus slightly rattled, feeling as though I'd forgotten something. A busy day lay ahead. My usual full load of teaching and then a trip to New Haven to speak with Negro alumni and recruit new students from among their sons. This trip had been arranged some time ago, and while I had planned for it carefully and worked hard on my speech, I confess to mixed feelings about it as well. I had been handpicked by Ted Fox some days ago to accompany him.

Fox has been with the Chelsea School for only ten years. At the time he joined us, there was intense pressure for the school to consider coeducation. It was argued that schools such as ours were an anachronism, raising a generation of misogynists who had no idea how to behave with women and little respect for them as equals in mind and spirit. This point of view is still held by many, though it is one I disagree with. I thought, further, that I might have been able to represent the school's interests quite well as a dean, or perhaps, even as headmaster. I made my interest in such a position known to the trustees at the time. They interviewed me, examined my credentials, and then decided that I was unsuited for an administrative position. They informed me of this in a meeting that I remember as profoundly uncomfortable. I was very angry for a time, like a fist clenched in my heart. But as Horace once observed, *Ira furor brevis est* ("Anger is a short madness"). My disappointment changed nothing. If I loved this school as I claimed to, it was up to me to accept the judgment of those who administered it and work to support them in their decisions in any way I could. In time I came to like and admire Ted Fox. I rarely thought about the fact that he was five years younger than I and had considerably less experience. I rarely thought about the fact that he was white and I was not. I simply continued in my work here, trying to uphold the standards I had set for myself. No matter if others didn't live by them. In Rome, public life consisted only of men. I imagine that the tenor of that life was much like the character of Chelsea—full of a surging energy and clarity. Fox shares this viewpoint and has a particular gift for articulating it to alumni, faculty, and students. At assembly after assembly, he spoke of the great traditions of men learning from men, of the importance of men's culture, of boys being cradled and nurtured by the rough-and-tumble of bumping up against each other's minds and bodies. He even spoke, though indirectly, of the sharpness it brought to a young mind not to have to deal on a constant basis with the mysteries of sex and the desire to impress or to win this or that girl. Whatever one's opinion before hearing him speak, it was hard—no, impossible—not to be moved by the force of his conviction and personality. I could see why the trustees had been impressed.

When he first came to the school, he took a proprietary sort of interest in me right away, which I will admit I found condescending but also oddly gratifying—as though he recognized in me what the trustees had not been able to. We often lunched together and talked at length of the great models for schools like Chelsea, the public schools of England and before that, in the distant past, the academies of Rome.

"There's nothing like it, Jerry," he said as he cut vigorously into his breaded chicken cutlet. "These boys might complain, but in the end, they're going to have an immersion in a culture that is going to make extraordinary men out of them. There are very few who have that. Very few indeed."

I greatly enjoyed these lunches. After all, some of my happiest times had been spent in the company of men, particularly men who used their minds and push me to do so as well—my lost friend Vaughn in college, Ted Fox here. Unfortunately, as Fox's tenure grew longer, our lunches became fewer. He had many obligations both out of town and with local alumni, so I began to see him less and less, though he always waved cordially when he saw me on campus. When he asked me to join him on this trip, I was both surprised and pleased. The way in which he asked me was characteristic of his general frankness and straightforward nature. He summoned me to his office, looking up from a morass of papers as I entered. "Please have a seat," he directed. As I sat, he began talking.

"As you know, Jerry, it's my job not only to maintain Chelsea as a first-rate boys' institution, but also to create a student body that is rich and diverse in ways that aren't just financial." He laughed slightly. "We have to do better than we've been doing. Some of our outside funding depends on it. As our only black faculty member, you are pivotal to our efforts to recruit more black students, as you always have been. I know you've been reluctant to participate in this sort of direct recruitment in the past, but I want to invite you to join me for a meeting with black alumni that we're having in New Haven next week. I need you, Jerry. I need you for the health of this initiative and of this school. Can I count on you?" His gaze was direct and unwavering.

I sat in silence for a moment. Then I spoke. "Are we having this conversation solely because of the color of my skin?" I said.

"Of course not. You're a veteran here and one of our most

valuable and respected faculty members," he replied. "This is something we must do, and I want you to be a part of it."

This little speech did not really eliminate my unease. Could he really have known me so long and not known how I felt about preferential outreach? "Well, of course, Ted. I want to do what's best for the school. . . ."

"Then I can count on you?"

I took a deep breath. "Of course. Tell me when we go to New Haven."

"Fantastic. I'll have Miss Carr give you details on the trip as we have them. Thanks for stopping by."

I emerged from his office and proceeded straight to the men's room. I splashed water on my face mechanically and wiped it off equally mechanically. I gazed at my face in the mirror without expression. What is it about this flesh that covers me that makes it a part of every transaction I conduct? Just when I think it is no longer seen, there it is once more, dictating the terms. I touched my face slowly, then rubbed harder and harder until I could feel my teeth through my lips, my skin shifting over my bones. My eyes stung. I would do what was expected of me, as always. Do what was best for Chelsea, as always. I stood there for a long time, looking at my face. No one else came in. I might have been alone on the earth.

It is hard for the children I teach every day to appreciate the extent to which the color of a man's skin informed his life when I was growing up. It dictated *everything,* from where one might live to the sort of work one might do to how long one might live. When I was in college it seemed, for a brief moment, that the words of Dr. King might come true and that this would at last become a country that operated on the democratic ideal that man has struggled for since the time of the Romans. But instead of using Dr. King's death as an occasion to continue to work for that ideal, we Negroes turned on each other with a fury that continues unabated. Just look around you. When heinous crimes are committed, who most often has committed them? When you view the squalor of our cities, who lives in the most hellish part? Who contributes most mightily to keeping it that way? Dr. King would weep if he could see what has happened since his death. And the children of that time live with the residue of our stubborn inability to let go of our pain even as things have changed. That is why it is so important to me that I be taken on my merits, whatever they are. I think that is why I have always struggled when I am confronted with a request such as Fox's. On the one hand, I have a lengthy tenure here and strong affection for the Chelsea School. Who better to represent it to any interested party? But at the same time there is the nagging suspicion that he has asked me simply so that he can put a brown face before the alumni he is trying to win over. Instead of letting those who are capable simply find their way here, as I did, we go trolling for money and students, using me as bait. I spent a good deal of time mulling over how I could in good conscience accept Fox's invitation, serve the school, and also make my own views clear. As the afternoon of our departure arrived, I thought that I had the answer.

New Haven is about an hour away from the school. At first, Fox and I spoke easily as he drove. We discussed various issues that had come up in the first few weeks of the school year. We agreed that this fall's crop of students were a little more raucous and less academically well prepared than their predecessors had been. We shared the kind of chat that teachers always have about students—this one isn't working as well as he might, this one is not as bright as he seemed at the interview, whereas this one is considerably brighter, isn't it amazing how this one is becoming such a leader? But after a while, there came a lengthy pause in the conversation. Jana's plea for young Mr. Bryson came into my mind, and I admit to a few moments of discomfort. We had driven a few more miles before I spoke.

"Has Miss Hansen approached you about the Bryson boy?" I finally said, straining for an air of ease.

"I'm glad you brought that up, Jerry," Fox replied. "I probably should have told all of his teachers beforehand. His parents were very reluctant to share the information, as was he. We decided to respect their wishes. Probably a mistake." He sighed. "In any event, Rashid hasn't really gone off the rails, but Jana is concerned. Do you know the whole story?"

"Miss Hansen just showed me an essay of his that indicated his brother had been killed."

"Yes. Well, if you saw that, you know the story. His brother was an exceptional young man, by all accounts. Had gotten a full scholarship to Mt. Herndon in upstate New York and showed signs of becoming a really remarkable writer. I think it was an attempted robbery that he was caught in. He wasn't involved, of course. We checked that out. The boy died on the street, I believe. Damned shame."

"Yes, awful." I paused, the words *we checked that out* echoing in my mind, then spoke again. "Well, what do you think is advisable?"

"To tell the truth, I think if we come on too strong, we'll scare Rashid right off. It's an enormous tragedy, and for him to have chosen to reveal it to Jana is quite a breakthrough. My impulse is to keep the door open, extend a hand as it were, but then let him come to us. Perhaps you might be able to build some trust with him as well." His eyes did not leave the road as he said this, but he spoke carefully, almost as if he was afraid of my reaction.

"I had thought perhaps I might try. He's rather difficult to reach in my class, though. Keeps to himself. Hasn't volunteered much."

"Yes, well, it's hard with these inner-city kids. Honestly, they sometimes arrive here with a complex of problems that we are just not equipped to deal with." He paused, seeming to carefully consider what he was going to say next. "I don't mind telling you, Jerry, just between you, me, and the fencepost, I'd rather we had more kids like Gerald Davis than like Rashid. Kids who are used to . . . well . . . a certain style, certain mores and behaviors. It'd make my job a hell of a lot easier." He laughed shortly. "I know that you'd agree with me, that's why I feel comfortable speaking frankly."

"Yes. Well, as you know, I quite agree. I'll do what I can, though. If you'd like."

The road ticked away underneath us.

We were silent as we pulled up to the Yale campus. New Haven is so different from the lightly populated area that surrounds the Chelsea School. Chelsea is nestled in about one hundred acres of rolling green hills. When one stands in the middle of campus, no city buildings are visible at all. New Haven, on the other hand, is small, gritty, and colored with the fatigued air of a decaying industrial city, out of which the campus rears up like a fortress. The college had availed us of the use of its alumni club, and we walked over to it, still without speaking.

We entered the room, which gave off the familiar, warm scent of leather and floor wax, similar to that of some of the older buildings at Chelsea. It was crowded with young Negro men of every size and shape. There were a few young boys and about twenty or thirty alumni from various years, mostly younger men from the 1970s and 1980s. Fox and I moved through the room, shaking hands briefly with the organizers of the event. None of the alumni spoke to us directly, although I saw a few nudge each other and nod a bit in Fox's direction or mine. I carefully composed my face to reveal nothing.

After a few minutes Fox stepped easily to the lectern, having been introduced by a young man from the Yale Club. As always, he commanded attention.

"I see a good many faces I recognize from recent years at

Chelsea. And I'm heartily glad to see them," he began. "Before Mr. Washington says his part, I wanted to say a few words. You know what the Chelsea School has meant in your lives. Obviously, you care enough to come out and discuss it with us on a pleasant October evening. I thought then, and think now, that by deciding to come to Chelsea, you gentlemen made a giant leap toward taking charge of your lives, breaking away from the pack, and living boldly. You chose the unpopular road of an academic life among men. I hope that your presence here tonight means that you found the experience worth it. I look forward to discussing with you how we can make it even better for our sons after us. Without further ado, I give you Mr. Jerome Washington."

I stepped up to the podium amid a smattering of applause. "Well," I began, my voice slightly ragged, "it's good to see so many faces from the past here today. And good to see a few that might join us in the future." I paused and looked at the boys in attendance before continuing. "For shaping the future is what we hope to do at Chelsea. And I think, by and large, we succeed. I think our success is due in large part to our adherence to principles and standards far older than we, far stricter than today's. The tradition of men being educated among men dates back to Greco-Roman civilization, which I'm sure you'll recall is my subject and my passion. There are those who say that the Greco-Roman civilization was the greatest ever to grace the planet. Though it's not currently a fashionable notion, I tend to agree." A murmur made its way around the room. "Obviously," I continued, "that doesn't take away from the greatness of other civilizations, the African, the Asian, and so forth. But there is a certain clarity of thought that persists in the Greco-Roman mind that can be found nowhere else. It is that tradition that I am proud to take part in passing on at the Chelsea School. I believe it has helped make you all the men you are today. I further believe that a crucial part of passing on this legacy is a single-sex education. Young men go about their lives at

Chelsea free to consider only the improvement of their minds and souls. In these difficult times, the timeless truths that have lived for hundreds of years are, I believe, the ones that will save us, if any will." The room was completely silent.

I spoke for a few more minutes about my affection for the school and then, almost without conscious thought, said, "You are, of course, aware that there are very few of us with darker skins at the Chelsea School. That is in part what this meeting is about. I ask you only to consider this as you look back at the education you received at Chelsea. You have received an education that has made you welcome wherever you go. You are no longer just Negro men, black men, what have you. You are Chelsea men. There is no finer imprimatur you can wear."

At first there was silence, then a thin, brief patter of applause as I sat down. Fox resumed his spot at the lectern without looking at me. He made an appeal for donations and applications from those interested, and then the floor was opened to questions. There was a short pause and then a tall, dark-skinned man, neatly groomed, stood up. I recognized him immediately, though his name escaped me—Darrell maybe?—something like that. He had attended Chelsea about fifteen years before and had studied Latin briefly, though he didn't make the full two years. He went on to become one of the school rabble-rousers, loudly proclaiming Latin a dead language and declaring the need for classes aimed specifically at Negro students. I remember trying to tell him at the time that he had much to learn from Chelsea and from the ancients, but he would have none of it. After he left my class, I had not thought he would come to much good and was not sad to see him leave the school—though he did make it to graduation. Now, however, he was clearly prosperous. Obviously the values that he so railed against had served him magnificently. He seemed to bear out my final words beautifully. His voice, when he began speaking, was clear and resonant.

"My name is Derrick Harper, and I'm pleased to be here, gentlemen. It's good to see you again," he said, "and I'm interested to have heard what you all have to say. But I've got to say this. When I attended Chelsea fifteen years ago, there were six other black students and one black faculty member—you, Mr. Washington, in fact. Neither of you has indicated that anything has changed in that regard. So as far as I can tell, it's still a school for white boys, run by white men. If that's the case, then I've got to confess my very strong reservations about it as a place for any son I might someday have. Mr. Washington seems not to share my concerns. I trust that you do, Mr. Fox."

Thick silence filled the room, and as I looked quickly at Fox, I could see his face reddening. After a moment, he cleared his throat and went to the lectern again. "I'm afraid that Jerry might have created an erroneous impression, Derrick. There may have been a time that it seemed that Chelsea was run only for white boys," he said slowly. "But rest assured that that time has passed. That's why we're here today. I won't deny that the Chelsea School has not had the best record in attracting and holding African American talent. Especially among the faculty. But that's exactly why Jerry and I are here tonight, to try to enlist your support as we move into the twenty-first century. Your sons can make the difference for us. Your dollars are the ones that are needed. We are willing to make the difference for you. Jerry was too intent on conveying what he loves most about the Chelsea School, but he definitely agrees with me. We were speaking about this very thing in the car on the way here, and he said to me, 'I'm glad you asked me to join you for this, Ted. Because God knows that we need more diversity at Chelsea. I hope that I can help achieve that.'" He turned to me with a broad, confident grin.

A nervous but hearty laugh echoed through the room. I could feel a foolish smile plastered to my face as I looked around the room and caught the eye of Derrick, the boy who had spoken up.

He was not smiling. He fixed me with an unwavering gaze. Fox's comments seemed to have loosened the tensions in the room considerably, but there was still some wariness. One young man asked exactly how we planned to change our recruitment efforts so that we could attract more black students. Fox ticked off a series of actions: a mailing to alumni and to certain Negro organizations, increased scholarship fund-raising, a more active relationship with race-specific scholarship agencies. He implied that I would be heavily involved in all these activities, producing satisfied nods from some of those present. I raised no objection. There were more questions, a few handshakes, and, in the end, a few checks pressed into Fox's hand—though not from Derrick Harper. He did have some words for me, however. He came up to me as I moved to gather up my things and join Fox to leave. "How are you, Mr. Washington?"

"I'm well, Derrick, I'm well. You're looking well yourself. What are you doing now?"

"I'm an attorney—I do a lot of housing rights work in Hartford."

"An attorney. Might I ask where you attended law school?"

"Howard, undergrad and law." He gave me a tight smile. "I needed a change after Chelsea."

"I see."

I busied myself buttoning my coat, and he spoke again. "Look, it's been a lot of years since the beef we had back then. We were coming from very different places, and I was just a kid. When you first spoke, you still sounded kind of shaky to me. But you're here, and according to Fox, you're coming around to seeing how it really is. I hope you can do the right thing and work to change that place. Bring it to what it could be."

"Mr. Harper, I assure you that I'm here because I love the school and support Mr. Fox's efforts to do whatever is necessary to keep it healthy. But I think it has achieved more, much more, than you're willing to concede. Your own life bears witness to that."

"I'd have to agree—but don't you see how much easier it would have been—for both of us—if we'd had some support? Some role models? Each other?"

I looked at him levelly. "I'm afraid, even now, that I fail to see why an accident of birth should have bound us together so firmly. You've prospered and done well with your education. Just as I have. I see that, and I'm glad. But I don't see how the fact that we're the same race gives us some special rights, some special bond. Why it has to determine everything. I'd like us to go beyond that. I believe that that's what all the struggle has been about."

Harper's face, which had worn a conciliatory expression, hardened. "I see I'm wrong about you changing. You're still just doing your job for the Man."

I did not reply. He shook his head, slowly, regretfully, and did not offer to shake my hand. "Good night, Mr. Washington." He paused. "Interesting to see you again." He turned and walked away.

The night had grown cool as Fox and I drove off. Silence prevailed for a number of miles. We left New Haven and entered the enveloping darkness of the chill country highway that led to the school before Fox spoke.

"We did all right back there," he said evenly. "Raised some good issues, heard some good ideas, even got a few donations." He paused. "I hope you don't think I spoke out of turn. Putting words in your mouth. I just gave voice to what I'm sure you're willing to do for the school. No matter how we might feel about it, the school has got to keep up with the times and diversify. It's critical to our survival as an institution. We've got to make a change. So I'm going to do it the best way I know how."

I turned to study his face as he peered intently at the road ahead. His expression remained opaque. I said nothing.

I felt as though I'd been made a fool of. I agree that the acts of the past were heinous. But men have always enslaved other men. Only we seem unable to let that past go or to allow it to truly strengthen us. Instead we turn on one another with it, competing with tales of suffering and woe.

It is that mentality that I find so troubling. And that mentality that I so badly wanted to speak against, to my people, the very people who practice it most. Fox had stripped me of my beliefs without so much as a nod. I knew why he had done it. I could even understand his motivation. But that did not make me any less uncomfortable.

Look at the Harper boy. He is a perfect example of what I refer to. There he stands, well-spoken, successful, affluent—all of which he owes in part to what he received at the Chelsea School. But he would deny his own son that same experience. Where is the sense in that?

As the miles rolled on, I felt a stirring of resolve. Perhaps I could reach out to the Bryson boy, help him to see what Harper couldn't see. Keep him from the edge of the crevasse that had claimed the life of my brother. Earlier, when I told Fox that he hadn't volunteered much in my class, it was in an effort to avoid tedious explanations of my theory about such boys to Fox. If he believed that Bryson had not been making much of an effort, he would not be disturbed by my reticence to help him. But now, after my encounter with Harper, I questioned my own decision. Perhaps the boy would be willing to follow my own strong example. I might have a chance to make a difference where I had not been able to before.

8

The Wall of Pain

RASHID HAD NOT been able to sleep through the night since Kofi's death. Almost every morning around three A.M. he would find himself awake, feeling as though he had been shoved by a cold, flat hand. His eyes popped open as though someone had called his name, and he lay there staring at the ceiling, his heart pounding. When he was at home, most times he could get out of bed and go sit in the living room, staring out the window and waiting for the gray dawn to gather, or watching an infomercial to distract himself. Sometimes he'd get to the doorway of his bedroom and find that one of his parents was already up, sitting in his place at the window. Then he made his way back to his room, to lie stiffly on his bed till his alarm went off. His thoughts were usually memories of Kofi or questions about him—Kofi laughing, Kofi bloody in the street, what Kofi's last words might have been, the look on his face as the bullet pierced bone. During the day,

Rashid found he could cope—Kofi's death always hovered there, a dark space in the corner of his mind, but he could push it away when he needed to. But at night it was unavoidable, burning his eyes and searing his throat.

Not much seemed to bother Gerald. He slept the sleep of a man who knew his place in the world, his breath soft and even, his sheets rustling occasionally. Sometimes Rashid wished he could talk to him, tell him what it was like not to be even able to fucking sleep. To be so tired all the time. So tired that his head felt full of cotton batting. Sometimes he wished he could tell him about the blood on the street, about the funeral, about how he wished he could talk to Kofi about school. But he couldn't.

Chelsea gave the boys very little free time during the school week, keeping them loaded with activities and schoolwork. But in the middle of each semester there came a short respite, separate from the traditional holidays like Thanksgiving and Christmas. Gerald invited Rashid home with him—"On me," he said—for the fall break, and Rashid, feeling awkward about the free ride but unable to afford a trip home, accepted.

"This boy said he'd pay your way for a visit?" said his father when Rashid called to tell them his plans.

"Yeah, Dad. It's okay. It was his idea. Him and his parents."

"And he's black?"

"Yes, Dad."

There was a long pause. "I guess it's all right, then. It seems a little funny, but if they can do it . . . Don't want you sitting up at school all by yourself while all your friends go off." His father's voice grew gruff. "And we can't afford to rent a car again just now. So you go on and have a good time."

"Thanks, Dad." As Rashid hung up, he realized that for the first time in months, his father had wished him well.

✴   ✴   ✴

Gerald's dad, a lawyer, picked them up at the airport. Their car was nice, but not more than Rashid had expected. Mr. Davis was a bluff, friendly sort, obviously crazy about his son and willing to like anyone he brought home as a friend. Rashid felt an odd twist in his heart at the long, manly hug Gerald and his father exchanged at the gate. But he swallowed twice and busied himself with his luggage, not wanting to look weird.

But then the house. Rashid had never had a friend who lived like this—a separate bedroom for each child and a lawn and so new, so new and quiet. No roach would dare live there.

Gerald, chatting to his father, didn't seem to notice Rashid's sudden discomfort as they walked into the house. Every room had thick, soft carpet, and everywhere Rashid looked, there were beautiful, obviously expensive things. African-looking paintings and sculptures on the wall and, well . . . it was really something. Something to stand in a house like this and know that it belonged to someone black. It's not like he didn't *know* this existed but damn . . . now that he was standing here . . . Damn.

"Rashid, I'm so pleased to meet you."

A voice like music cut into his silence. Rashid turned around and there was the most beautiful black woman he'd ever seen smiling at him. She was older, a mom's age, like forty or something, but her skin was smooth, like chocolate cream, and she had the warmest brown eyes and a short haircut that made her look like she'd stepped out of one of his mother's issues of *Essence*. A girl of about ten, still just a kid but with the promise of being just as beautiful, stood next to her, staring at him. "I'm Gerald's mother. And this is his sister, Kim."

"Nice to meet you, Mrs. Davis. Hi, Kim." He hoped he didn't look too thunderstruck. He'd never met anyone's mother who looked like her.

"Gerald, why don't you show Rashid your room?"

Gerald picked up his bag and said, "Come on, man," and they went upstairs, their feet hushed by the carpet.

"Well, here it is, man. My domain—when I'm home, anyway. You can have that bed." He tossed his bags down wearily and flopped onto the bed after them. "It's nice to be home."

"Yeah. It must be." He paused. "This is a nice room, man."

Gerald sat up and fixed him with a penetrating look. Rashid gazed back, unconsciously smoothing the soft mudcloth printed quilt on his bed with his hand. After a moment or two, Gerald spoke, a bit uncertainly. "It's all right, I guess. Beats the dorm, anyway." He jumped up. "You wanna shoot some hoops before dinner?"

The weekend went by. They went to a ball game with Gerald's dad. They hung out and played Dreamcast with some of Gerald's old friends from home. They watched television—no cable in the dorms at the school, so MTV seemed like a joyous, raunchy missive from some forgotten civilization. Gerald teased his sister about her newly gangling arms and legs. Gerald's mom asked Rashid a lot of polite questions about where in Brooklyn he was from and did he like school and what did his parents do? (She did look a little surprised when he said they worked for the MTA.)

The weekend passed in an increasingly pleasant daze. On the last night, they all sat down to dinner together—Gerald's mother bringing the food to the table with a look of shy pleasure, Gerald's dad smiling proudly, occasionally interjecting a comment. They were really nice people. Rashid had finally relaxed. He felt more at ease than he had in weeks. They were having chicken with some kind of sauce. It looked good. Rashid picked it up with his hands, just the way that he had every single time he'd eaten chicken his entire life. As he brought it to his mouth and took the first bite, he realized that everyone else at the table was using a knife and fork. Even Kim. He put his food down quietly. His hands and mouth felt oily, and his face was hot. Gerald caught his eye briefly, but his expression was unreadable. There was a minute—it felt like an hour—when it seemed that everyone was looking at him. Then Gerald made a joke about something, and the moment passed. But the heat in Rashid's face remained for the rest of the evening.

Now, lying awake in this strange, prosperous bed, he remembered an incident from earlier in the school year. After English class one day, Rashid had said that he'd never heard of this Hemingway guy. "You didn't read any of his stories in eighth grade or anything?" Gerald said.

"No," said Rashid, suddenly embarrassed.

"Wow. I thought everybody had to read *The Old Man and the Sea.*" A pause as the two regarded each other. Then Gerald spoke, grinning. "Well, it don't matter, cuz. Book ain't that good anyway. And you know who he is now, right?"

"Right."

Gerald never said "ain't" around his parents. And his parents spoke as clearly and precisely as any white people. Rashid rolled over, wanting to groan. His face was pressed into the pillow, his hands between his legs. Was there nowhere he belonged? At least there was one way to get back to sleep. He did it quickly, without a sound, without much pleasure. The night was very quiet as he finished. It was nearly four-thirty A.M.

Gerald seemed to have forgotten the incident at dinner by the next day, so Rashid said nothing more about it, though he felt a little sick whenever it crossed his mind. Their trip back to school was uneventful, though Rashid found that he couldn't stop thinking about the easy, confident manner of Gerald's parents. As opposed to his, who walked around looking like they expected to be hit any second. He wished he didn't feel that way, too.

Rashid found it harder and harder to be quiet about what was inside him once he got back to school. And stuff kept happening to push him. Like in that class before midterm break where Ms. Hansen read Hendrickson's essay about his grandmother. Rashid felt as though he were going to burst into tears at any moment the whole rest of that day. He'd been in a bad mood even before class started because of that mess with Washington—and then he'd had to listen to these white-bread punks whine about losing this and that and how sad it was that their hundred-year-old grandmother died. What did they know? What did they know about really losing someone, way before they were supposed to be gone? That's why he finally wrote that thing when Ms. Hansen asked him to. He couldn't carry the weight by himself anymore. He left it in her box on a day when he didn't have her class so he wouldn't have to talk to her about it. He just had to get it out.

Before he'd come up to Chelsea, his parents had called him into the living room, where they were watching *Diagnosis: Murder,* and made him sit down with them. "So, Rashid, you're off to school in just a few days," said his father. His eyes left the screen only briefly to glance into his remaining son's eyes. "Your mother and I, we don't feel . . ." He trailed off.

"What Daddy is trying to say," his mother chimed in, "is that we don't want to tell everyone up at that school about Kofi. It's not a secret exactly but we don't see any reason to walk in there and announce that your brother was killed, either."

Her eyes filled with tears. Rashid looked from one to the other of his parents, then he spoke. "There's nothing to be ashamed of. I'm going to tell if people ask."

His mother turned back to the television. "If they ask. But I don't see any reason to announce it. We've said that to the headmaster and the admissions people."

Rashid turned to the television, his chest tightening. He'd said there was nothing to be ashamed of. But why did he feel guilty? He felt guilty even for drawing breath. And he *was* ashamed. That's why he told no one.

He supposed he ought to tell them about the essay. But it was easy enough not to. Right after he got back from Gerald's, he talked to his mother on the phone. She asked about his visit. He told her he had had fun, that they'd fed him well, and that Gerald's parents were very nice. He didn't say, You're supposed to eat chicken with a knife and fork. He didn't say, Gerald's mother looks like a model and their house looks like a TV show. He didn't say, Gerald's sister is alive. He didn't say, I wrote about Kofi because my heart is crumbling in my chest. He didn't say, Mama, I miss you. He hung up the phone at the end of the conversation. He was holding the receiver so tightly that his hand hurt.

The day after he'd handed in his paper, he felt every eye in the school on him—though in fact Ms. Hansen hadn't sought him out to speak with him and no one else knew about it. Still, the only place he felt comfortable all day was in the barn.

He hadn't planned on taking this course when he'd come to visit, and he knew that none of his boys back home would even half believe it, but the truth was that he had developed a real affection for the big, black cows. This course probably wouldn't do him any good after he left Chelsea. But he was comfortable in the barn. The cows asked nothing of him, nothing but that he bring them hay and feed. That he could do. Today, he didn't have to deal with the other boys much because it was his day in the stalls, a duty each boy took alone. The cows mooed noisily as he entered the barn.

"What up, y'all? It's chow time." He wrestled a large bag of feed off the stack and tore it open with a knife that hung nearby. The lowing grew more excited, and the cows began to shift and shuffle in their pens. Rashid walked slowly among them, pouring feed into troughs. When he got to his favorite one, the cow they called Mr. T because of the protuberant ridge of fur on her back, he stopped and rubbed her there for a minute. The cow was unmoved by this show of affection, but for some reason of her own, she did not bellow like the others for food, just looked at him with large, liquid brown eyes. After he filled her trough, he slid down the wall opposite her, into the coarse, loose hay scattered throughout the barn. The only sounds that could be heard were the noisy exhalations and mastications of the cows and the ragged, tearing sobs of the boy. The sounds went on for a long time.

Rashid was cold and cramped by the time he struggled to his feet. The cows ignored him. His face was lightly dusted with chaff. He brushed the back of his hand roughly across his eyes and sighed. He had never felt so alone in his life. The only thing he could hear was the beginning-to-be-bitter wind sighing through the trees across the road. He looked at his watch. Almost lunchtime. He'd been in the barn for nearly two hours and missed two classes, Latin among them. He started walking back to campus, his mind completely blank.

By the time he got back to the cafeteria, everyone had gone into lunch already. The din hit his ears as soon as he entered and took his place in line. His heart was tight in his chest, and he could hear his breath in his ears. He saw Gerald sitting in the corner where they usually sat, surrounded by the mix of black, Asian, and white guys that they sat with. Rashid could tell from where he was standing that Gerald was telling some long story. Every face was turned to him, expectant and laughing. Rashid carried his tray to the table as though it were laden with crystal. Gerald acknowledged him briefly: "What's up, cuz? Didn't see you after history today."

"I cut, man. Couldn't deal."

Gerald raised his eyebrows slightly and turned back to the others at the table. "So anyway . . ." He continued his story, some long thing about his exploits with a hometown honey. The other boys at the table hung on every word as though they had been in that dark basement themselves, lights down, clothes half off, breath mingling warmly with hers. Rashid only half listened—he'd heard this one before. Gerald was just trying to keep it live at the table. He seemed to feel that was his function at meals. For his part, Rashid responded to comments directed toward him during lunch with the absolute minimum number of words necessary and ate rapidly. The food tasted of ash. He caught Gerald giving him a couple of sidelong looks, but he acted like he didn't see him. Finally lunch was over. He was just about to leave the table when—oh, shit—Mr. Washington approached them. "Mr. Bryson?"

"Yes, sir?"

"We missed you in class this morning." The table had fallen into absolute silence. "I'd like to have a word with you if I may."

Rashid's stomach dropped into his shoes, but what could he do? "Okay, Mr. Washington. Just let me clear up my stuff here."

He could feel the other guys at the table gazing at him nervously as he picked up his tray. Mr. Washington stood without speaking to them, waiting for him. They walked out through the leaded glass doors together and headed down the path that led back to the classroom buildings.

"I suppose you're wondering why I wanted to speak to you."

"I'm really sorry about class this morning, Mr. Washington. I just . . . I had something I had to do with the cows for Animal Husbandry, and it took a lot longer than I thought it would."

"Yes. The cows. Do you enjoy the cows?"

He's lost his mind, thought Rashid, *but I better just play along.* "Yeah . . . I mean, yes. I like them. I'm from the city and didn't ever get to deal with big animals like that. It's . . . well, they're sort of calm. It's nice, I guess."

"I remember feeling that way when I was young. Down south." Mr. Washington seemed to drop into a momentary reverie, then clapped a hand on Rashid's shoulder so firmly that it made him jump, resting it there for a moment. "Mr. Bryson. I learned of your brother's misfortune, and I wanted to caution you not to let your loss interfere with your studies here." He paused for a moment. When he continued, his voice was husky. "I have felt sadness much as yours. But I always remembered that I had been given a rare opportunity, one that very few Negroes are granted. Just as you have been. It is important that you make the most of it. If I am hard on you in class, it is out of my belief that knowledge fought for is knowledge best remembered. I would suggest, as you go through your time here at Chelsea, that you adopt the attitude of the Stoics, maintaining a disciplined mind that nothing can harm. I think that you will find that to be the best course as you pursue your studies here."

Mr. Washington's hand remained on Rashid's shoulder throughout this speech, tightening slightly as he reached points that he wanted to emphasize, but his gaze was focused on the middle distance, as though he couldn't bear to look Rashid in the eye. Rashid didn't know what freaked him out more—having Washington know about Kofi, that hand on his shoulder, or the peculiar way he was talking. He was too stunned to ask a single question—it was crazy to think that no one else would ever find out about Kofi anyway. Mr. Washington seemed to think that he was helping—but his eyes were far away. It was as if he was talking to someone else. "Um . . . okay, Mr. Washington. I know that this is a great chance. I don't intend to blow it."

"One thing more." *What more could there be?* thought Rashid. "You have a great gift, Mr. Bryson. I have never seen a natural runner like you. I think with the proper coaching, you could excel to an extraordinary degree. Even perhaps compete at the highest level. I'd like to work with you a little outside the team practices, if I may."

By now, they had reached the buildings and boys were beginning to surge past them on both sides. They stood, facing each other. "You would?" said Rashid. He heard his voice squeak a little, but he couldn't control it.

"Absolutely. Come by my office so we can discuss some extra workout times." Mr. Washington paused. "I might even run along with you sometimes. That can be a great encouragement."

Rashid stood speechless, which Washington seemed to take as assent. "I'm glad we had this talk," he said, sticking his hand out to shake. It was cold and dry, unexpectedly callused. "I'll see you in class tomorrow. I don't expect this morning's incident to be repeated."

"No, sir."

With that, Washington turned and walked toward his office. There was a roaring inside Rashid's head. He stood there for a long time after the man had gone.

Rashid went through the rest of the day in a kind of a fog. He went to classes to avoid the trouble he'd be in if he didn't go, but he was so distracted that he couldn't really hear. A gifted runner? Extra workout times? The highest levels? He liked running, the smoothness of his stride, the way he didn't have to think, the way it felt to have the tape snap across his chest—ping—and everyone cheering. But how could he even consider more running—as hard as his schoolwork was? And if it meant more time with Wooden Washington . . . He couldn't imagine it. His legs turned to stone at the thought, and his eyes filled with tears. He kept feeling Washington's hand on his shoulder, hearing his voice going on, remembering himself crying in the barn. He didn't even go to dinner. He couldn't eat. When Gerald came in about seven, he was sitting on his bed, staring at the gray-green wall opposite him. Gerald threw his backpack on his bed, took a long look at Rashid, and came to a decision. He spoke.

"What is up with you, man? You ain't said two words to me since you got back from wherever it is you went this morning, and you been acting beyond weird for longer than that. Last couple of days, really. Since we got back from my folks' house. And then Washington wants to speak to you. What is going on?"

That did it. More tears came to Rashid's eyes, but this time he let them fall. He felt something shifting inside of him. He sat up and his mouth opened to set free some words. He didn't know what they would be until he spoke them. "My brother is dead. He's been dead for a year. More than a year." He looked steadily at his feet but he could hear the creak as Gerald sat down on his own bed.

"What? You had a brother? What?"

Rashid nodded. His eyes were burning, and he brought his hands up to keep the tears, the very blood, from flowing out of them. His hands were scalded. Gerald didn't move, but Rashid could feel his eyes on him. There was no sound but Rashid's ragged breath. Then Gerald's question: "What happened?"

What happened. It was eight on a sultry July evening, after dinner. Kofi and Rashid were sitting in their airless living room, silent under the fan's useless whir. Neither boy moved more than necessary, just turned the pages of the books they were reading— trying to read. After a while, Kofi spoke. "Man, it's too hot. I'ma run down to the corner and get a Coke or something. You wanna come?"

"No." Rashid didn't feel like moving.

"Well, I can't sit here anymore. You want anything?"

"Naw. I'm all right, I guess."

Kofi yelled to their mother that he was going to run to the corner, that he would be right back. She cautioned him not to stop anywhere and asked him to pick up some milk. He left. That was the end. The next time Rashid saw Kofi, he was on his back in a pool of blood. His mother's screams could be heard for half a block. Rashid hadn't even looked at him as he'd walked out the door. Why should he have? He was coming right back.

Gerald listened as Rashid talked. He didn't interrupt. He asked no questions. He sat without seeming to breathe. When Rashid was done, he did something he'd never done before. He got up and walked over to Rashid's bed, sat on it, and put his arm around his friend. They sat like that for a long time, while tears streamed down Rashid's face. The room was very quiet.

"You could have told me sooner, man," Gerald said after a while.

"No, I couldn't. I couldn't tell anybody."

Gerald nodded. "Well, what happened? Why you telling me now?"

"That thing that we had to write for English class. That essay that Hendrickson wrote. I felt like the top of my head was going to come off. Ms. Hansen asked me to write something and I wrote about Kofi. Now I just wish I could get it back. Fuck. Then somehow Washington found out. I don't know, maybe she told him or something. You know how teachers are. Or maybe Fox told him. Anyway, that's what he wanted to talk to me about." He brushed fiercely at his eyes. "And he was so *weird,* man. Telling me to be like some kind of damn Roman and that I was lucky to have this chance, I shouldn't blow it. And he kept rubbing my shoulder. The guy's a freak, man. You know what I'm sayin'?"

Gerald was silent for a long time before he spoke. "Washington didn't try anything faggy, did he?"

"No, no, not like that. The whole thing was just weird. He was trying to give me some kind of pep talk, and he was just . . . It was like he was mad at me or something. Like he was trying to get me to shape up from something I did to him and he was trying to be sympathetic at the same time. I don't know how to explain it. It was just fucked up."

"Yeah, well, they don't call him Wooden Washington for nothing." Gerald paused before speaking again. "Listen," he said, his voice a little ragged. "I know . . . I know that we haven't had the same kind of lives. I saw you looking around my house, bro. And I know you've been through some shit I only know about from CDs and TV shows. But I'm glad you told me about your brother, man. That's a lot to carry by yourself."

Rashid snuffled and wiped his eyes with the back of his hand. He nodded and then, in the silence that had suddenly grown awkward, scooted off the bed and rummaged in his drawer for something to wipe his face with. For the first time in a week, his stomach didn't hurt. He could feel Gerald's steady gaze on him as he pulled out a worn handkerchief. "Thanks, man, for listening and all," he said without looking up.

"No problem." Gerald climbed off the bed, suddenly brisk, his voice a little too loud. "Let's go see if it's anything left in the Coke machine. Those knuckleheads probably drank up everything by now."

The boys left the room together. You would have had to look closely to see the sorrow in their eyes.

9

Speed

LONG-DISTANCE RUNNING is largely about pain and the transcendence of that pain. The pain, of course, is obvious the first time one runs anything more than a quarter mile or so. What at first perhaps felt liberating and easy begins to start offering a twinge in the foot there, a tightening of the calf here. As you continue, your lungs begin to cry out for more air, every rock on the roadway becomes an insult, sharp beneath your feet. Your whole body gradually becomes taut as a rubber band, begging only for relief, and then, just when you cannot bear another minute, it comes. You are suddenly above the pain, outside your body, and a strange and fragile joy comes over you. It doesn't last long, and you cannot force it to come. But the effort toward it is one that brings me back to running day after day after day.

When you run competitively, another element enters the picture: simple fear. The fear before every race that this will be the time that your legs give out, this will be the time that everyone runs past you, this will be the time that you throw up before you finish. Humiliation. Pain. Loss. This will be the time. One has to transcend that, too. It's not really something one can explain to the boys. They have to find their own way through it. All I hoped to do was to offer the Bryson boy some assistance.

He took me up on my offer to work with him individually, although he kept a wary attitude. He always did what I asked, but I felt he was holding something in abeyance, some fear or concern regarding me. We worked around it, but it remained, present and undeniable. Still, I found that working with him was a source of great pleasure. His initial poor condition was thoroughly eradicated by this point, and he could easily cover the 3.1-mile cross-country course in nineteen or twenty minutes. We were working to bring him well under that—somewhere around seventeen or eighteen. I thought that he had the potential to break our course record of 16:37 by several seconds. I had talked to him about that, and about the potential he had beyond that as well. Gifts are not given to be thrown away. This I know. I tried to impart some of my knowledge of life to him as well in this time we spent together. I told him of how I was accepted into Harvard, my excitement at arriving, and my hard work while there.

"That's a good school," he ventured.

"It was. It still maintains a fine reputation, but . . ."

He looked at me, confused. "But what?"

"Should you be fortunate enough to attend such an institution, Mr. Bryson, I hope that you will realize the pitfalls of a kind of victim mentality that a lot of young men and women like yourself have adopted in recent years. By sticking close to one another and reinforcing each other's dubious ideals . . . well, I've seen a good many young men like you go by the wayside. I hope that you won't be one of them."

He looked at me for a moment, then busied himself stretching his hamstrings. "I don't intend to go by the wayside, Mr. Washington," he said quietly.

I went on. "Of course there were injustices—there still are quite often—but the best way for us to transcend them is to keep pushing forward, keep achieving, not yelling for some ill-conceived change. Or for a handout. Do you see what I mean?" I paused, and he said nothing in reply. "You have a great gift, and I think, a good mind. I know you can use them both to achieve some real success."

He nodded, looked at me seriously, and then said, "Are we done for today, Mr. Washington?"

I let him go after that. I believe that he was listening, that the abruptness of his change of subject was a function only of his youth. One thing I've learned in many years of spending time around boys this age is that they never know what to say. Particularly to men like me, men in positions of authority. Either they are too bold and achieve a rare kind of obnoxiousness or they are simply mute, content to keep their thoughts to themselves. But they are listening. Despite my initial reserve about him, I believed that Bryson was making an effort.

On this day, as we worked together, there was not so much talk. I wanted to keep moving, to shake off the residue of my recent trip to New Haven. I drove the boy rather hard in sprint after sprint, but he never yielded. He came huffing up to me after some wind sprints, his eyes dark with fatigue. His face was shining with sweat, and his hair bobbed around his face. "Now what, Mr. Washington?"

"I think we can finish today with a longer run. Five miles, perhaps?" He groaned. "Now, Mr. Bryson, no theatrics. I'll be joining you today. There's a reason to cheer up, eh?"

He looked a bit startled but then smiled at me, warily. We busied ourselves stretching out after that. I usually prefer that my running be a solitary endeavor, but today I was oddly eager to test myself against this boy.

"All right, then, are you ready?" He nodded. "Let's go."

We took off over the gentle, rising path that ran behind the barn. We didn't speak. Only the sounds of our breath and our shoes hitting the earth filled the crystalline air. For the first few miles, we ran at a companionable jog, neither of us speaking. The trees rolled past and our breath shot cold puffs before us, rhythmically. The boy's hair flopped annoyingly at every step, but I tried to put it out of my mind. I had not run with him before and found it remarkable to study him as he moved along. It was as if there were some small machinery at his core that allowed an unusual degree of fluidity to his movement. Nothing was wasted or jerky or excessive. I found that as I attempted to match his stride, I became more graceful in my running as well. But it did not feel natural to me. I had to think, to be conscious of my limbs, before I could even begin to approximate a stride like his. That is, I suppose, the difference between an inborn talent and a willed one. The latter cannot be maintained indefinitely.

Before long I realized that we had already come four miles. "Last mile, Mr. Bryson. Let's make it a good one, shall we?" I quickened my pace, as did he. We didn't speak, our breath coming harder and harder.

There comes a moment when you decide to truly compete against someone that your mind ceases to function conventionally at all. One becomes only windmilling feet, flying arms, the will to win. I entered this space as we ran the last 500 yards or so. I was pushing myself as hard as I could, harder than I have in years. My breath was loud in my ears. The boy was clearly pushing himself, too, but I kept on his shoulder until we were roughly a 220 from the finish. Then my legs gave out. There is that moment, too. When one has run as fast as one possibly can and the body simply says, "Enough." It is much as it has been described, like hitting a wall. I didn't fall. Thank God. The boy kept up his pace and finished well ahead of me, easily. I jogged the last few yards, fighting the nausea that comes when you've run as fast as you can for a lit-tle too long. Bryson jogged back toward me with a smile, one of the first I'd seen from him. "Not bad, Mr. Washington. I thought you had me there for a minute."

"No."

"Well, that was fun anyway. Are we done for the day?"

"Yes." I was still having difficulty talking.

"Okay, then. See you later," he said. He jogged back toward the campus and the locker rooms, the picture of grace. I stood there, trying to catch my breath, for a long time after he'd gone.

When I first arrived at this school, not long after the upheavals of the 1960s, Henry Murdoch, who was then head of the Classics Department, pulled me into his office. "Look here, Washington," he said, "I'm going to be frank. I didn't want you in this depart-ment, and I didn't particularly want you in this school. There's been too much agitation coming from outside, pandering to your kind. The headmaster had the final say, but I'll say this to you. You put one foot wrong, deliver one subpar performance, and I'll be only too glad to see you out the door. Do we understand each other?"

He did not raise his voice during this speech, nor did he show any signs of outrage or anger. He used much the same tone of voice that he might have used to inquire about my trip up to the school and my move into faculty housing. I said nothing for a moment. Then finally, "I think you'll find that my work far exceeds your exacting standards, Mr. Murdoch," I said. "I under-stand you perfectly."

"Good. It's time for your first class, then."

I left his office and went to the men's room. I went quickly into a stall and vomited. I then came out and washed my face. As I looked at myself in the mirror, I felt a sudden coldness wrap itself around my heart. The water dripped from the darkness of my skin, each drop clear and separate. The words *I'm not leaving* came clear and separate in my mind, as on a sign or a billboard. I squared my shoulders and walked out of the room. I told no one about Murdoch's comments. I knew where I stood.

Some might call me foolish, being so determined to stay after being treated like that. But I felt that as long as I stayed in Boston, working with poor Negro boys who had little chance of making good, of rising beyond their station in life, that my chances of making any sort of real impact on the powerful of this land was minimal. Here, they would see me. They would have no choice but to give me my due. I had not thought of this story in years, but it returned to me after I caught my breath and half jogged/half walked back to the school.

As I passed the parking lot, I saw Jana walking toward her car. She smiled and raised her hand to wave, enthusiastic and sweet. "Looks like you've been running," she said as I approached.

"I have. Actually, I had a bit of a race with young Mr. Bryson."

She grinned, obviously a little startled. "Do tell. Who won?"

"I'm afraid youth triumphed," I said.

"Once again," she said.

"Once again."

We stood in awkward silence for a moment. "You've been working privately with him quite a lot. Do you think it's helping?"

"Well, his running is definitely improving. I should think he has a good shot at the school record sometime soon."

"And the rest? What we talked about?"

"Well, he hasn't broken down in tears and confessed all. But we're talking. I'm telling him a bit of my experience in the hope that it inspires him. I believe I'm making headway."

She paused, seeming to consider whether to say something more, then said, "I'm glad." She looked away briefly. "I guess I'd better be going. I'll see you tomorrow. I understand you're one of my fellow chaperones at this shindig we're having."

"Ah yes, the fall dance. Couldn't get out of it this year, I'm afraid."

"Oh, come on," she said, suddenly flirtatious again. "It'll be fun. Maybe they'll even play some music we know."

"Maybe."

"I'd better go. I'll see you."

She looked at me a long moment. I had that sudden feeling one has in the moments before a first kiss, that everything is narrowing to one small point. I felt breathless again, though I'd stopped running some time ago. "I'll see you tomorrow," I said.

She continued to her car. Neither of us had said anything about my taking her hand, about the palpable current between us. It is so hard to talk about the body.

That is, I suppose, the nature of the flesh. When one is a boy, like these boys at Chelsea, one's flesh is so insistent—it is constantly in the way, constantly asserting its dictates. Feet too big, arms gangling out of jackets, hair appearing overnight on parts of your body where there was none before, genitals over which you have no evident control, spurting and rising at odd, inconvenient times, at the sight of some longed-for skin, the turn of a head, the back of a neck. You might share a dance with a girl, have a short conversation, and her presence is stamped on you indelibly, part of your flesh. The fingers that brushed your arm. The careless laugh that entered your soul. The eyes the color of moss-covered stones underwater that softened briefly as they looked at you. All those moments sink into one's flesh. I could tell you exactly where the moles are on Jennifer Hargraves's back. I could tell you the texture of Alice Murray's hair—she was the girl who sat next to me in sixth-grade English. I could tell you of the iron smell of my mother when she came home from a day's work, cleaning powder and fatigue and the sour tang of effort ill rewarded. And now, like a boy again, I could tell you about the play of dark and light through Jana's hair, the rings, just two, that she wears. One is amber, shot through with some small white lines the color of vanilla ice cream, and one is a small, ruby-colored stone that shines slightly as she pushes a hand through her hair. I have spent so much time, so much effort, setting my flesh aside. I don't even look at myself as I step out of the shower. It is as though I am afraid to see my own flesh. I suppose I am afraid to see it as it is, unused, untouched, unloved. I sometimes feel that if I could rip it from my bones, I would. I would leave only what's clear and pure there for others to see. Not this flesh that covers me, but the muscled heart that beats within.

The telephone rang as I finished showering and dressing. It was Jon Sasser. We talked for a few minutes of this and that, the logistics for an upcoming meet, how certain boys' times were improving or not. Then he asked, "How'd your practice go with Rashid today?"

"Well, I think. The boy is coming along."

"I'm glad you're taking the extra time with him. I think it's going to pay off by the end of the season." He paused. "Do you think he wants to go as far as he can? Does he really love this?"

I was silent a few minutes, considering. I thought of the boy's wariness in our practices; how opaque his expression had been until the moment he beat me in our race. Then his face had glowed with a barely suppressed joy, the gleam of the victor. The hint of a gentle smile around the lips. The impulse to throw his arms into the air. I could feel it—and I won't deny that I had wanted to be the one to feel that way, to show him that I had learned a thing or two in my life. That it was that knowledge that was allowing me to win. But he was so young and so talented. A gift from God. How could he not love it? How could he not want to exercise it to the fullest? "I think he does. I think he'll go the distance."

"How far do you think he can go?"

I thought of his loping, leonine stride, the ease with which he ran past me. I looked at the picture of Bikila on my wall, shoeless in victory. "I think he can go as far as he wants to. He's got the ability. It's a matter of will."

"I know. That's what I worry about. It's hard with boys. You know."

"I know. But I think we can hold on to him."

"Right, then. I'll see you tomorrow."

"All right." In the distance, I could hear the cows lowing as evening fell.

10

A Woman's Life

ON A COOL November evening, I stood under the showerhead, feeling the water course smoothly through my hair and down my back as I readied for a high school dance, of all things. I had been pressed into service as a chaperone by Ted Fox himself. "Good chance for you to see the boys at play, Jana," he said in his bluff manner. "And to make sure they don't play too much." He chuckled at his own mild joke. I had never chaperoned a dance before— the big schools I taught at didn't have them. Too hard to control and staff.

I emerged from the shower and wrapped a towel around myself without looking in the mirror—age and too much solitude, I suppose. I'm thinking of getting a cat, for God's sake. I wear the same lipstick shade I've worn for the last fifteen years, my hair is long and dark, the same. I'm afraid to change, I guess, is what it is. The way I look is the way I look.

The phone rang and I jumped to answer it, tucking my towel in as I went. "Hello?"

"Hi, Jana. It's me." Cal. My heart started racing.

"Cal? What on earth are you calling for?"

"I . . . well . . . I had something I wanted to tell you. It's good news, really. I wanted you to hear it from me." I could imagine him, nervously biting his left thumbnail as he talked, shifting from foot to foot. Habits I used to find endearing. "What's up?"

"Caitlin and I are getting married. I don't expect you to come or anything, but I didn't want you to hear it from Sarah." The words were conciliatory, but his voice sounded angry. Like he was daring me to be hysterical or accusing. Married. Married. He was married to me. But in the end that hadn't been worth a damn. Caitlin would find that out soon enough.

"Well, when's the big day?" I tried to keep my voice from shaking.

"We haven't decided yet. Um. We'll let you know." He paused. "You're okay, right?"

"Never better, Cal. Never better. Listen, I've gotta go. I have something on tonight and—"

"Sure, I understand. Take care of yourself."

Once his news was delivered he was all tenderness and solicitude. My stomach tightened, and incredibly, my eyes filled with tears. "Good-bye," I said.

That was the end of our conversation. I sat on the edge of the bed for a few minutes after hanging up the phone, feeling oddly breathless. I had an impulse to tell Jerome about it, to see his great brown eyes soften in sympathy and desire. I have been divorced for four years. I have no claim on Cal, nor he on me. I felt sick, pressing the heels of my hands into my eyes to comfort myself, to calm down. Okay. Okay. Time to dress.

I dried myself quickly. Didn't pay to linger, to take a close look at the delicate tracery of new lines and sags and freckles, so different from Caitlin's firm, fleshy youth. I chose a black dress with a semiplunging neckline that Sarah had given me and I had sworn I would never wear. I suddenly, deeply, did not want to look like a teacher. The crepey shoes and slightly out-of-date clothing. To that end, I put my hair up as well, into a smooth French twist, much more high style than my usual efficient look. I listened to Marvin Gaye as I got ready, occasionally singing along: "Believe half of what you see, / Son, and none of what you hear . . ."

The night was brilliant with stars and beginning to be cold as I pulled up to the school's parking lot. I was deliberately not thinking of Cal. The gym windows glowed brightly against the dark blue of the night surrounding them. I could hear a faint thump, thump of music as I walked up to the doors and entered. Knots of boys, separate from knots of girls, stood in various corners. A bright-eyed freshman with a halo of blond curls sat behind an old card table, stamping hands. I extended my hand for a stamp, smiling while I did it, and asked him where the chaperones were. He directed me to a spot in the corner of the gym.

The music thrummed and pumped—I didn't know who the singer was, no guitars in it at all, another sign of time passing. I found myself standing next to Helen; Bob Harmon, the gym teacher; and Jerome. He looked . . . well, he looked handsome in a slightly too formal dark suit and a white shirt that set off his skin. I found myself thinking about the hollow at the base of his throat. But I just said, "Hi, Jerome. How's it going?"

"Good. The natives are not too restless as yet." He smiled and for the briefest moment looked at me the way a starving man looks at a steak. I felt unutterably gratified—and grateful to Sarah for this doggone dress. "Can I get you some punch or something to drink?"

"Punch would be great. Thanks."

He was back in a moment, and we stood silently next to each other for a few minutes, the music washing over us, the faint smell of old sweat in the air. I could feel the heat his skin gave off. He shifted a little bit, brushed my arm accidentally, shifted away again with an awkward smile. A few kids danced confidently in the center of the room, but for the most part one corner of the large room was full of boys talking to one another and shifting from foot to foot, casting occasional glances toward the equally chatty cluster of girls from Langton Day, the nearest girls' school. A few balloons drifted lazily across the floor, and some of the boys got into an impromptu balloon-tossing match.

"So does this pick up any later on?" I asked Helen, smiling a little.

"Oh, you know. There's always a couple of kids sneaking out to get high and usually some groping in the corners—which is our job to prevent from getting too hot and heavy. But it's never really bad. They know they're being watched, after all. Our big moment is coming up," she went on.

"How so?"

"We—all the chaperones—are supposed to get out there and cut a rug when they put on 'Signed, Sealed, Delivered.'" said Helen. "Why that song, I don't know. Imagining we'll all be sent away and the inmates can take over the asylum, I suppose."

"You think?"

Helen just smiled enigmatically. And the dance went on. The kids were starting to pair up more and dance together. Song after song I didn't know came over the speakers. After a while, there was one that was purely male—some hip-hop thing, a dense collage of sound, a black man's voice rhyming assertively over it. The sound instantly reminded me of Cleveland, of boarded-up businesses and too-big high schools. I heard a small roar from a corner of the gym and saw Rashid, Gerald, and Sean Cho skid to the middle of the dance floor, not even stopping to attempt to gather up any girls. They were responding only to the brutal energy of the song. Rashid was clearly the leader, smiling broadly and, for once, relaxed as they formed a hooting, yelling, stomping line, dancing fiercely, not looking for a reaction. The other kids moved away from them, forming an approving circle, and they moved in the middle of it, thinking only about the music. It must be tiring to be so careful all the time. It must feel wonderful to just break out. I watched with pleasure and turned to Jerome, grinning, wanting to share it. His face had gone completely opaque, his eyes focused intently on Rashid.

"Oh, come on, Jerome, they're just having a good time," I said, to jolt him into lightening up a little.

He smiled at me briefly. "I know . . . I just haven't seen this kind of . . . performance from our boys before."

"Well, it's a new world. All boys want to be hip-hop heroes now. Haven't you heard?"

"I have." A pause. "But as you know, I don't love it." He smiled at me more fully and the tension was broken as the song ended, the stomping boys yelling and rubbing each other's heads gleefully. They looked so happy, especially Rashid. It made it easy not to think anymore about the look on Jerome's face, not to worry about what it might mean.

The boys dispersed, the music continued, and suddenly there it was: that crystalline, thudding opening break, followed by Stevie's "Ooh yeah, babe . . ." booming through the gym. The kid who was DJ'ing put it on reverb so that the hooting and yelling could really build up: "Teachers! Teachers! Teachers! Teachers!" On impulse I grabbed Jerome's hand in one of mine and hit the floor. Helen and the rest of the chaperones followed.

I hadn't danced in public in years. Literally years. But the old, well-loved song rang through the gym, and I let it take me. I looked at Jerome, laughing. He was a surprisingly good dancer, fluid and easy. Despite his formal manners, he had the look of a man who did a little dancing alone in his living room every once in a while, just like me. Helen was stiff, but game; Bob hammered it up for the kids. The students encircled us, hollering wildly. I felt my hair coming undone. I reached up and took out the pins, enjoying the eyes on me, the movie-star theatricality of the gesture. After I did it, Jerome took my hand and spun me into one smooth twist—like we were both in high school ourselves. I laughed and spun away from him as the kids roared. We grinned at each other and his hand was so tight on mine and I felt this highway open up inside me and I was driving down it as fast as I could. I was so tired of being alone, so tired of keeping my chin up, so tired of controlling it and resisting this desire, this wanting, this man who thought I was so beautiful. Who thought that about me anymore? Why should I say no to it? Why not just say yes? I closed my eyes and let Stevie wash over me, let that gorgeous break in the song carry me away. The voices were sweet in my ears. I was free.

I lifted my hair off the back of my neck as the music ended and looked Jerome right in the eyes. We stood there for a long moment, gazing at each other. I leaned toward him under the babble of happy voices, the pound of the new record that was playing. "I'd like to go have a drink somewhere when this is over," I said. I didn't feel awkward, I didn't feel afraid, I only felt like I finally knew what I wanted.

"I'd like that very much," he said. We slid apart.

The dance went on for another hour. I got a lot of laughing compliments from students—"All right, Ms. H!" "Way to go, Ms. H!" Jerome did not talk to me again, although we kept catching each other's eyes. The last song had finally been played and I was making my way toward the door when Jerome caught my elbow. "Jana?"

"Yes?"

"Where should I meet you?"

"How about Brandywine's in fifteen, twenty minutes."

"That's just off Main?"

"Yeah." I shoved my hands under my loosened hair again, behind my neck. I was acting like a teenager, trying to get him worked up. "I'll see you there in a bit, then."

In the parking lot, I put on a little more lipstick. Same old color. I pulled down my dress and brushed at it quickly. I pushed an image of Cal the day he left out of my mind. I was ready. Jerome was already sitting at a small table, a glass of red wine in front of him. "Hi."

"Hello." So formal, even in this situation. "I took the liberty of ordering." He smiled, a little sheepishly. "I felt rather in need of a drink."

I sat down, ordered. He played with a packet of sugar, his hands turning it over so quickly that it was almost a blur. The confidence I felt in the gym vanished like so much smoke. Now that we were sitting across from one another, there seemed to be no way to talk. I wasn't even sure what I wanted to say. "Well," I finally said, a little too loudly. "It's been quite an evening."

"Yes."

"You're a good dancer." *How stupid is that?* I thought.

"Am I?" he said. "It's been so long since I've done anything even moderately like that. I confess to being a bit stunned." He paused, then looked at me directly. "You bring that out in me. Surprises. I'm not sure I like it." The sugar packet whirled in his dark, smooth hands. Our wine sat before us, waiting.

"Yes. Well. It's mutual."

More silence. We both looked at the table. Blond wood intended to look expensive and tasteful, but probably from some monster midprice outlet like IKEA.

"I have been intending to say that when I took your hand when you came to see me, that I didn't mean anything by it," he said. "I have been intending to say that I think of you only as a colleague." He paused and looked away. "But I think you know now that that isn't true. Though this feeling is completely unexpected. And not one I feel we need to act upon." He paused again, looking pained. "No need for that . . . it would be quite inappropriate."

His hands kept whirling, and I reached out and covered them with my own, to quiet them. He looked at me, startled, but he didn't pull away. "Let's act upon it. Appropriateness isn't everything," I said. And I didn't let go.

He tasted slightly of wine and of something else undefinable, chalky and sweet. His one act of aggressiveness was that he started kissing me the minute we got through the door, like he was drowning, like he'd been thinking about it for a long, long time and was afraid that if he stopped, I would vanish. I had to pull away, to take his hand and lead him to the bedroom, to collect myself for a minute while we walked. I don't know if he even saw the room, my carefully chosen African-print bedspread, the pictures of Sarah, the clothes piled on a chair in the corner. He was looking only at me. I turned around. "Unhook this, would you?" The way I might have to Cal. Or someone else I'd been with a long time. But then I turned back around so he could see me when I took the dress off. He bit his lip when I did it, not to draw blood, but anxiously, like a boy might. I stood a little ways away from him. No words yet, but he stepped just a bit closer. He was still fully dressed. "It's all right." I let him take my bra off. His hands were shaking. I looked down at my own breasts to see what he might see. The lines and sags, the spread of my hips. I didn't want to look up. I'd grown too old for Cal. Who's to say, when presented the goods, that Jerome wouldn't feel the same way?

I felt his hand under my chin, and he lifted my face to his. The first words he'd said to me since we left the bar: "My God. I don't know if I've ever seen anything so beautiful. My God." Just the least bit of a southern accent in his voice. All formality gone. I had the strangest feeling, as if I was going to cry, as if we were both going to. But I helped him take his jacket off and his shirt and everything else. He left his glasses on.

Once that was done, it was easier. All the kissing and licking and stroking, it's the same, the feel of another's flesh after a long time away. I was entranced by the contrast of our skins, both a little weather-beaten, the worse for time. But him so dark and me so light, it was lovely. And when he slid inside me, his face buried in my neck, murmuring some words I couldn't hear, I felt such joy. Just like on the dance floor. I was free again, at last.

Afterward, I was oddly calm. It was Saturday night, which meant there was Sunday to deal with, and he couldn't seem to keep his hands off me. One hand made its way sleepily down my back as we regarded each other. He looked like a man who couldn't believe his luck. I couldn't believe mine, either. "So," I said.

"So."

"So thanks. I . . . thanks."

"It was my pleasure." He grinned, suddenly boyish. Sex seemed to have really loosened him up. "And yours, I hope."

"Oh, yes. I mean, of course." I fell silent again. "My ex-husband is getting remarried. He called and told me before the dance." Jerome's hand stopped moving. "I don't know why I told you that. I just thought of it. I don't know. Do you care? It's not why I wanted to be with you. I just thought of it somehow."

I was babbling. He propped himself up on one elbow, brought a finger to my lips. "I don't care."

"What?"

"I feel so privileged to have had this night. This night where I have behaved utterly out of character. Where I . . . I didn't worry about what was appropriate for once. Where I got something I wanted so badly—" His voice broke, softened. He lay back on the pillow; closed his eyes; spoke. "I don't care why it happened. If you don't love me. But I don't want to stop just yet. Don't ask me to. Please."

What could I say? I rested my head on his chest and let him stroke my hair. It was a little difficult to breathe. The room was very quiet. It wasn't long before we fell asleep, each to our own uneasy dreams.

I wish this whole thing didn't sound quite so adolescent, but there you are. It started at a high school dance, after all. Sunday morning, I made coffee and English muffins, which he praised lavishly, and he admired my apartment and my taste in books and my pictures of Sarah. I asked him if he ever wished he'd had children, and he said that he had them in a way. The boys were enough for him. I smiled and gave him some more coffee. "Did you ever teach anywhere else?" I asked.

"I used to teach in the Boston public schools," he said.

"You did?" My voice squeaked a little, which sounded stupid, but I *was* stunned. Boston public? In the seventies? That meant busing, poor black and white kids, intense hostility, the whole nine.

"You sound shocked," he said with a laugh, taking another muffin.

"Well, Jerome, come on. I thought you'd spent your whole career in these rarefied environs. Teaching there must have been pretty tough back then."

"It was." His eyes went flat and dark.

"Why'd you leave?" I pressed. I couldn't help it. We'd slept together now, after all.

"I . . . it simply became too difficult. Personally and professionally. I thought it best if I moved on." He started buttering his muffin with great intensity, and I knew we were done with that topic.

It was awkward after that. He was solicitous and affectionate still, but the way he'd clammed up brought Helen's warning back to me full force. We didn't talk about the night before. We didn't talk much at all. But as he left, at around noon, leaving us both to our empty days, he held me so tightly, like a drowning man, and kissed me so deeply that I was suddenly feeling like I was the one who was in over my head. We didn't say anything about seeing each other again. Like this. Or like last night. I started crying not long after he left. It took a long time to stop.

All of the English teachers at Chelsea worked with individual students on their freshman-year chapel talks. The teachers chose the students rather than vice versa because, it was hoped, we would be more mature about it and even the kids no one liked would end up with someone to advise them. I'd picked Rashid long before he'd told me about his brother, and we were scheduled to meet on the Monday after the dance. On Sunday I pulled myself together after a while, made my weekly phone call to Sarah, told her a heavily edited version of what I'd been doing over the weekend; called Tina, one of my oldest friends from college, told her the unedited version, cried some more (wasn't sure that was possible), and, bucked up a bit by her sympathy and kindness, finished the day with a long bath and an Agatha Christie mystery I hadn't read before, which was soothing in its undemanding predictability. I did listen to Stevie Wonder while I was reading, though. And when I put the book down, I had an absolutely physical memory of the way I'd felt as he'd moved inside me, slow and deliberate and so full of longing. The same swoop in the stomach, the same longing for it to go on and on without having to think. I was glad to see Monday morning dawn.

I hadn't spoken to Rashid concerning the essay he wrote about his brother, even though it had been a couple of weeks since he'd given it to me. He'd been so terrified since then. He practically ran out of the room the instant class was over. Before, he had tended to be one of the last boys to leave, kind of the way Jason was. I decided that I was just going to have to talk to him. He was never going to come to me. But I didn't know how he'd react. So I was bit nervous when I heard his hesitant knock on my office door, late in the day. "Ms. Hansen?"

"Hi, Rashid. Come on in."

He entered and sat warily on the edge of a chair. "So, we've got to discuss your chapel talk. How's it going?" I asked.

The boy relaxed slightly—clearly he'd been afraid I'd pounce on him about the essay right away. "Um, okay. I never . . . I mean, I haven't done anything like this before, but I think it's going okay."

"Well, what's your subject?"

He looked uncomfortable. "Um, integration, I guess."

I was startled. I hadn't heard that word used by anybody in nearly twenty years. "Racial integration?" He nodded. "What about it?"

"Well, I'm not against it, obviously, or I wouldn't be here, right? But there's some problems with it that I just want to talk to people about. How this place isn't really integrated enough. We— I mean people like me—are just here to round out somebody else's experience. That's what it feels like, anyway. You know what I'm sayin'?"

"You really think that's the only reason you're here?"

He sighed. "Not the only reason. No. But it's a big one." He paused. "People look at me like I'm in some kind of freak show. Some people." His dark eyes softened. "You don't. But other people do. Those are the ones I want to talk to."

I was silent, touched by his faith in me. "Do you have a draft of your talk?" I said.

"Yeah . . . I mean, yes. I know I was supposed to bring it. Here it is."

I took the slightly wrinkled paper. Even though it had been done on a computer, it was marked with a few cross-outs and changed words. I read carefully. "Well. This is a very fine speech. You're going to make some people very angry, though. Are you sure this is what you want to say?"

His eyes were unwavering. "Yes."

"And you're ready to tell everyone about your brother?"

"Yes."

"Then there isn't much more I can say." I paused, swallowed, spun my ring briefly around my finger. "I did want to talk to you about the essay you put in my box, though."

"I thought you might."

"It was beautifully written—which isn't really the point. And I'm terribly sorry about your brother—which also isn't really the point. I just wanted you to know that I'm on your side. If you need to talk, or if it all gets to be too much, or if you need help with schoolwork—anything. I'm here. I think you like to work things out on your own, so I won't offer more than that. But I'm offering that."

He gazed at me steadily, his eyes a little less steely. "Okay. Thanks." He fell silent again.

I took a breath. "I understand you've been spending a little time with Mr. Washington as well. Extra practices and things. Is that helping?" *If you only knew, kid,* I thought.

A shutter came down behind his eyes. "I guess. My times are getting better, anyway." A small smile. "We raced the other day and I beat him."

"He told me. Good for you."

He scooted back in his chair, pleased. "I don't know. We don't talk that much. About school stuff. He's always trying to . . . to get me to be like him, I think." He paused, looked fearful, as though he'd said too much. Then he decided to go on. "Yeah. To get me to be like him. I don't think I can do that."

Once again I wasn't breathing quite right. "No reason you should. You need to be who you are. That's all we can expect from you." I paused. "I know he wants to help, though. If he can. Do you want to talk about anything else? Ask me anything?"

"No. I'm done."

"Then I guess we're finished. Remember what I said, though."

"I will." He took the draft of the speech from me and stood to leave. I turned back to my desk. But at the door, he paused. "Ms. Hansen?"

"Yes." I half turned, facing him.

"You think I belong here?"

I looked dead into his eyes, seeing how much hung on my answer. "Yes, I do. I wish there were more kids like you."

"You wouldn't lie to me, would you?"

"No, I wouldn't."

"Washington . . . You know why I feel funny around him? Because I don't think he wants me here." His voice was thick with anger and something else—sadness, I think.

I knew as a teacher, I should rise to Jerome's defense. But I couldn't. I suddenly remembered the look on his face when the boys were dancing. I said nothing, and Rashid went on. "I saw you with him at the dance. That's why I need to know where you stand. I need to know who's got my back."

I nodded. The silence in the room grew larger. "You can trust me, Rashid," I finally said.

"I hope so," he said. Without another word, he left, the door closing softly behind him.

"You can," I murmured into the space where he'd been. But I couldn't think of a reason he should believe me.

11

The Failures of the Flesh

I MEANT WHAT I'd said to her: I do not care why it happened, what brought us together. But this is what I did not say: I don't know if I can bear its ending.

That is, I suppose, why I've deemed it best to keep my heart to myself for these many years. A life of perfect solitude was the jewel that I had. And now it bears a flaw I cannot avoid seeing, a breach I cannot repair. I would give anything to touch her one more time. I never thought I would feel that way again. But there it is. I cannot close the door I have opened.

After I got home Sunday, I changed into my running clothes and headed out. I barely warmed up. I ran for miles—I don't know how far—far enough that I was gasping and aching and finally incapable of thought by the time I returned home. I sat on my front step for a long time after my run, watching the light shift and change before me. Then I went into the house, showered, dressed, prepared dinner, ate without tasting, fought a blinding impulse to call her, put on a Stevie Wonder album, blinked back unreasoning tears. Thus ended my day.

Monday was better. I'd read for a while Sunday night when I couldn't sleep and had somehow managed to get myself somewhat in hand. The prospect of work was calming. Things would be the same there. And I'd find some way to avoid her. I was not prepared to render our interactions at school bland and normal. Not yet.

I did manage to avoid her all day (though that required that I eat lunch in my office), but I had forgotten that this Monday was our November faculty meeting. The school's faculty meets once a month. As you might expect, it is an event largely filled with routine moments and lengthy discussions of minutiae, enlivened by the occasional ideological debate or school scandal. At these meetings, people tend to group themselves by department. The members of the English Department sit by the window. Jana gave me a slight, awkward smile from the window seat where she sat but did not invite me to join her. Clichéd though it is, my heart was pounding so rapidly that I felt ill. I sat down quickly, hoping no one noticed my discomfort. I usually sit alone, not far from the English teachers, since I constitute an entire department. As I took my seat this time, I was acutely aware of Jana sitting behind me and slightly to my left. I fancied I could hear her breathing.

Ted Fox strode in shortly, folders under his right arm and graying hair disarranged, wearing his usual preoccupied look. He sat at the table in front of the room, spread the folders before him, and looked up, eyes widened slightly, as if he was surprised to find us there waiting. "Right, then, gentlemen—and ladies, of course— let's get to it." He then proceeded to describe, in detail, a number of small bureaucratic matters that required our attention—attendance sheets filled out incorrectly, the importance of signing in and out of school on the clipboard left in the faculty lounge, the routine upcoming visit from members of the independent school board of accreditation. My attention wandered, and I could see my fellow faculty members shifting in their seats. None of what Fox was saying invited the slightest response.

After he had droned on in this vein for a few more minutes, he closed the files before him and pushed the various papers into a neat pile. He cleared his throat and gave the assembled faculty the benefit of his penetrating blue gaze. "This brings us to our main topic of the day, ladies and gentlemen," he said firmly. "Some of you may have heard that Jerry Washington and I paid a visit to New Haven recently to meet with some of our African-American alumni and friends. Many of them expressed grave concern about the current state of our enrollment of black students. Or, to be frank, the lack thereof. As I'm sure you all know, we have a miserable retention rate with these young men, and we are having a harder and harder time attracting them at all—even as boys' schools begin to come back into favor. What I want to hear from you today is not arguments or rationalizations, but some bold, clear thinking on what we can do to change this. Certain of our funding sources have demanded that we at least show an effort toward change in the very near future. What's more, greater diversity is where this nation is headed. I don't intend for this school to be left behind. Your thoughts, anyone?"

Stony silence descended. One or two people looked quickly at me, then away. The backs of my hands tingled, and I could feel my breath moving tightly in and out of my lungs. The issue of Chelsea's racial makeup had never before been spoken of quite this bluntly. There seemed to be no immediate way to respond. The first voice to emerge from the silence was that of Jack Brodie, the chemistry teacher.

"Ted, what do you mean, 'certain of our funding sources'?"

Fox reddened slightly and then decided to answer. "Well, do you all remember Brendan Hastings?"

There was a general murmur of agreement. Hastings was one

of Chelsea's most prominent alumni. An unremarkable student, he had gone on to develop a popular Internet search engine called Howl (after the Allen Ginsberg poem, which he greatly admired). It had made him wildly wealthy. Fox went on.

"Well, Hastings has taken a great interest in matters of diversity—perhaps because his wife is black—I don't know. In any event, he's buying a home on the East Coast, and not long after my trip to New Haven with Jerry, he expressed an interest in making a substantial gift to the school—very substantial—but only if we improve our numbers in this area." He paused. "I think you all know about our current fiscal crunch. Enrollment and endowment are slipping. We're up against it. Hastings's gift is a much needed one—a gift I can't pass up."

Fox's frankness stunned the room into silence. There had been much talk of late of the school's dire financial straits, but to pin our hopes so explicitly on one man and his one cause—I hardly knew what to say. Jana was the first to speak.

"So you're only doing this to get money?" she said, her voice quavering slightly.

"No," Fox said levelly. "Not only. But I thought it best to be utterly candid at the outset. I would be lying if I didn't say that Hastings's offer has lit a fire under me on this issue. It's one we should have addressed long ago."

"You got that right," said Jana a bit sarcastically.

Fox looked at her coolly. "Thanks for your vote of confidence. Now if I could hear some concrete suggestions on how we should go about making this much needed change?"

Jana spoke again, though she still sounded a little angry. "One thing that might help with the issue is a little old-fashioned outreach. In my time here, which is admittedly rather short, I haven't had a good sense of us sending the black students we *do* have out into their communities. With some faculty, of course. Has that been tried? It seems an obvious first step."

Fox looked at me evenly. "We have done that in the past," he said, his voice level. "But it's been a number of years since we put a great deal of effort into recruitment with the faculty." His eyes never left my face. At that moment, I knew I was to be involved in any future recruitment plan—regardless of what my feelings about it might be.

"We did try it several years ago," I said, my voice tinny in my own ears. "It was not entirely successful, but I am convinced—I should say, Mr. Fox has convinced me—that if we redouble our efforts, they might bear more fruit in the future." I smiled slightly.

Bob Harmon spoke up. A good many of the black boys in the school played on the Chelsea basketball team—which he coached. "Let me speak frankly, Ted," he said, his fair skin reddening as he continued. "I probably spend more time with more of the black kids here than any of the rest of you. I see how hard it is for some of them to fit in here. It's a great chance for a boy, coming here. But it's not for everybody. I think we need to be very careful about who we recruit—so we don't see the levels of academic difficulty that I've seen from some of the kids on my team. I just think we need to be careful." He trailed off a little uncertainly.

"Careful?!" This, angrily, from Tom Kelly, perhaps our youngest faculty member, who taught Spanish. "If we were any more careful, there wouldn't be any black students here at all. Is that the kind of care you want to take, Bob? Careful to keep them out of here unless they can help the team?"

Harmon sputtered, "That's not what I meant . . ." And suddenly I heard my own voice chiming in.

"If I may be so bold, I think that Bob has something of a point. We all know that not every boy thrives in an environment like Chelsea's. I think it is our duty to select young men who can truly profit from the experience."

"And none of those young men are black?" Jana said, a little sarcastically. She was looking directly at me.

Fox jumped in. "Please, ladies and gentlemen. There is no point in us getting into some sort of turf war over this issue. For one thing, it's not up for debate. As I've said, this is something that we as a school are going to *do,* not discuss. We are going to get to at least ten percent black students by 2005. It's as simple—and difficult—as that."

I heard Jana's voice behind me again. "I'd like to add that I don't think that getting to *ten* percent is even such great shakes—although it would be doing better than we're doing now. I can't believe there's no one else in here who thinks that." There were some nods and murmurs of assent from Kelly and a few others. Harmon crossed his arms across his chest, his mouth pulled down.

Fox spoke again. "Now I'd like some constructive conversation about this issue. And I want it now." A brief, chastised silence, then various voices were raised, suggestions were made, at first timidly, then with greater and greater vigor. Most of my colleagues, though they had been quiet during the confrontation, seemed to feel as Jana did, that further diversifying the school was a wise course of action, and suggested numerous ways we might do so. No one looked at me. I could feel people willing their eyes not to drift my way.

At last the meeting ended. The tension that had built up in the room dissipated somewhat as we dispersed, but I still felt as though I had been bound with piano wire for an hour. Jana fell into step with me as we left the building. After what seemed an eternity she said, "How are you?"

At the sound of her voice I found I could look at her. Her eyes were gentle and sad. Rather as mine were, I suppose. "I have had better days," I said.

"Me too."

We fell silent. We had arrived at the parking lot. She looked around quickly, as though someone might have followed us. But there was no one. "Come talk to me for a minute," she said. She opened her car door, got in, reached over to let me in. Once again she was in charge. I got in.

Once I was seated, we both stared out the window for a minute. Finally I found my voice. "Jana. I don't know if I can stand this." My God. I'd had no idea I was going to say that. So desperate. Had I lost control completely? I clenched my hands into fists on the car seat. I could smell her grassy perfume. It filled the car.

"I know," she said. "But I think we'll have to. Don't you? I mean . . . we just can't . . ." She sighed. "I mean, for one thing, we work together in this tiny school. And it was . . . nice, it was great but—" Her voice caught. "It just . . . happened." She stopped, pressed the heels of her hands to her eyes, swallowed twice before she could speak again. "I was listening to you in there, and watching you and thinking, *I hardly know him at all.* You can't really think so little of a boy like Rashid, can you?"

I could not have been more shocked if she had reached across the seat and slapped me. "What in God's name has this got to do with the Bryson boy?"

She looked at me. Her eyes were intensely green. "Do you see how you can't even say his name? His name is Rashid."

My hands clenched even tighter. I struggled to keep my voice measured. "All right. His name is Rashid. But what does that have to do with what's happened between us?"

She gazed out the windshield, not looking at me. "He doesn't trust you. He came to see me today to work on his chapel talk, and he thinks you don't want him here. And . . . after watching how uncomfortable you were in there today at the thought, even the very thought of having more boys like him in this school, I . . . I'm not convinced that he's wrong. I'm sorry. It's hard to explain, but that's part of why I'm not sure we can go on. I had a boy like him in my old school . . . I lost him. I just can't be with you knowing you feel as you do. I just can't." She looked out the window on her side.

"What is it you see in him, anyway?" I said suddenly, surprised to hear real heat in my voice. "Why are you so convinced he does belong here? Because his brother was killed?" I drew a deep breath. "That alone doesn't make him deserving of what we offer here. You have to work for that. Having a brother killed . . . that earns you nothing. You hear me? Nothing."

She turned away from the window and gazed at me keenly for a minute that seemed without end. Then her eyes widened. "This happened to you. This happened to you. Didn't it?" Her voice did not change inflection. Now it was my turn to look away, my eyes stinging.

"My brother was killed when I was teaching in Boston. He was holding up a store. I . . ." But there was nothing else to say.

"Jerome, I'm so sorry." She reached across the seat for my hand. "I'm so sorry."

"Yes. Well. I left the public schools after he died. There didn't seem to be much point. After that. I couldn't save him. I couldn't help any of them. And they wouldn't help themselves." At those words, her hand, her whole body, stiffened and then moved away from mine. She removed her hand. A bitter drawing away.

"That's how you see it?"

I looked her full in the face. "It's the only way I know how to see it."

"Jerome . . . I . . . I'm sorry about your brother. I don't presume to know what might have helped him, but don't you see . . . you have to give people a chance. They can't make it if you don't. Supporting Rashid . . . it's a chance to try to put things right. Why are you throwing that away?"

"I'm not throwing anything away."

"Yes, you are. All you see is some ridiculous statistic or some ridiculous theory you cribbed from the Romans or something. Don't you see? Don't you see him—who *this* boy is?" I just looked at her. "You don't, do you? Well. Your loss." She put the car key in the ignition, looked straight out the windshield. "You should probably go now," she said without looking at me.

I didn't move. I remembered how her breasts had felt under my hands. I felt, briefly, that I might actually lose my mind. I thought of hitting her. But that would not be appropriate. It would not display the kind of decorum I have spent my life achieving. I drew a long, shuddering breath and got out of the car without speaking. She drove away without looking back. I stood there, the cold pulling at my bones. "We forget our pleasures, we remember our sufferings." Cicero said that. I could smell snow in the air, bitter and sharp. A long night lay ahead.

Oratory skill was one of the hallmarks of a man in ancient Rome. Decisions that shifted the course of history were based on speeches that were made in public forums. Even in the history of this country, there have been moments—the Lincoln-Douglas debates, the Gettysburg address, John F. Kennedy's inaugural address, Dr. King's "I Have a Dream" speech—when the well-placed words of a man have swept the nation to a higher plane. This is the noble impulse behind the Chelsea School's long tradition of training our young men in public speaking through the forum of a chapel talk. The young men here will be the Plinys and the Lincolns of the next age. It is part of our job to prepare them for the mantle they will soon assume. You would be a bit surprised if I told you the names of some of the prominent men I have seen as boys, stumbling through their first efforts at public speaking. Often, it is the boys who appear the most confident, even cocky, when standing before their lockers with their friends who stammer through their brief speeches with looks of cold terror on their faces. Sometimes, though, the confident ones are just as at ease on stage as off. They reel off facts and figures, joyfully persuade, stand without shifting uneasily from foot to foot.

Sometimes the life of privilege that they have led brings them to a level of mastery that nothing can break. They are fourteen. They believe nothing will ever go wrong in their lives and that they deserve—perhaps even have earned—all that they have. They will never die or suffer. Nothing will ever be taken from them. All that foolish belief resides in the ten-minute gloss of their speeches.

But that's not most of the boys. Most of them are simply boys. They'd rather die than stand there before us, defending their thoughts about anything.

Their topics are generally reflective of the concerns of the young. They tend to be broad—I remember one young man who proudly stood before us and announced that he would be discussing the entire history of science; another who said that he would be enlightening us on the subject of space interest and exploration from its very earliest times. Some boys try to provoke scandal with their talks, filling their speeches with weak sexual puns or controversial topics—topics they know Fox will not appreciate—like the boy who argued for the legalization of marijuana and then pretended to a theatrical mock inhalation on what appeared to be a joint. It was later found to be shredded tissue wrapped in cigarette paper, but by then the damage had been done. That boy was expelled—I should say that he was, in general, a troublemaker. Lesser offenders are generally chastised quietly afterward by Fox and show up later in the school year with a hangdog look on their faces, offering dutiful, well-researched, reasonable speeches for the second attempts they've been forced to make.

Over the years, I have heard hundreds of these speeches. I have been struck—and saddened—as time has passed, by the continual diminution of basic skills of self-expression among the young men we teach. So many of them now affect the stance of young hoodlums, mumbling into the microphone, never making eye contact, shuffling their feet vaguely back and forth for their brief time on stage. I have grown to expect such behavior, though I do not approve of it.

The room was full of its usual rustlings of paper and coughing of restless boys as we awaited young Bryson's arrival on the stage. I spotted two sophomores to my right passing notes back and forth and stopped them with a single cold look. They sank back in their chairs, nervous looks on their faces. After a few minutes, Bryson appeared on the stage, adjusted the microphone to his level, looked out over the assembled faces briefly, and began to speak. His voice was uncertain, and I anticipated a performance as tedious and unfocused as others I had witnessed—perhaps more so.

"Most of you know me. Well, most of you think you know me. You look at my hair and you think I'm into hip-hop. Which I am. You see me with a basketball in gym class and you think I'll be real good. Which I am not. You see me running cross-country and I'm real good at that and you think, 'Well, he's just a natural athlete. They're all really good runners, aren't they? They learn how to run dodging those bullets and running from the cops.' You don't see all the time I spend in practice, how hard I work at it. That I've never committed a crime in my life. Neither had my brother." He paused. A deep breath, so that his voice truly carried as he spoke his next words. "You hear that my brother, Kofi, was shot and killed in the street a year and a half ago and you think that kind of thing happens all the time to guys like me. That all we do is sit in our ghettos and shoot each other." There was a collective gasp at this, but Bryson continued undaunted. "You believe all this because you never look outside these walls. I know people like you. People like a lot of you. You think you're so different. But you're not. Your prison is fancier—you've got the cars, you've got the cash—but not wanting to hear about anything that's gonna make you think? That's the same. I've seen guys like that here. Some of them are students." He paused and drew another deep breath. "Some of them are teachers. They might know all about the best bike or the best computer or some civilization that's been dead for a thousand years. But they don't know me. They think they do—but all they know is what is locked up in their own closed minds. That's what I wanted to talk to you all about today. It's time you all really got educated."

He went on in this vein for the rest of his allotted time. He informed us that the school ought to be, by his reckoning, at least 40 percent "people of color" (ridiculous term—we might as well go back to "colored people"). He informed us that this world that was Chelsea was one that was nearly extinct, and good riddance to it. He and those like him were the wave of the future. He went on: "Change is going to come about. If you're ready, you'll get out of the way. If you're not, it's going to run you right over."

Though, as I said, he began uncertainly, by the end of his speech these words of Cicero's came to me: "No rarer thing than a finished orator can be discovered among the sons of men." Bryson was a mesmerizing speaker. He stood easily at the lectern, his hands punctuating his most important points as though he had been born to the stage. His voice rose and fell in cadence so that just at the moment when we might have drifted away, he would snatch us back with some trick of the timbre of his voice—like an old-time Baptist preacher. I had never seen such control in one so young. And I had never heard such nonsense in my life. He was spitting in the face of the very place that might help him develop this gift and get somewhere in his thus far benighted life. He was spitting in *my* face. "Some civilization a thousand years old." When I thought of all the talks I'd had with him, the hours of extra practice and special care, the effort to get him *not* to claim some kind of victim status . . . and it all meant absolutely nothing to him. He was determined to throw his gifts away. My stomach contracted with disbelief.

His effect on the boys was electric. Some sat up nodding and looking properly chastened. Others looked as contemptuous as I felt. Some seemed simply baffled. Fox's face was red and his hands were folded tightly in his lap, but he betrayed no other emotion. "The future is in our hands. It's time that this school steps up and leads—not follows—based on some ancient idea of what manhood is about," concluded Bryson. "It's time."

Absolute silence followed. Then the sound of one pair of hands clapping. I looked around—it was Gerald Davis, Bryson's friend, who now rose to his feet, applauding even more vigorously. He was followed, slowly at first and then with growing vigor, by all the Negro students and then a great many of the white ones. Some boys, among them Max Harrison and Ben Gould, remained stubbornly in their seats, staring defiantly at the floor, their faces red. But all in all, slightly more than half of the student body stood, accompanied by a few faculty members— Jana among them. I saw Fox give her a tight-lipped look as he walked to the podium to dismiss the assembly. Bryson still stood there, a slight, hard smile on his face, his hands resting lightly on the lectern. He looked much older than fourteen.

"All right, gentlemen. Let's have a little decorum, please." Turning to Bryson, he said, "Thank you, Mr. Bryson, for that most . . . unusual chapel talk. We will give it all due consideration. Gentlemen, I believe it is time for your classes. Onward!" The boys filed out, abuzz.

Today, as I walked out of the auditorium among the boys, I felt only as though I didn't know them at all. I was not unaware that the world had changed. But how could it have changed so that a boy like Bryson would be able to persuade with nationalist claptrap of the sort I hadn't heard since I'd left Harvard thirty-five years ago? What had shifted? Nothing. Who was in power? The sons of those who were in power thirty-five years ago. He could stand there and spout his nonsense, but what made him think that his way would lead to any real change? He was fourteen. He didn't know what it was like to be denied access to anything because of his skin. He didn't know that the only way to win them over was to concede. To let them know that what they wanted was what you wanted. Simply to live quietly.

I felt I had to get outside, if only for a moment, before my class, to try to compose my thoughts. Jana was standing in the doorway that I stepped out of. A light snow had dusted the greenness of the grass, and the end of her nose was slightly reddened by the cold. The campus looked very beautiful.

"Some speech, huh?" she said.

"Quite." The air was sharp in my lungs. "You knew what he was going to say, didn't you?"

"Yes. Of course."

"And you didn't try to stop him? Make him see reason?"

"He was being true to his experience. The point of these speeches is for the boys to learn to articulate their own positions clearly, isn't it?"

"But what he had to say . . ."

"Is what he had to say. Look, Jerome, this is who this boy is. If you don't see that, well, then I can't help you."

She turned sharply and walked away. I almost called out her name. But there was no point. There was no getting her back now, I knew. And somehow that boy had driven us to it. I thought of his raucous cries during that ridiculous display with his friends at the dance. Not even music. Just noise. Destruction and tearing apart. That was all he knew. I went back inside, my eyes stinging. The glass of the door was cold under my hand.

My first class of the day was Latin 1. As I entered, the quiet hum of conversation that had filled the room dropped to silence. Bryson was in his usual seat in the back of the classroom. I looked at him evenly as I stepped to the front of the room. *I am not going to sink to his level,* I thought. I even managed a cordial smile at the boys. "Well, gentlemen, let's get started, shall we?" I flipped my text open to the day's lesson.

We made our way slowly through the day's translation. As is

my custom, I called on various boys to allow them to try their hand. I will admit, I try to keep them slightly off balance, sometimes calling on someone who hasn't volunteered, sometimes going only for the boys who have raised their hands. Since Mr. Bryson's initial objections to my overlooking him, I had begun to be more conscientious about calling on him as well, not wanting to be perceived as unfair. It was also important that he do well in my class in order to continue to participate in cross-country. Once I did start calling on him and had a chance to deal with more of his written work, I found that he was an average student. Not particularly gifted in Latin translation, but within acceptable boundaries for a boy of his age.

He sat with his gaze directed out the window, his legs planted insolently. "Mr. Bryson." My voice came out more sharply than I had intended.

"Yes, Mr. Washington?" He looked rather guileless. But I knew better now.

"I'd appreciate it if you would bring your mind down from whatever elevated plane it was on and rejoin us here in the room." Some of the boys laughed. I ignored their chuckles. "Since, as you showed us this morning, you are possessed of an extraordinary degree of wisdom, would you be so kind as to favor us with your version of this phrase: *Diligentia maximum etiam mediocris ingeni subsidium.*"

"'Diligence is the most . . .' I . . . I don't know the rest. Sir." His eyes were wide but defiant, his voice contemptuous.

"'Diligence is a very great help to even a mediocre intelligence.' Seneca said that. They are words I believe you could heartily benefit from, Mr. Bryson. Perhaps a little more time with your books and a little less time on your speeches would be in order." Again, a moment's laughter from some of the boys, a cowed silence from others. I ignored them all, turning away from him. I could feel his wounded gaze following me. "Let's move on, gentlemen."

I taught the rest of the class without incident and without calling on him again. I said in conclusion shortly before the end of the period, "Before I end for the day, I wanted to let you gentlemen know that I'll have your midterm exams back to you by tomorrow's class. Are there any questions about today's work or the assignment for tomorrow?"

Bryson's hand went up, the only one. I couldn't very well ignore it. "I wonder, Mr. Washington, if I could ask if people thought that my chapel talk this morning had anything to do with this class in particular? We're supposed to ask people what they think of our talks when we make them, right?" He said this with what I perceived to be slight sarcasm.

"We've ended a bit early, so I suppose we might take a few minutes to discuss that now, though we don't do that as a matter of course." My voice sounded harsh and constricted in my ears. "I think your talk this morning presented some particular challenges for those who opt to study Latin. For example, if you believe it is so narrowing and irrelevant to your experience to study this language, what brought you to this class?"

His bravado faded for a moment, and his voice was husky as he answered, "My brother took it at his school. And I didn't say it was . . . what did you say, 'narrowing' . . . I said only taking that, only sticking with what you know . . . that's stupid. I came here so I wouldn't do that. And turns out, it's not that different. People never want to get out of the box."

At this, he looked directly at me. Needless to say, I did not respond directly but spoke to the class as a whole. "I think perhaps that you are selling the traditions of this school a little short, Mr. Bryson. Any other thoughts, gentlemen?"

"Well, I don't really see what's wrong with the school now," said Josh Bernstein. "I mean, they take the people who pass the test, right?"

Bryson took his eyes from mine for a moment. "Yeah, man,

but who gets to take the test? Who even gets to know about this school? Not the brothers where I come from. And a lot of them are smart enough to come here." He paused. "I mean, look at Mr. Washington here. Would you say that he isn't qualified to teach what he's teaching? He obviously passed the test." He looked back at me, his eyes flat and glittering.

I'd obviously passed the test. The words hit me like separate daggers, sharp and individual. It was clearly a moment for me to speak. Every boy in the class focused his gaze on me. The words of the former head of this department danced through my mind. *I didn't want you here anyway. Too many of your kind agitating as it is.* "I suppose I have," I said after a while. "But not without great effort and great struggle. I've earned whatever I have."

Bryson regarded me coolly. "With no help?"

"None that was unwarranted. None that I did not make some effort to be worthy of. None that I treated with contempt."

I looked at my watch. The period, mercifully, was over. "It's time for your next class, gentlemen. I will see you tomorrow."

The students filed out, some darting quick looks at me or at Bryson as they left. Bryson walked past my desk, paused, and looked directly at me, his eyes like coal—black and fathomless. "See you at practice, Mr. W." I simply nodded, unable to speak.

Isaiah had that look in his eyes. The same coal black anger that I see in young Mr. Bryson. As Isaiah drifted away and away from us, his eyes became angrier and more distant. He began to affect the street style of the day—a large Afro, tight silky shirts made out of some synthetic material, wide-legged, low-waisted pants. And when he spoke, he never looked either me or my mother in the eye. He regarded me as something of an oddity. Little professor, he'd call me.

"Hey, little professor. Got that nose stuck in a book again, I see. What you think's in there that's gonna help you out here on these streets?" he said once when he was about sixteen, sitting insolently on the other side of the kitchen table where I studied. I did not look up. "I'm talking to you, professor," he said, his voice raised just a threatening notch.

I looked up, annoyed and, for the first time, a little afraid. "I'm trying to finish this assignment. It's due tomorrow, and I don't want to be late."

"Don't want to be late," he said in a mocking tone. "What the fuck difference do it make if you're late or not? What do you think finishing this shit is going to do for you, boy?"

My voice rose to meet his. "I think it might get me out of here. I think it might improve my mind and teach me about something besides hanging out on street corners and drinking cheap wine. I think it might . . ."

My words trailed off as Isaiah rose to his feet. Though he was two years younger, he had lost the slightness of his youth and now looked more like our father, tall and bulky and threatening. He could have flattened me with one blow. "Think you better than me, huh? Well, come on, then. Show me who the real man is. Show me."

I looked up. This brother I had once known, whom I had shared a bed with until just a few years before, whose smells and habits and tastes had been as familiar to me as my own, was now a stranger. When we were little, before we left Georgia, we used to sit together on our ragged front porch, our dusty legs touching, and see how many june bugs we could catch in a jar on a summer evening. One. Two. Three. Four. Our breaths would mingle as we leaned over the jar, our heads touching, our skins one against the other. Sometimes on those nights, as darkness fell and the world was silent, I didn't know for sure where Isaiah ended and I began. We were just one brown boy, one breath, one flesh.

The moment that he stood before me, hands clenched to fists, breath coming hard as I rose to meet him, contained all those moments gone and all the moments we would never have. I stood there. My hands were open. My book was resting on the table. Isaiah spoke again. "Think you a man now, huh? You better show me."

But his hands were unclenching, and as I stared into his eyes, I saw, just for the scarcest fraction of a moment, the gentle boy who watched crows in deserted lots and caught june bugs with me on hot Georgia nights. "Isaiah," I said.

His face crumpled briefly, then he turned and walked quickly from the room, his platform shoes making a ridiculous clatter against the floor. My throat was tight with tears. I stood there for a long time. And I did not cry.

It had been many years since I thought of that moment. School long over for the day, I sat in the chill silence of my living room, remembering. All that I have struggled so hard to put behind me, to eliminate, to leave in order to achieve whatever small status I have gained in this world. Everything I have, I have earned by dint of my own hard work, my careful elimination of anything or anyone that might hold me back. My brother, my mother, my life before here, are nothing compared to what I hold in my hands at Chelsea—a line into the power that great ideas and great traditions hold.

I rose from my living room chair, and as is my habit, made some strong tea to drink as I graded my papers. It was going to be a long night. These exams were a significant part of every boy's grade for the semester, and I took particular care with them. Jana's face flashed before me for a moment, but, as I had been doing all day, I suppressed the thought quickly. A man must set aside what he cannot have. After that morning's class and my uncomfortable encounters with both her and with Bryson, the day had passed uneventfully. By the grace of God, I managed to avoid any con-versations about the morning's speech with anyone else, though I gathered from what I overheard in the halls that his stance and his revelation about his brother were the talk of the school. I opted to spend most of the day appearing to be absorbed in work in my office. I am used to being alone. I begged off cross-country practice, claiming a headache.

Now, tea in hand, I pulled the papers toward me with a sigh. More and more I find that the most basic rules of grammar and logic are lost even on those the boys who are interested, making their study of Latin grueling and their work discouraging for me. I finished the first few quickly—they were some of the better students, and the mistakes they'd made were easy to note and correct. Then came Bryson's test.

From the start, I had been fairly rigorous in grading his work. I wanted him to know that he could expect no breaks from me simply because we were of the same race. He had taken the stringent grading in reasonably good stride and always showed an effort to correct what had been wrong previously. But now, I found I was looking at his work through new eyes. As my pen moved over his translation, I found error after error, mostly the result of sloppy thinking. The paper was hatchmarked with red by the time I finished. I looked it over for a long time. Stopped to sample my tea. "It is said that man is wisest who can decide for himself what needs to be done." Cicero. Then, with a deep breath of resolution, I firmly wrote a D– across the top. I hoped that this would begin to teach him the importance of careful thought and of being grateful for the chance he'd been given.

I gazed out the window, drinking my tea. I remembered my excitement upon first watching him run. I remembered the moment that we raced against each other, my feelings—both joy and sorrow—as he passed me by. For no reason I could readily discern, my eyes stung. But with a few swift blinks, I turned back to my work. "The earth produces nothing worse than an ungrateful man." Ausonius said that. How bitterly I knew it now.

12

Boys to Men

As Rashid said these words in his chapel talk—"You hear my brother, Kofi, was shot and killed"—a dull roaring began in his ears. It muffled the applause and made it hard to see people getting to their feet. It made his movements feel jerky and unconnected as he accepted people's words of congratulation or as he avoided the glares of the guys who thought he was just some affirmative action radical, in the school on a quota. When Washington called him out during class, asking him to translate and ragging on him when he got it wrong, it got so loud that he thought he might lose his mind. But it quieted when he spoke up and got into that little beef with him. Then he felt strong again for a minute—the way he had behind that podium. After class, though, the roaring came back.

He was at lunch, waiting for Gerald, resisting the impulse to shake his head or hit his ears, the way you do when you get out of a pool, when Josh Bernstein, from his Latin class, came up to his table. "Can I sit down?"

"Sure. I guess. It ain't . . . I mean, nobody else is sitting here yet."

Bernstein seemed to have something on his mind. He fiddled with his knife and fork for a minute, then spoke. "Listen, Rashid. I know that you think that a lot of us are just . . . that we've got a lot of ideas about this stuff and about you, but . . . well, I thought what you did today took a lot of guts. More than I have, anyway." He paused. "And that's really sad about your brother." He laughed nervously now. "I know we haven't talked much. But I wanted you to know . . . what I was thinking. Not everybody's the same here."

The roaring in Rashid's head got very quiet. "Thanks, man. I appreciate that."

A moment's silence hung between them, then Gerald came up to the table, "Yo, R. You. Are. The. Man! You rocked the house today. Everybody's talking about it."

They both turned to Gerald, and the moment was over; the conversation went on, flitting from Rashid's speech to the terror of waiting for midterm results to whatever. No one talked about Kofi. But for a little while, Rashid felt at rest, at ease. Quiet. If only it could stay this way.

That night, another shock. He was in his room, studying, like always, when there was a knock at the door. "Phone for you, Bryson."

For him? It was never for him. But he got up and went to answer it.

"Hi, son." His mother's voice. She had called him.

"Ma? I . . . What's wrong?" he asked sharply.

"Nothing's wrong, Rashid. I can't call my son?"

Rashid was silent. She sighed and went on. "I know that I don't usually make the call, but tonight I had the funniest feeling. I felt like I needed to talk to you. Isn't that funny?"

"Yeah."

"So. You all right?"

His hand was so tight around the receiver that it was starting to hurt. He pressed his lips to the mouthpiece. "Mama. I told. I told," he whispered.

"Told what, Rashid?'

"I told about Kofi. I know you and Daddy didn't want me to, but I couldn't stand it anymore, Mama. I couldn't stand it. So I told everybody. I made a speech."

She was silent. For one minute, two, more. Rashid thought about buildings collapsing, tidal waves. The roaring in his ears returned.

"Well," she said after an eternity, her voice shaking. "Well." A long, shuddering breath. "You know, Rashid. You're my boy, too. You couldn't do anything that would make me ashamed of you. I wish . . . Your daddy and I . . . it's just been so hard. But I know you wouldn't do anything to make us ashamed. I don't know why we thought you would." She was silent again. Then, as if to herself, "We got nothing to be ashamed of." A whisper.

Rashid's eyes were full of tears, but he did not let them fall. He was grateful for the old-fashioned door on the phone room. He wrapped the phone cord around and around his finger.

"Don't you miss him, Mama?"

"Every day, son. Every day."

"Me too."

"Well, we all really loved him." She paused. "But I've been thinking that we've got to take better care of what's left. That matters, too. So I'm going to try to do that. You try too."

"I will, Mama." Silence. "Do you want to know what I said, Mama? I could send you a copy of the speech. It . . . it's too hard to say over the phone."

Her voice over the wires was ragged but strong. "I'd love that. And so would your daddy. Don't you call us this Sunday. We'll call you. All right?" She laughed a little. "We've started going back to church. It helps a little. And here I am planning to call you twice in one week. Looks like I might be trying to get myself together after all—" Her voice broke off in a sob. "I'll talk to you real soon, baby. Real soon."

Rashid sat in the phone room for he didn't know how long. Till his eyes were dry. He swallowed a few times, then got up and went back to his work. There was still so much to do.

The next day, Mr. Fox approached him in the hall. He was walking to Latin class, his head down, his mind blank, when he heard his name called. "Mr. Bryson, I'd like to speak with you for a moment."

He looked up, startled. Was he going to get yelled at about his speech?

"Yes?" He resisted the impulse to start shifting from foot to foot, but just barely.

"Mr. Bryson, we're starting a program of outreach into some of the city schools, and we are recruiting some students to join some of our faculty on speaking visits to some of them. I was impressed by your ease in front of a crowd during your chapel talk and so I thought you'd do a fine job on such a trip. The trip needn't—and shouldn't—interfere too drastically with your schoolwork."

"What would I have to do?"

"Just talk. Tell some young men much like yourself of your experience here. Why you chose it. What the benefits are for you. Why they might consider it. Pretty basic stuff. Do you feel prepared for such a task?"

Tell some young men of his experience here. Tell them about being surrounded by rich white boys twenty-four hours a day. Tell them about feeling the color of your skin every second as something strange to them, that they'd seen only in positions of servitude or entertainment. Tell them about the schoolwork that made your brain literally ache—but then the brief moments when it all came clear and the world seemed bigger and you saw the light within what you were reading and wondered why that couldn't happen at your old school. Tell them about looking around at the dances for one girl who looked like the girls you knew back home—round and brown skinned and glossy with bravado. Tell them what it's like to never see that face. Tell them about everybody wanting something from you—the coaches wanting you to run and run, even when you weren't sure how you felt about it; the teachers wanting you to speak up in class, even when you weren't sure what they were talking about; your parents wanting you to do them proud, even when you weren't sure that you could. Tell them about the weight of needing to succeed, knowing that so much rests on it and feeling afraid. Tell them what it's like to know that for everything you're getting from this place, you're giving something up. Tell them what it's like here. Do you feel prepared? "I think I could do that, Mr. Fox. I think I would do a good job."

"Excellent. I thought as much. I'll let you know the date of the first trip soon. Thanks for your help, Mr. Bryson. It's much appreciated."

Fox started to walk down the hallway when Rashid called after him, "Mr. Fox, who else will be going on the trip?"

The older man took a few steps back toward Rashid, ticking off names on his fingers. "Some of the other students—Sean Cho and your friend Gerald Davis. And a couple of the faculty members, Mr. Washington and Ms. Hansen, I think, will be the ones who join you on your first trip. You'll be visiting a school in New York City. Your hometown, yes?"

"Yeah. I mean, yes."

"Well, perhaps you'd like to let your parents know that you'll be there. In any event, you'd better head along, young man. It's nearly time for your next class. I'll speak with you soon."

Rashid turned to walk to his Latin class, his chest tight. It felt that way always now, but even more so before Latin. The thought of driving to New York with Washington and having to act like everything was all right for a whole day made him sick. But he couldn't say no. As sick as he felt, he still had this deep, inescapable feeling that to leave this school would be death. That it would kill him as surely as being home had killed Kofi. He feared that to refuse any request—especially one from the head-master—could lead to his having to leave. So he set himself to do what was asked of him and kept quiet about the knife in his heart.

The worst thing about that knife was that the serrated edge was distracting him from the work he needed to do to stay at Chelsea. He tried to read, but the words swam before him in a red mist. He did homework, wrote papers, parsed verbs, but it was all so hard. His assignments from all his teachers kept coming back to him littered with red marks, *see me*s, errors. He was hanging on, but it felt like just barely.

Latin was the worst. They had just finished midterms, and he needed to do well. He'd studied his head off, going over and over the material. He'd felt okay going into the test. Not great, but okay. Up until now, he had been consistently getting Cs and sometimes even a B on his regular work, despite hordes of frantic red-ink corrections. Even when he hadn't got something *wrong* exactly, Washington seemed to find some little thing that could have been done better or more smoothly or with more thought or care or something. Basically, he seemed to feel that Rashid just wasn't right. And after that scene yesterday . . . He gazed at Washington with slitted eyes. His ears were ringing.

"Well, gentlemen. I have your midterms for you. There are many of you who will need to bear down in order to bring your final grade up for the year. At this time of year, I generally make myself available for questions and discussions of some of the material we've covered. I hope that you all will take advantage of my availability as you see fit. I think once I return these tests, you'll have a better idea of whether or not you need to speak with me." He passed the papers to the students, facedown. Rashid didn't turn his over for a few moments. When he did, his throat tightened abruptly. If it hadn't, he might have cried out. A D– was staring him in the face. Next to it was a terse comment: "You may see me if you wish, but basically, you need to apply yourself to more careful study."

Rashid stared at the page until the words began to run together. More careful study. That's all he'd been trying to do since he got here. And Washington was giving him no credit at all. Rashid looked up at the teacher, who gave him an icy glance. If he hadn't been in a classroom full of boys, he might have broken down and cried. But since he was in a classroom, he got up, gathered his books and the test with the horrible note, and walked to Washington's desk. "Mr. Washington?"

"Yes, Mr. Bryson?"

"Mr. Fox talked to me today. He wants me to go on a recruiting trip into the city with you and Ms. Hansen and some other students. I guess we'll be going to some schools like the one I came from. Looking for some more guys like me."

Rashid could feel the edge in his voice as he said this last. And from the look on his face, he knew that Washington heard it, too. They might have been standing on a street corner, shattered glass under their feet, the whir of traffic going by. The hum of privilege seemed to vanish, the quietly lovely campus, the beautifully appointed classroom with enough unbroken, undamaged chairs and room for everyone, the textbooks that were current and not destroyed by overuse and obsolescence—all that seemed to disappear in that moment. They were two black men, dark hard skin about the same shade. The same angry look in their eyes. Silence rose up between them.

Washington broke first. He looked down at his desk, arranging papers quickly and stuffing them into his briefcase. "Very well, then. Perhaps you will avail yourself sometime soon of the opportunity to discuss your work with me. Or at least to apply yourself to it with a bit more enthusiasm. I want you to take advantage of the chances you've been given."

"I will."

Washington left the room first. Rashid followed behind him a few steps, but then turned to go his own way, back to his locker. *Who's going to help me?* he thought. But then he thought that maybe there was no help for him. That however this played out, he would have to play it out alone.

Gerald came up behind him at his locker and got him in a fast headlock. "What up, G?"

Rashid felt the heat behind his eyes and the tightness in his throat quickly shoot down to his stomach. He was back in control. "Nothing, man. Nothing at all."

"How was Washington today?"

"The same." The big, determined roundness of the D, the definite little slash following it. The same. Gerald was speaking again.

"Listen, man, did Fox speak to you?" he said.

"About this trip? Yeah, he did. You gonna do it?"

"Yeah. You?"

"Hell, yeah."

Gerald shifted his backpack swiftly from one shoulder to the other. "He had that look, you know? That look like 'do this or I'll kill you.'"

Rashid felt his lips curve up in a slight smile. He felt oddly insubstantial, his backpack shifting on his back, each foot hitting the carpet soundlessly. Extended speech seemed a grave effort, and he thought he could feel the crumpled test at the bottom of his backpack burning through to somehow sear his flesh. It seemed a miracle to him that no one else could see the fire. His voice, when he spoke, sounded faraway and odd to him. "Yeah, I'm going. I'm going."

He could hear Gerald talking about when they were supposed to go and what all they might talk about. He could hear himself giving what he supposed were appropriate answers. He just remembered Washington's eyes on him. The coldness of them.

Without warning, Sean Cho came up behind Gerald and Rashid and ran into them with his arms outstretched, shoving them both forward a few steps, laughing. "Why, it's the minority outreach committee," he said gleefully. "Planning your new strategy, kids?"

"Shut the fuck up, Cho. You know you're going on this little boat ride, too," said Gerald. His voice had taken on the teasing aggressiveness that he affected in public. "'Sides, it's like Rashid here said—we could use a little color up in here."

Sean laughed. "Don't I know it? To tell the truth, I was a little surprised Fox asked me along for the ride." He looked suddenly embarrassed, his smile fading. "I mean, there's a lot more guys like me here than guys like you."

Rashid looked at him evenly. "Well, in the city, the best schools are half Asian as it is. I guess Fox didn't want to pass that up, either."

The boys were briefly silent. Then Sean spoke. "I didn't run into you guys to get all heavy, actually. I wanted to invite you for a little nature walk." He waggled his eyebrows. "If you're free this period."

Rashid felt the knot in his stomach loosen. "I could definitely use a nature walk. Let's go."

Gerald shot a surprised look at Rashid but nodded after a moment. "Cool, I got this period free, too." The boys returned to their lockers, got their coats, and pushed through the school's front doors at the same time. They teased and joked as they walked into the dense woods surrounding the tennis courts. The air was tense with cold, sharp and glassy, and as they walked away from the school, gradually the only sounds to be heard were their heavy hiking boots breaching the light crust of snow and ice on the ground and their voices bouncing through the air. Their breath puffed before them. After a while, they came to a small clearing, not far from the barn, that was littered with cigarette butts and the tag ends of joints. A few large rocks were arranged into a rough circle of seats. Sean dug around in his overstuffed backpack for a while and finally produced the small, soft bag of pot. He rolled a joint, quickly and expertly, picking the seeds out carefully. He held it up for brief admiration when he was done and then said, "Nature. Nothing quite like it." Gerald and Rashid both laughed as he lit up, took a hit, and passed the joint to Rashid.

After the first couple of hits, Rashid's head started to feel light and full of air. Latin class seemed very far away, and the test in his backpack—the one that just a few minutes ago seemed as though it would burn right through to his skin—no longer even bothered him particularly. The dusting of snow on the ground took on a delicate glow. He felt as though he could see each flake if he only looked carefully enough. It had been a long time since he'd smoked—he'd done it only a couple of times back home and hadn't done it at all at Chelsea—but the feeling of warmth swaddled him like a blanket from his childhood. Everything that had been so difficult began to shift and slip easily away, the edges softening and blurring. His friends looked particularly kind and beautiful to him. They talked for a while of many things in a circular, laughing way—football, music, girls, reading, music, girls. After a little while, Gerald and Sean were laughing about some girl who had been at the last dance they had had with Langton Day, the one where Washington hit the dance floor. "Yo, did you see that girl? That one, what's her name, Sheila Jackson? You couldn't miss her. She was like the best-looking honey in the place," said Gerald.

"And she only danced with Josh McGovern," said Sean. "She wouldn't be caught dead with the likes of you, Davis. Thinks all the Negroes other than her doctor daddy and all us Korean folks are here on scholarship while our folks back home run grocery stores or rob banks."

"I know it," said Gerald. "But damn, she was fine."

They sealed their agreement with another hearty toke. "Do you ever feel like you can't stand it?" said Rashid as he passed off, his voice constricted by smoke. He didn't know what he was going to say until he had said it.

"Can't stand what? Not getting any? Hell, yeah."

Gerald and Sean both giggled madly and high-fived each other. Rashid felt his high taking on a crazy, uncomfortable edge. "No, I mean everything. This whole damn school. Sometimes I feel like . . ." He jumped up and kicked the rock he had been sitting on as hard as he could. Gerald and Sean watched him, their breath chill puffs of air before them. "Damn, now I'm bringing us all down. Let me just shut the fuck up."

The giggling stopped, and the boys sat in silence. The air was a lot colder. But that wasn't something that anyone could do anything about. "It's cold out here," remarked Sean. Without any more words, the silly good feeling dissipating, they buried the roach and stood, intending to head back to campus.

As they walked, Rashid squinted against the brilliant sunshine. It hurt his eyes. The brown and fading green of the grass under the dusting of snow was weirdly blinding. He looked toward the barn. It throbbed red against a brown-and-white backdrop, outlined by a comically blue sky. The cows were nowhere to be seen—it was too cold for their tastes. He imagined that they were huddled in the barn, their warm, bovine breath adding to the thick hay-and-cow-manure smell. The uncomfortable hyperawareness that he'd briefly lost when they were first getting high was coming back. He could feel the cold earth through his boots as he ground small things to death beneath them. "I'm too high to go to my next fucking class," he said finally. His voice seemed to come from a very long way off.

"Me too," said Gerald. Sean just nodded.

"Well, what are we gonna do, then?" said Rashid. "I'm fucking freezing."

The boys stood for a moment, their breath puffing out before them. "We could go to the barn—do the ropes course," Gerald suggested after a few moments of silence. Sean and Rashid caught each other's eyes with a "dare ya" look, then all three boys took off running, back toward the great red barn on the hill.

They stood breathless once they pulled open the heavy wooden door, a little shocked at what they were proposing to do. In addition to the six cows that lived there, the barn housed an elaborate obstacle course constructed of ropes, tires, and ladders called the ropes course, part of the school's outdoor leadership class. Before graduation, it was expected that every boy who came through Chelsea would not only be able to acquit himself ably in the academic program at any university he might attend, but would also have taken this class and done the ropes at least once. The ropes course was intended to give the young men a strong sense of teamwork and mastery over their bodies. It was not intended to be used unsupervised by stoned teenagers. The boys gleefully shucked their heavy backpacks and fat, shiny down coats and ran, howling, toward the ropes. The cows shifted uneasily in their stalls—it was usually quiet during the day. They were used to hearing only themselves in the barn.

Gerald was the first one up. He shinned up the rope easily, his soccer-honed legs making quick work of the climb. Then Sean followed, laughing and yelling, "Oh, shit!" all the way. Both boys made their way across the tightrope strung over a loosely woven net a little more nervously. Sean slipped once, causing all three hearts to leap into mouths, but he righted himself with a confident laugh. When they reached the platform at the end of the tightrope, they called raucously for Rashid to climb the hell up.

He stood at the foot of the rope for a minute, watching it sway.

Even once he'd reached out and grabbed it to still it, it continued to feel as though it was swaying under his hand. He started to climb anyway. Feathery sharp bits stung his hands as he climbed. The world whirled away beneath him, the hay-covered floor growing smaller and fainter. Now he was up to the tightrope and reaching out, one hand, the other, one knee, the other. He eased across the rope, suddenly scared. He looked across at his friends, who gazed at him expectantly, eagerly. He didn't feel high at all anymore, just clear and calm for the first time in many days. He inched forward a bit more. One hand, then the other, one knee, then the other. When his hand slipped, then his knee, and he began falling, twisting through the air, his biggest surprise was that there was no surprise. Only the cool shock of the barn's air moving swiftly past his face. He could dimly hear the shouts of his friends. He thought he probably ought to be more frightened. But in an odd way, as he plunged toward the ragged net below the rope, he felt only relief. It was so good to let go.

He hit the net on all fours, felt it give beneath his weight with a loud creak and sag, felt an odd, sharp, twisting sensation in his left ankle where it got caught in the mesh. It didn't really hurt but it was such a peculiar feeling that he cried out: "Fuck!" Gerald and Sean, who had watched silently, suddenly shouted, "We're coming, man," and scooted down the course as fast as they could. Rashid struggled to sit up. "Fuck," he said again.

Gerald reached him first. "Are you all right, man? Jesus Christ."

Sean stood right behind him. Together, they got Rashid to his feet. He shook his head. He had never felt so awful in his life, sick with sorrow and the fading paranoid remains of his high. He could put his full weight on his leg, but only with difficulty. "Y'all better take me back to the dorm. I gotta get myself together. Fuck."

The boys progressed down the short road to the dorms, jumping at every noise, praying no one would see them. No one did, a miracle. They didn't speak. Rashid had to hop every so often, get the weight off his leg. He threw his arms around Gerald's and Sean's necks to get up the stairs. They helped him into bed and stuck pillows under his ankle. Then they all slumped into the various corners of the room, Gerald biting the edge of his thumb. Rashid's leg didn't hurt so much propped up, and unbelievably, he felt himself falling asleep. *I miss my brother, y'all. Do you know that?* He thought he might have spoken aloud, but he wasn't sure.

When he woke up, the light had shifted to late afternoon gold. His leg hurt and his head hurt and his mouth tasted of ash and dirt. Gerald came into the room as he lay looking at the ceiling, dry-eyed.

"I think I need to go to the doctor. My ankle really hurts."

"I thought you might. Well, I'll help you." Gerald paused. "What are you gonna tell him?"

Rashid smiled bitterly. "That I'm a motherfuckin' idiot." He sighed. "I'll tell him that I went out to do some sprints or something by myself and tripped. I ain't gonna fuck you guys up, too. Can you help me into my running stuff?"

"Yeah. Sure." So Gerald got everything out of the drawers and helped him change clothes, tenderly, like his own mother might have done. "Think this is the end of the season for you?"

"Yeah, probably." A moment passed while he realized that he was relieved by this. "You know, I don't even care. Not totally. Sasser and Washington were more into it for me than I was really into it. You know? It was just too much."

"Yeah." Gerald finished tying Rashid's shoe silently, then looked up, his gaze penetrating. "You got anything else you want to tell me?"

Rashid thought about the midterm, about his conversation with his mother. But he was too tired, and his leg hurt too much. Not now. Maybe later. "Naw, G. Just help me get over to the infirmary, okay? I . . . That's all. That's all for now."

13

Long, Strange Trip

I GUESS I SHOULD say that I was not prepared for the sorrow that ending things with Jerome caused me. It was particularly strange, of course, because they hadn't really even gotten started. Even so, it was like that night had opened up some kind of dam. I was crying as though I was a teenage girl after her first breakup—privately, frequently, and with great drama. For his part, he still watched me. All the time. I didn't sit with him at lunch anymore, but his darting glances followed me wherever I chose to sit. When I walked past his room at dismissal time, the same gaze followed me, persistent, longing. But I didn't return it—sometimes with an effort. And after Rashid's speech, I knew that I had to keep my resolve. There was no point in letting him think something could happen that couldn't. Could. Not. Happen. Again.

Needless to say, I didn't tell my daughter that I had been acting younger than she was lately. Cal had told her about his remarriage, and she brought it up gingerly, like a fish she was holding by the tail. "So Daddy told you?"

"Yes, honey."

"Well, I'm not going to call her Mom or anything."

Good, I thought. But I said, "Nobody expects that. But you don't have to take care of me about this. I'm okay."

"Are you really, Mom?"

"Well, it's not my idea of a day at the beach, but your father and I are not married anymore. I have to respect his decision. Even if you're angry, I think you should go to the wedding. Don't feel bad about it on my account. He's still your father." How reasonable I sounded.

"Okay. I mean, I'm thinking about it. I'll let you know." She hesitated. "Mom, do you ever think about getting married again? Dating somebody?"

"Oh, honey . . ." I decided to tell her the truth, as much of it as seemed reasonable. "Of course I do. But I haven't found anybody . . . good. I'm an old lady, you know."

"Oh, Mom, you are not. I bet you could find somebody. Like through a club or something. A book group maybe."

She was so young. "That's a good idea, sweetie. Maybe I'll try it."

"You should." Problem solved.

"All right, sugar bear. I'll talk with you later. Love you."

"Love you too, Mom. Bye." So that was that. Wish it was that easy.

I knew that Rashid's speech was like lobbing a bomb into a crowd. But I hadn't expected him to toss it with such panache. Fox came up to me later that very morning and asked me to take a walk with him. I resisted an impulse to giggle, thinking of all the Mafia movies wherein wiseguys had been asked to take a walk from which they'd never returned, and fell into step with him.

"Bryson caused quite a stir with that speech today," he said.

"I'd say so." I paused. "I think it's good for the students to challenge each other in that way, though. Myself."

"And what did you think of what he had to say, Ms. Hansen?" Being cute. He'd seen me stand up, for God's sake. And he'd heard me in the faculty meeting.

"I think you know perfectly well what I'm going to say, but if you insist. I think that while he's young and wants everything to happen right away, he's got a point that we ignore at our peril. You know that, Ted." I paused, then plunged ahead. "It wouldn't hurt to diversify the faculty a little bit, either."

Fox looked at me sharply as they reached the door of his office and he opened it, then stood back so I could enter before him. "One thing at a time, Jana, one thing at a time."

"Why? Why is it always one thing at a time?" I was surprising myself, but I suddenly really wanted to know. I was sick of pussyfooting around.

"Because this institution is nearly one hundred years old, and there are a great many people who would happily see it not live another hundred years." Fox's voice took on a mournful edge. "We are guardians of the values of another time, Jana. And while I can't say I wholly disagree with you or young Mr. Bryson, the changes you desire have to be made thoughtfully, in a way that will last and that will honor the great traditions of the Chelsea School. I can't just open the floodgates. But, in fact, I wanted to ask you today to help shove the door open just a little bit wider."

That's how I found myself recruited to go to Parkside Academy, a small charter high school in Brooklyn, to troll for some likely candidates. With Jerome. And Rashid. Jesus. I couldn't refuse—there'd be no way to explain it. We were just going to have to act like adults. If that was possible. We were to leave in a week.

I was thinking about all this as I got ready for my first class of the day, freshman English, the one that Rashid was in, on the Monday after his speech. I was still worried about him, how he'd respond to having gone public the way he had. Giving me that piece he wrote, that was one thing. But making that speech—that had to have cost him, throwing his story before the whole student body like that. He'd done okay on his English midterm—I gave him a slightly generous B, so he was in good shape in my class—but I didn't know how he was doing otherwise. I shuffled through the papers, preparing to give them back to the boys. We didn't meet on Fridays, so they'd had to wait out the weekend for their grades. They were suitably quiet and nervous in the few minutes before class. I was startled as the door banged open and Rashid swung through on crutches. I gasped. "Rashid, what happened?"

He looked away from me, his eyes a little hooded. "I fell while I was running by myself Friday. It's not a big thing. I just twisted my ankle. School doctor said I should be all right in a couple of weeks."

"That's awful. I'm sorry."

"Yeah. Well."

"Will you be able to finish out the cross-country season?"

"No. I can't run again for a couple of months." His expression was carefully neutral.

"Goodness. Well, sit down. Do you need to prop it up?"

"No, I'll be okay. Thanks." He struggled over to his seat.

Given that this was a classroom full of fourteen-year-old boys, crutches and limps and casts were frequent guests, but I felt uneasy with the way that Rashid described his fall. He looked out the window for the entire class, his expression flat and unreadable. When I passed back the midterms, he looked, well, terrified. He was visibly relieved after he saw the grade. When class was over, I called him up to my desk. "Rashid, come to my office with me. I need your help with something." A look of annoyance came across his face quickly but just as quickly fled.

We walked slowly down the hallway together, not talking. The hall was filled with the sealike rumble of boys' voices and catcalls. Every now and then, the door would swing open as someone went in or out, and there would be a rush of cold air. I fought the impulse to just start talking—but I knew that Rashid might simply bolt if I approached him too soon or in the wrong way. When we got to the office, Rashid sat down gingerly and then finally looked me full in the face. "So, what do you need help with, Ms. Hansen?"

I took a deep breath as I sat. "I need help understanding what's going on with you. You hardly paid attention at all in class today, and you've hurt your leg, and ruined the rest of your cross-country season. Plus, you seem kind of frightened. I want to help. What's going on, Rashid?"

His eyes widened slightly during this little speech, but he didn't interrupt. He tapped his good foot, considering. "I'm cool, Ms. H," he said after a few minutes. "I just tripped, and I'm working as hard as I can on my schoolwork. I'm all right."

"I don't believe that." I paused. "And I'm a little pissed that you would sit there and try to tell me that when it's obvious that everything is not all right."

Using the word *pissed* had the effect I'd hoped for. He looked startled. Then, so suddenly that it was as if a wind had passed through the room, his hard-guy veneer was gone. "Ever since I made that speech, I feel like everybody's looking at me," he said brokenly. "Everybody's like 'Ooh, your brother got killed.' I can't concentrate. I don't know why I thought it would be better once I told. It didn't do any good at my old school. I don't know why I thought it would help." He rubbed the back of his hand fiercely across his eyes. "I wasn't thinking. Now . . . This thing with my leg. It was just stupid. I don't really mind about the running, but it was just stupid." He sat back in the chair, biting his lip. I felt my heart contract under my ribs. I wanted to hug him but instead sat quietly, watching him pick at his pant leg and breathe.

"So what do you think we should do?" I said after a long silence.

"I dunno." He sat up and looked at me, speaking more clearly. "I don't know. I want to stay here, even though . . . even though it's really hard. I don't know what to do."

"What really happened to your leg?"

His gaze went flat again. Wrong tack. "Like I said, I fell. I'm going to be fine."

Okay, okay, don't press there, I thought. "Well, do you think it would help to have some tutoring, spend some extra time on the subjects that are giving you trouble?"

He snorted. "Every subject is giving me trouble. It ain't . . . There isn't that much tutoring in the world."

I sighed and straightened my back. "Look, Rashid, I can't imagine how it must feel to have your brother die like that. I think you've been incredibly brave to talk about it. But don't you think he'd want you to get help if you need it? To stay here, if that's what you want? I want you to stay here. And not just because of your running. I don't care if you never run cross-country again. But I want you to be here and get what you can out of it. I think I can help—and I will, if you'll let me."

He looked at me appraisingly for a long time. "I'll think about it. I appreciate the offer, Ms. Hansen." He paused. "I really do." He got up to leave, but I remained seated, gazing at him. "I'll see you in class tomorrow. And we have that trip to get some more brothers up in here next week. You're going, right?"

"Right."

"Should be something. Thanks. I'll see you." He left, the door click firm and final behind him. I sat there for a long time. *That didn't exactly work, did it?* I thought. I wasn't sure what I had expected. Maybe that he would fall into my arms and sob out his gratitude. Well. No. Or at least that he would accept the help I offered and not drown willingly. And he said he had to think about taking it. I had a sudden flash of irritation. How could he hesitate? Unbidden, and oddly, Jerome's face came into my mind. The hunted look he'd had after the faculty meeting about diversity. Exasperated and suddenly sad, I started getting organized for my next class.

I went to check my mailbox before going to the classroom, and there in his neat hand, was a note from Jerome. "Please, if you can, come talk to me after classes today. I have something I need to discuss with you. J.W." If I'd been standing in front of a locker, a backpack over my shoulder, the moment would have been complete. I was so lost in thought that I jumped when Helen came up behind me. "Jana, how are you? Have a good weekend?"

I stuffed the note into my pocket. "Pretty good, pretty good. How are you?"

"About as well as can be expected. Say, are you all right? You look like you've seen a ghost."

"Oh, I'm okay. Just a little distracted, that's all. Have you seen Rashid Bryson today? He's on crutches."

Helen looked at me for a minute but then clearly decided to follow my lead and change the subject. "No. Really?"

"Yes. He's out for the rest of the cross-country season."

"Jerome and Jon will be upset about that, eh? How about his speech Wednesday?"

"Oh, he's something. Didn't you think he was right?"

"Sure—but what an idealist. This is an old, old boys' school—or hasn't he noticed?" Her eyes turned serious. "Haven't you?"

"Oh, yeah. I've noticed. And how."

"See you at lunch?"

"Definitely."

Somehow I made it through the rest of the day without making a fool of myself. Lunch with Helen was even fun, though I caught her giving me speculative looks a couple of times. But I kept my mouth shut. I liked her a lot, but I didn't know her *that* well. I couldn't lose the feeling that she'd probably figure it out on her own anyway. I made my way to Jerome's office at three, right before he would have to head out to practice. I comforted myself with the fact that we'd be in his office. No big scenes likely there.

He was bent over tying his running shoes as I came to the door. I stood outside for a moment, looking at the graceful curve of his back and hands as he worked, absorbed in this small task. I closed my eyes for a minute, took a deep breath, knocked. He sat up and moved quickly to the door once he saw it was me.

"Jana." A little bit breathless.

"I got your note. You had something you wanted to talk about?" Why did my voice sound so damn funny?

"Yes. Well. Fox has asked me to go on this recruiting trip next week, and of course, I said yes, but I know that you're going as well, and I thought if we spoke first, we might avoid any awkwardness." He smiled, bitterly. "Well, at this point, I guess it has become impossible to avoid *all* awkwardness. But . . ." He trailed off.

"Oh, Jerome . . . it'll be fine. We can't very well beg off. How would we ever explain? Look . . ." I swallowed. Looked at the books on his bookshelf, so neatly arranged. "We'll just behave like the adults we presumably are. All right?" I looked back at him. That same damn look. When was he going to stop giving me that same damn look? "All right?"

"All right."

"I'm sorry about Rashid." When I said this, his whole body tightened; an unmistakable look of fear and caution crossed his face. I didn't know what to make of it, so I went on. "I know you guys are going to miss him the end of the season."

"What do you mean?" He picked up his stopwatch, started playing with the buttons.

"Haven't you seen him?"

"Jana, what in God's name are you talking about?" His voice was flat, a little angry.

"I thought Jon would have told you or something. Rashid's on crutches. He twisted his ankle, somehow. He told me he won't be able to finish the season."

Jerome dropped into his seat so suddenly that I thought for a minute he'd had a heart attack. "Are you telling me the truth?"

"Jesus, Jerome, why would I make up something like that?"

He buried his face in his hands. Without thinking, I knelt in front of him, took his hands in mine. "Jerome, what is it? Please . . . are you all right?"

He looked up, more composed now. "I . . . I'm sorry. It was just a shock to hear about it like that. The team is very dependent on him. You know yourself how good he is. I . . . I just hate to see him lose this opportunity." He paused, drew in a great breath. "I hate to see him throw it away."

"Jerome, it was an accident. He's only a boy." I let go of his hands, stood up.

"There are no accidents, Jana. There is only what men do. I learned that when *my* brother was killed." He drew another long, shuddering breath, rose to his feet, looked at me for an infinite minute. Then he walked out, leaving me standing in his office, my hands at my sides.

I slept badly the night before the trip to New York—I'd gone to bed feeling fuddled and sad about Jerome, then had dreamed about Cal for the first time in years. Dreamed not just about him, but about making love to him. My hands roaming over his back, pulling him deeper and deeper inside of me, laughing afterward and then doing it again. Maybe a different position this time—try everything. We had nothing but time. In my dream, we had just finished and were lying together, warm and a little sweaty and both young again. He was gazing at me, about to say something, something that was going to make everything clear. But he never said it. I woke up feeling more lost than I had since the first days after we separated. "Jesus," I said aloud, "Jesus Christ. What is going *on* with me?" I was usually one to bound into the shower almost before the alarm clock's ring had died away, but today I lay flat on my back, the heels of my hands pressed into my eyes for quite a while, my mind racing like a gerbil on a wheel.

After my visit to Jerome's office last week, we didn't talk again. Helen told me that Jon Sasser was upset when he heard about Rashid, but he wanted the boy to recover fully for next year and he just wanted the team to finish as well as they could this season. I wished I could put Jerome's reaction out of my mind, but I wasn't able to. The look in his eyes as he left . . . it was like something had been done to him specifically. I couldn't understand it. But it didn't make the idea of two hours in a van with them any more appealing. I groaned, then pushed the sheets aside.

I did my morning things—yoga, washed my hair in the shower to the learned yammer of NPR, looked quickly through the arts section of the paper while drinking my coffee. As long as I was moving, the peculiar dread in my stomach was at bay. Driving to school, I sang along with the radio, self-consciously, as loudly as I could.

Jerome and the boys were gathered around the van, waiting for me, their faces delicately illuminated by the gray early morning light. Jerome was wearing a navy topcoat and khaki pants. The boys, Gerald, Sean, and Rashid, were wearing pants that were as baggy as the dress code would let them get away with—which is to say not very—and the neon-bright down coats that were de rigueur among the boys. Rashid leaned on his crutches fairly easily—he looked as though he'd gotten more used to them. They all looked eager and nervous. I suddenly felt extremely white—not a feeling I had all that much at Chelsea. "Hi, all," I said, bounding out of the car with teacherly enthusiasm. "You look ready to take on the world."

The boys laughed, and Jerome allowed himself a small smile. He didn't look directly at me. "I guess we're all here now. Let's get going, shall we?" he said. They piled into the van, the boys oddly quiet but moving with that gawky alacrity that only teenagers seem to have. I climbed into the front seat next to Jerome. "How are you this morning?" he asked.

"Good. A little nervous."

"Well. Glad to hear I'm not alone." He started the car without saying more and pulled out onto the road. I tried not to look at his hands. For a moment, the only sound was the gravel beneath the wheels. We had all been briefed by Fox and by Bill Corliss, the admissions director, on how to present ourselves and how to behave once we arrived at the school, but no one had briefed us on how to behave in the van going to New York. It was very quiet for several miles.

Rashid was the first to speak, his voice shy and quiet. "My parents are coming today."

I turned around, surprised. "Why, Rashid, that's great. Why didn't you tell us sooner?"

"Wasn't sure till last night. I talked to them. This school we're going to is right near Banneker, my old school. My parents wanted me to go to Parkside, too, maybe. They have one of those lotteries, but I didn't get in. And then Kofi got killed and, well . . ." He trailed off.

"Well, I really look forward to meeting them. That's great that they're coming."

The boys all nodded and made affirmative sounds, and Jerome said, "That will be nice," in a noncommittal, distracted tone.

Silence again. Why do women always have to be the ones to keep the conversational ball rolling? Annoyed, I did my girlish duty. "So, you guys all ready? Know what you're going to say?"

Gerald and Sean looked at me gratefully and said yes, they both had a few remarks all ready. Jerome nodded gravely, then added, "I'm looking forward to encouraging a few young men like yourselves to consider a Chelsea education." He didn't sound entirely convinced of this but seemed to feel it was the right thing to say.

The van was silent for a few minutes more, then Sean mercifully broke the quiet with a story about some silly thing one of the other boys on the soccer team had done, and the tension was broken. The boys made a collective decision to relax into just being boys, not worrying about us, and their voices began rising and falling in a rhythmic cadence of bravado and laughter. Some incomprehensible talk passed between them about some hip-hop group—one song in particular was "the bomb," according to Rashid's learned opinion. I smiled a little to myself at Jerome's expression on hearing that—he'd obviously never heard that particular term of praise before. Then the boys segued into groaning about a recent math test. Gerald raised his voice gleefully: "Do you all plot about how you're going to torture us with those things? I mean, really, Mr. Washington. Do those tests have to be that hard?"

"It's just a way of gauging the curve of your learning, Gerald. They're not meant to torture."

The boys all laughed. "Well, that's sure how it ends up," added Rashid, an edge in his voice. I turned around—his eyes were fixed on Jerome.

"I grade according to the dictates of my conscience and the quality of my student's work. Those who work well, apply themselves, and do what's necessary will see the fruits of their labors rewarded. Those who don't, will not."

"Mm-hmm," said Rashid. There was no mistaking the contempt in his voice.

"I'm starving," I burst out. "Let's pull off up here, get something at McDonald's—my treat." I felt like my head was going to explode, like everything was resting on me. They both fell silent as we pulled off, but the morning's earlier tension was back.

Once we were in the McDonald's I excused myself to go to the bathroom. I threw water on my face. Took a deep breath. I had a sudden image of Rashid swinging on Jerome with his crutch; Jerome slamming the boy to the ground with one blow. What was going on? What was going on? I couldn't even ask. The boys were all right there. I could only try to keep us all afloat.

Once we got back into the van, things were a little better—although I couldn't help noticing that Jerome and Rashid did not speak. Gerald and Sean kept up a stream of nervous patter that carried us into the city. I was grateful I wasn't the only one struggling to keep it together. We arrived in New York on their sea of talk.

I hadn't been in New York in a couple of years, but as someone once said, it is always and never the same. The densely packed streets, swarming with bodies of all different heights, ages, colors, needs. Everybody in New York needs something. All those needs, all those lives, all those thoughts, coming together on one slender island, some land across bridges, buildings reaching for the sky. It's a wonder to me that it doesn't explode. The subway keeps running, the buses inch along. Those who have work go to it. It all keeps humming as though by some kind of secret pact. And that humming, that energy, fills you as soon as you enter. Some people hate it; I could see Jerome tensing up as the streets became more and more crowded. But Rashid relaxed. And I felt my own breath come a little easier. I couldn't live like this, in a place like this. But I could appreciate it. I wanted to open the windows, let in the bitter smells of cheap roasted meat and burnt chestnut shells.

"Are your doors locked, gentlemen?" Jerome's voice was slightly strained.

There was a moment's silence, then the thudding of locks and Rashid's voice. "What do you think's going to happen, Mr. Washington? Think we can't drive through New York without getting killed?"

"No, I'm just advising everyone to be prudent. You are all under my charge, after all. Mine and Miss Hansen's."

"I think Mr. Washington is right. A city's a city," I said in a sudden impulse to protect him. He shot me a grateful look.

"We're not all muggers," Rashid muttered. "You oughta know that."

Jerome's hands tightened briefly on the wheel and a muscle in his jaw jumped, but he didn't speak. I watched him for a moment but then realized that he wasn't going to say anything more. A few minutes later, a battered brown livery car came speeding out of nowhere, narrowly avoiding us. Jerome burst out, "Dammit to hell," with such ferocity that we all looked at him, startled. I fought a momentary impulse to slide my hand across his back— just to help him calm down.

After that, everyone was quiet. We were over the Manhattan Bridge and approaching Fort Greene. Flatbush Avenue was hectic with traffic and packed on all sides with dingy buildings fronted by bright signs. People scuttled to and fro through the chill gray air on errands. It was late enough in the morning that the streets were mostly crowded either with tired-looking mothers and young kids or men who had no place to go and hadn't had such a place in some time. As we turned off Flatbush, the boys stared out the windows, fascinated. If Rashid felt either pride or discomfort in returning to his old neighborhood, he didn't show it. Miraculously, Jerome found a parking place without too much difficulty and we all quickly climbed out of the van.

The school we entered was in a building that had once been very beautiful and imposing but was now weathered by dirt and the press of smaller, less distinguished buildings all around it.

Wire fencing obscured the graceful old ironwork that surrounded the school. But when I looked more closely, I could see that the stairs were clean, and as we entered, we were greeted by a warm smile from the security guard, a black woman about sixty or so. There were always women like her in the schools I worked at in Cleveland. They were always standing behind the scenes of most events that made life more pleasant in neighborhoods like this. Her voice was raspy and vaguely southern: "Y'all must be from that school up in Connecticut. We've been waiting for you. Go right on into the principal's office."

Banners reading "Respect—It's What We're About" and "Learning Makes Us Strong Leaders" festooned the hallway, and bold, hand-painted murals decorated the walls. There was a slight smell of sweat and industrial disinfectant in the hallway—that closed-in odor of a city school. But I didn't feel endangered here. The place didn't feel like a prison. It was relatively quiet—the students weren't free to roam the hallways between classes as they were at Chelsea. There was no place inviting for them to roam even if they'd had the chance.

We found the main office, and a harried-looking secretary pointed out the principal's small inner office and we went over. The principal's name was Mr. Hendricks. He was tall and dark skinned, with close-cut hair and an imposing manner. He was talking to a man and woman, both a little overweight, with medium brown skin and tired eyes. They all turned as we entered, and the woman in the couple broke out into a broad smile. Her eyes stayed sad, though. "Rashid, baby. How are you?"

Rashid swung forward on his crutches, was pulled into an awkward sort of embrace by each of them in turn. We stood, feeling awkward ourselves. Finally, Rashid turned away and said, embarrassed, "Everybody, this is my parents, Mr. and Mrs. Bryson. Mama, Daddy, this is Ms. Hansen and Mr. Washington and Gerald and Sean." They nodded at us briefly.

"Look at you on these crutches, boy," said Mrs. Bryson. "Are you sure you're all right?"

"I'm fine, Ma. Really." So impatient. I thought of Sarah at fourteen.

"I'm Walter Hendricks," said the principal, rising to greet us with his hand outstretched and ending the scene. Taking his hand was like being embraced—warm and surrounding. I imagined he ran the whole school that way—with a mixture of cordiality and command. "We're pleased to have you gentlemen—and of course, this lady—here," he went on. "We have quite a few boys who could greatly benefit from the education that Chelsea offers. You're due to speak soon. Let me take you to the auditorium. But first let me get your names again. I didn't quite catch them before. You are . . ." he said, extending a hand toward Jerome. Jerome introduced himself, then let the boys and me each do the same.

"Well, I was just talking to Mr. and Mrs. Bryson here about Kofi." He turned to them with a brief look of deep sorrow. They both looked at the floor, looking for all the world like shy versions of their son. "I'm acquainted with the folks up at Mt. Herndon. Some of our students go on to that school as well. And of course we heard what happened to your brother. I was so sorry about that. He sounded like a young man of great promise."

"He was," said Rashid. His voice was ragged, but his eyes were clear.

"That's right," said his father.

"Just like Rashid," said his mother, looking steadily at him. He turned, looked startled, held her gaze for a long moment. She smiled, even though her eyes were full of tears.

"Well," said Hendricks. "We're proud to have you here, son. Very proud." He turned to the rest of the group. "Let's go up and see the boys."

I couldn't help comparing Hendricks's easy empathetic way with Rashid to the tortured attempts I'd made to offer him help.

Maybe if I just relaxed a little bit. I concentrated on the boys' backs as they made their way to the auditorium.

Hendricks led us into a large room, small by auditorium standards but set up to serve that purpose. He offered us each paper cups of water and places to sit in the front of the room, Jerome and me on opposite ends, the boys in the middle. He got Mr. and Mrs. Bryson settled in the front row of seats so they could see. We had not been sitting for more than five minutes when the noise began.

Boys, almost all black or Hispanic with a smattering of Asian kids, all shapes and sizes, poured into the room, seething with sound. There wasn't any actual shouting or bad behavior, just the noisy, talkative rush of a bunch of teenage boys together. The room clattered with the sound of chairs being shifted around, notebooks opened, heavy hiking boots hitting the floor. There was no carpet here to mute the sounds, no vast expanse of grounds outdoors for their energy to funnel out to, no sense of a larger destiny waiting to be granted. There was only now. So now was where all of their noise and energy went. I caught Jerome looking at me, and I quickly mouthed, "Here goes nothing," which brought a slight smile from him. After an effusive introduction by Mr. Hendricks, Jerome stood up to speak.

I hadn't seen Jerome speak before students before, never having sat in on one of his classes. I wasn't surprised by how formal his manner was—that's the way he was—but now for the first time, I could see how hard that must make life at Chelsea for him, though he'd never admit it. We live in a casual age, and he was not a casual man. He hadn't slept with me casually, he didn't take teaching casually, he wasn't going to speak to these kids casually. How exhausting that must be.

He was losing this crowd, I could see, even though they had obviously been told to behave and Hendricks stood in the back of the room, an impassive, daunting presence. But when kids aren't listening, even if they aren't actually throwing spitballs and whispering, a teacher can tell. Jerome knew it, too—he seemed to end his ringing remarks, full of references to the kind of man Chelsea would make them—a little sooner than he might have. And he sat down with a slight sigh.

I kept my remarks brief and simply introduced the boys. The kids in the audience perked up a bit when I spoke, probably because they knew it wouldn't last long. Gerald and Sean each acquitted themselves well, briefly saying what they liked about Chelsea and what they didn't in simple but inviting terms. Then Rashid stepped to the microphone, as easily as he had before his chapel talk that day. I felt the skin on the backs of my hands tighten.

"I used to live not too far from here. I went to Banneker, I.S. Fifty-two. Didn't get in here on the lottery." The boys laughed. "My brother was killed not far from here. Just going to the corner for a Coke, minding his own business. Wasn't killed by a white man, either—just another brother who wanted what he had. After that, I started thinking." A long pause. He looked directly at his parents, who gazed at him, rapt. The room breathed silence. "I looked at my brother lying in his coffin, and the only thing I could think was that I didn't want to end up the same way. And I was afraid that the only way to avoid ending up the same way was to get away from this city. I found some stuff about Chelsea in my brother's things, and it was like he was showing me what to do. I checked it out. It was nothing like my life. Nothing like the life I had then. After Kofi got killed, that's what I wanted. Now that I have it . . ." He trailed off, his voice ragged. A deep breath, and then, "Now that I have it, I sometimes think I can see how my life can be, what do they call it, a testament to his. If I can learn to deal, to really deal with the world like it is—not like it is just in this neighborhood, but like it is where the power is, like it is everywhere that things are not fair— then maybe I can make my life worth enough for both of us. I don't love Chelsea. But it's teaching me that. You have to decide for yourselves if that's something you want to learn." He sat down.

The room was as quiet as stone. Jerome stared straight ahead, his expression unreadable. After a moment, I got up and walked to the podium. "Thank you, Rashid, for sharing your feelings so eloquently and honestly. I'd like to think that Chelsea helped you learn how to present yourself that way—but I'm not sure we can take credit for that." I turned to the audience. "Are there any questions?"

The audience asked the kinds of questions you'd expect from twelve- and thirteen-year-olds. They asked if there were any girls' schools nearby. They asked if the homework was hard. They asked if there were substitutes when a teacher was out (there was an excited murmur of approval through the room when it was revealed that when a teacher was absent, his or her classes were canceled for the day). They asked if there were a lot of black students. Rashid's parents looked too moved to speak. Finally, the bell rang and the boys filed out—they were much more orderly now than they had been upon entering. Jerome had been quiet and preoccupied during the entire question-and-answer session, letting me and the boys do most of the talking. Now, as Hendricks approached them, he focused his attention back into the room with a visible effort.

"Thank you so much. All of you," said the principal, his eyes lingering for an extra moment on Rashid. "You know how kids are—never want to let on that they're that interested in anything. But I think you really reached some of these boys. Your presence here meant a lot. To all of us."

"Thank you for having us," Jerome said. "It's truly been a pleasure to be here." His voice had a funny, hollow sound, but maybe I imagined it.

Mr. and Mrs. Bryson came up to us, brushed past us without seeing, and both wordlessly went up to Rashid. First one, then the other, hugged him for a long, long time. After a while, Mrs. Bryson turned to me and Jerome and said, "Do you all have to get back right away? We'd . . . we'd like to have you all over for a bit, if we could." I couldn't miss the look of surprise in Rashid's eyes but looked quickly away from him to Mrs. Bryson.

"That would be lovely," I said emphatically, my tone of voice daring Jerome to try to stop me.

"Certainly," he said, a bit less emphatically. The boys looked tickled, Rashid a little panicked. We said our good-byes to Mr. Hendricks, then left all together, our feet clattering on the stairs.

The Brysons' apartment was in a brownstone just a few blocks away from Parkside. Rashid accepted a hand on the front stoop but once inside struggled up himself, leaning heavily on the banister and refusing his mother's and father's anxious offers of help. The apartment was a narrow two-bedroom, cluttered with fabric flowers, framed stenciled quotes from the Bible, and pictures of the boys everywhere. A big, new-looking TV sat in one corner in one of those glossy black-and-gold home entertainment centers, and the house smelled clean but faintly of air freshener. It felt a little bit like a shrine, but not unpleasantly so. Right over the sofa was an enormous photo of the boys together: Rashid, his hair still short, not yet dreadlocked; and Kofi, laughing and confident, a little darker skinned than Rashid, a little handsomer, with horn-rimmed glasses that gave him a curiously professorial air.

Mrs. Bryson saw me looking at the picture and her eyes teared up. "Those are my boys. My boys."

"They're beautiful."

"Yes. They are." She twisted her hands a moment, looking at the picture and then quickly at me. She looked as though she wanted to ask me something but then thought better of it.

The boys and Jerome entered the room behind me, and everyone perched nervously on the sofa and chairs crammed around the glass-and-wood coffee table. Mrs. Bryson disappeared into the kitchen and came out with Ritz crackers and yellow cheese and a bottle of Coke and glasses for everyone. Small talk was difficult, but the boys acquitted themselves pretty well. They responded politely to Mr. and Mrs. Bryson's questions about their schoolwork and how they liked the school and offered some funny little stories of things that had happened during the year. Jerome, oddly, didn't speak at all. He just looked around, a glass of soda in his elegant hand, his eyes quiet and waiting.

"The house looks nice, Ma," said Rashid during a lull in the conversation.

"Well, I've been trying to get myself together a little." She smiled ruefully. "Henry and me. . . . after Kofi . . . well, we let things go. But since Rashid has gotten up to you all's school and is doing his best, we got to thinking that maybe we could try a little harder, too. It's just so hard." She sighed, looked out the window. "Some days it's hard to even get up out that bed." Mr. Bryson placed his hand on her knee, and she looked back into the room. "Listen to me. I'm sorry. This isn't what we invited you all here for." She smiled, brightly, falsely, around the room.

Rashid was silent during her words, his eyes growing wide and his jaw clenching and unclenching. Sean, Gerald, and even Jerome appeared to have been struck dumb. Before I could even think about it, I was on my feet, moving to Rashid's side.

"Don't worry, Mrs. Bryson," I said. I put my arm around his shoulder, feeling goofy, theatrical, but knowing that he needed to be touched right now. "We're glad to be here. And we're glad to know Rashid. You're right to be proud of him. He's a really . . . a fine student and a terrific young man."

I looked at Jerome, waiting for a similar accolade, for him to say something, for God's sake. He looked at me, his eyes opaque. "You have to say what you believe, of course, Jana. For my part, I wish that he would do all that he is capable of," he said slowly, very softly. "I'm afraid that he can be so angry. It sometimes gets in the way."

The Brysons looked at Jerome, confused. Under my hands, I felt Rashid's shoulders rise, his fists clench. I pushed down on them, lightly, quickly, willing him to know what I meant; I spoke up, my voice loud, loud enough, I hoped, to drown out the echo of Jerome's words. "Well, anger that's out of hand is never good, is it? But I don't think that's Rashid's problem." I looked at Jerome quickly. My heart was pounding. "I don't think that's his problem at all. Listen, boys, Mr. and Mrs. Bryson. We've got to get back. Thank you for all your kindness—and for the snack."

I smiled, my face stiff, moved to the Brysons, hugged them both quickly, lightly. Sean and Gerald, to my surprise, did the same, without prompting. Jerome shook their hands, murmured good-bye. They did the same. Everyone acted as though nothing had happened. Rashid swung over to his parents on his crutches. He looked his father dead in the eye.

"I wish I could stay tonight, Daddy. But I've got some stuff I've got to take care of back at school. I'ma be home on the next break, though, for sure. For sure." Then he hugged his father for a long, long time. Then his mother. We stood by the door. I felt as though I was witnessing something that was a long time coming. Jerome walked out in front of me. I could not imagine what he was thinking. We left without saying any more. I looked at his back and remembered my hands on it, his hands on me. But the memory brought me no warmth now, no pleasure. We stepped out onto the street into air that had become sharply cold. He looked at me as he held the door. But I didn't meet his eyes.

14

The Bomb

RASHID WAS A LITTLE surprised at how easy it was to keep quiet about what had really happened to his leg. Everyone—his parents, his teachers, Mr. Sasser, everyone—accepted his story as he told it. The doctor even complimented him on his initiative at trying to get in a little extra practice, even as he told him, with a slight downturn of the mouth, that his running days were over for this year.

Rashid kept his face neutral at this news, but he found his breath coming easier almost immediately. No more hanging out with Washington. No more anxious eyes fixed on him, waiting for him to break the tape and carry them to victory. One less thing to do; to worry about failing at. He thought he liked running—he did like winning—but now that he was out of this particular race, there was no mistaking this feeling: it was relief.

He felt much the same relief as he heard Washington's

oblique, knifelike words to his parents on the day of their trip to New York. "Wish he would do all that he is capable of." "He can be so angry." "It gets in the way." In that moment, despite the anger that made his hands clench, his breath come hard, things suddenly became very clear. He was hated, but it wasn't his problem. Like that moment after he lost his grip on the rope and he could see everything so brittle and sharp, as though cut out and laid against a background of white paper. He felt Ms. Hansen's hands on his shoulders, their gentle, encouraging warmth. He looked into his father's eyes. And he wasn't afraid anymore. There was nothing to be afraid of.

That night, he showed Gerald his Latin test after they got back to their rooms.

"Whoa," said Gerald, his eyes widening as he looked at the crumpled paper. "My boy went wild with the red pen. D minus! Is this gonna flunk you out that class?"

"I don't know," Rashid said. "But it doesn't feel right. You know how much I study for Latin. I can't believe this midterm is that messed up."

Gerald was silent for a minute, considering. "Why didn't you tell me? We even talked about midterms."

Rashid was suddenly ashamed. Why hadn't he told? "I don't know. Thought I could handle it on my own. I didn't know what to do. I was so fucking mad." He paused. "I got it back the day I fell." His voice was quiet.

Gerald received this news in silence, then spoke. "I thought you didn't seem right that day. I'm sorry, man." He shook the paper again, briskly. "Now what are we gonna do about this?"

They talked late into the night.

The next morning, the boys were in front of Josh Bernstein's door by seven A.M. Josh came to the door still wearing the T-shirt and shorts that he slept in, his hair sticking up. He looked owlish, about ten years old. "What the hell do you guys want?" he said grumpily, running his hand through his hair.

"We need to see your Latin midterm," said Rashid, shoving into the room.

"Why, for God's sake?"

"You did all right on it, right? You usually do," said Rashid.

"Yeah, I got a B. But what's that got to do—"

"I just need to check something out. Come on, man, you said you were in my corner just the other day."

Josh rubbed his face sleepily, smiled. "I am. But I wasn't expecting any surprise visits at the crack of dawn."

Rashid laughed a little and said, "Sorry, man. It's important."

Josh went to his desk, an eerie haven of order in his chaotic room, rummaged through some papers, and found it. Gerald and Rashid took it from him and, without a word, flopped onto Josh's unmade bed, looking anxiously from his test paper to Rashid's crumpled one.

Josh looked at them, puzzled. "What are you guys doing?"

"Uh-huh, uh-huh. That's right," said Gerald, not answering him but looking intently at the two papers and circling something on Rashid's with a pen he had jammed in his back pocket. "That's right, too. And that. Damn, R. You deserved at least a C on this—maybe better."

"Are you sure?"

"Hell, yes. Bernstein has the same answers as you on at least three of these, and a couple of the translations are, you know, not exactly the same but close enough he could have given them to you. I'm sure."

Josh looked from one boy to the other again and finally near yelled, "What are you *talking* about?"

"I got a D minus on the midterm. But it turns out . . ." Rashid took a deep breath. "It turns out that maybe Mr. Washington don't see so good. Or don't translate so good. At least when it comes to me."

"Let me see those." Josh snatched the papers from Gerald, stood looking at them for a few minutes. "Shit. You're right. Shit." He looked at Rashid. "What are you going to do?"

What was he going to do? Run screaming from this place, never to return? At least at home, the enemy was straight with you. Or was he going to go to Washington's office and wait there for him, and when he came in, catch him over the head with one of his crutches? The satisfying crunch of metal against bone, the sweet feeling of liberation. Or was he going to stand his ground? He thought of Kofi's face, his voice telling him, "It's no joke going to this school. It's no joke."

"I'm going to get what I deserve. That's what I'm going to do," said Rashid.

Gerald and Josh both nodded without saying anything. The room smelled of sweat and sleep, close and a little dank. Rashid's breath came hard in his throat. His hands were tight around the grips of his crutches.

It was like a checklist in his mind, what he needed to do now. He talked to his mother first, then his father. He even told them about his fall—they surprised him by not being mad, just sad that he was feeling so awful. They were shocked, disbelieving at first when he told them about Washington; but the more he talked the more he convinced them.

"You know," his father said after a while, "that brother didn't seem to like you much."

"He doesn't, Dad."

"Well, can't everybody like you. Can't everybody do what's right, either." He sighed. "Lord knows we've learned about that, the last couple of years." Rashid was silent. His father went on, his voice ragged across the miles. "You and your brother, you're both strong. Got a lot of spirit. You've gotta be strong now. You do what's right."

"Yes, Daddy."

"Your mama and I love you very much. We always have."

"I know."

"All right, then." He paused. "Call us after you've talked to the people you need to talk to up there. We'll find some way to come up if you need us. Okay?"

"Okay, Daddy." Rashid clutched the phone. He felt as though he'd been saved from drowning.

He stayed after English class to talk to Ms. Hansen. His stomach was gurgling and leaping the way it did before a meet. He was afraid he'd have to run out and go use the bathroom like some baby before he spoke to her, but once he got up to the desk, her eyes were clear and calm, and he felt better just to look at her. She had big dark circles under her eyes, and her hair looked kind of messed up, like she'd been running her hands through it a lot. "Ms. Hansen?"

"Yes, Rashid?"

"You said . . . you said I should tell you if I needed help with . . . with anything."

"That's right."

He wasn't sure, for a moment, if he'd be able to say the next words he needed to say. "Well, I do. I . . . Mr. Washington . . . he . . ." All his assurance suddenly seemed to vanish. He lifted a hand from his crutch, stroked quickly at one of his eyes with the heel of his hand. He swallowed. "I need you to look at these Latin midterms. I think Mr. Washington is trying to flunk me out of here." There. It was out. Now he would know where she stood. He laid the papers on the desk before her.

She didn't look surprised, didn't offer a protest or an exclamation. She just said, "Why don't I get you a chair, Rashid? This room is free for a little while."

She did that and he sat and she looked at the papers carefully, comparing, chewing her lip. She pushed her hair behind her ear once. Rashid stared out the window when he wasn't looking at her. Finally she spoke.

"I think you're right, Rashid. Josh's test isn't that much better than yours. I think we need to speak to Mr. Washington about this." She paused, leaned her elbow on the desk and her head on her hand, closing her eyes for a minute. "And to Mr. Fox." She lifted her head and looked straight into his eyes, took his hand. Her skin was dry and thin; he could feel the large bones underneath. "I'll help you." They sat like that for a long time.

By the time he was done talking with her, the school day was over. They had decided to speak to Mr. Fox the next day and set up a meeting with him and with Washington. Rashid felt curiously empty now that it was done, although his stomach still jumped around a bit, nervously. He went outside, thinking only of getting some fresh air, no particular plan in mind. He swung along the road to the barn and the cross-country field on his crutches, enjoying the cold crispness of the air. His armpits hurt—there was still another week before he'd be off the crutches, and he couldn't wait. Almost before he knew it, he had walked all the way out to where the cross-country team practiced. He saw Washington standing with a stopwatch, outlined against the blue sky, Mr. Sasser standing a few feet away. He could hear the shouts of his former teammates. He suddenly knew he was where he needed to be. He moved closer, close enough for Washington to hear him. "Hey, Mr. Washington." Almost a shout.

The man looked up, startled, then walked toward the boy warily, the way you might toward a dog you didn't know. Mr. Sasser watched from a distance. He took a few steps toward them, but Washington gestured him away. "Mr. Bryson, what brings you out here? You can't serve us very well in your current condition."

"I know about you."

"What?"

"I said I know about you. You motherfucker." His voice was a low hum. Sasser couldn't hear. He didn't even know he was going to say it. But it was all right. Washington was silent, clearly too stunned to respond. "You spend all your time talking about honor and justice, and you'll do any goddamn thing you can to get my black ass out of this school. You'll do any goddamn thing you can. I don't know who *fucked* with you to get you so royally fucked up, but you know what . . . I don't care. You're not getting me out of here. I'm not getting beat down. You got that?" He felt calm. Unafraid. They stared into each other's eyes. Then Rashid drew a deep breath. Went on. "You know one other thing? The really sad thing? As far as they're concerned, there ain't . . . there *isn't* any difference between us. You're just another nigger."

Washington slapped him full in the face, so hard and so fast that he didn't have a second to think, a second to react, even a second to regret his words. He was just down, his crutches flying out from under him. And then, almost as fast, Washington was kneeling over him, trying to help him up and apologizing frantically, and calling him some other name—Isaiah, it sounded like.

Rashid got to his feet unsteadily, without Washington's help, and stood for a moment regarding him. His eyes were filled with tears, a muscle in his jaw jumping furiously. "My name's not Isaiah. I don't even know who the hell Isaiah is. My name's Rashid. Rashid Bryson. You know that."

"I do know that. I'm so sorry. I don't know . . ."

Rashid rubbed his cheek absently, massaging away the sting. "It's a lot you don't know. I see that now." His voice was gentle but confident, not angry anymore. "Look what they've done to you." He took a deep breath. "Look what you've done to yourself." Mr. Sasser was just a few feet away now, a look of horror on his face. Rashid spoke up, more loudly. "It's okay, Mr. Sasser. It's all over now."

15

What's Going On

EVEN ONCE IT had faded into the past, washing away and away from me, I still had trouble believing it. He had been my lover, after all. You like to think you know a person before you allow them that. Know the worst thing they would do. But I didn't. He hit a child. A child in his care. There was some talk that Rashid had said or done something first. But what could it have been? What could have provoked something like that? I will never understand it.

I never have found out exactly what happened that day. I never spoke to Jerome about it—he vanished from the campus like smoke. Rashid and I have become friends, good friends, in the year since Jerome left. But that is one thing he has never told me. And I have never asked. He doesn't know about my relationship with Jerome. I sometimes think he suspects that something was going on but, like me, feels that some things are better left unsaid.

We talk about many other things. He is astonishingly mature—sometimes I forget that I'm talking to a fifteen-year-old. He loves to tell me about his life back in Brooklyn, before he came here, though he still doesn't say much about Kofi. He did tell me that Kofi loved to read—especially Toni Morrison. And that he played the saxophone—one his parents had saved for more than a year to buy. Rashid has it now; he's thinking of taking lessons. His mother and father have been up to visit once or twice on various parent occasions—we've been out to eat. It's touching to see the three of them together. They are like people slowly being born again—not the same, but alive.

Once this whole business with Jerome was over and Rashid came out in the right, it seemed to set something free in him. He took my help after that, the tutors, the suggestions. His grades crept up and he became more confident in class, a better student. He began to reach out to other boys as well; his hard shell peeled away. He even made a few friends besides Gerald, who remained his best buddy. Oh, the stupid ones still avoided him, and the place didn't become a bastion of racial harmony overnight—but he stuck it out and let what was good touch him. That's worth something, isn't it? I think it is.

He was in my office the other day, interesting to talk to and funny and charming, and as we wound down I said, "You know, Rashid, a year ago, did you ever think that you'd be happy here? Happy the way you are right now?"

A serious look came over his face. He was silent for a long time. "I didn't think I could ever be happy again. I didn't think it was right . . . after Kofi, you know."

"Yes."

"But it's not giving him anything if I'm not, you know? He's not here either way." He paused again. "Happy's not the right word anyway. I'm . . . not afraid. I'm where I have to be. I used to be scared all the time. 24–7. But now . . . I'm not running anymore. That's all. Doesn't get you anywhere anyway."

"I suppose that's right, Rashid."

He looked thoughtful. "I went to church with my parents when I was home over Christmas. It was weird—I hadn't been in so long. Everybody was looking at me."

"Was that hard?"

"A little. But then when everybody was singing and I started singing too and then I remembered Kofi's voice—he could really sing, almost like he could have got a record contract or something—and it was all right. I'm not sure I'm ready to go back to church. I don't know what I think of the whole deal anymore. But it was nice to remember him. That was nice. I don't know. I still miss him. But now . . ."

"Now you're not running anymore."

"No." He paused again. "Only gotta stick this place out another two and a half years." He smiled. "My folks would kill me if I left now, anyway." He stood to go. "And I don't really want to. I'll see you later, Ms. Hansen."

"Later, Rashid." And with that, he left.

I told Helen about this conversation that evening while we were having dinner at my house. We'd taken to having dinner together once a week, first my place, then hers. It had happened gradually, without any great declarations of friendship. It just was. We were planning this summer to take that trip to Ghana that she had proposed more than a year ago. "That boy is really something else," she said, expertly twirling her spaghetti onto her fork. "We're lucky to have him."

"Oh, I know it. Not too many kids could have taken what he did from Jerome."

"That's for sure." Helen fell silent for a moment, concentrating on her food. "Have you talked with him? Jerome, I mean."

I sipped quickly from my wineglass. "No. I hear he's living a couple of towns over. But no."

Helen was quiet again, then spoke. "You slept with him. Didn't you." It wasn't a question. I dropped my fork.

"What?" My voice was loud, a little shrill.

"You slept with Jerome. Don't worry. It's okay. I haven't told anyone. And I never will."

Her gaze on me was warm and serious. I could hear my heart in my ears. "Jesus, Helen. That's a hell of a bomb to drop. Why'd you say it like that?"

"Because I didn't think you'd ever tell me, and I couldn't figure out any way to ask. And I wanted you to know that it's all right. You can trust me."

My eyes stung. "I do trust you. I don't know. The whole thing was so confusing. It still is."

"You can talk to me. If you want to." So I did.

It was late when she left. We embraced at the door and she said, "Next time I'll tell the deep, dark secret." We both laughed.

After she was gone I leaned against the door for a moment, trying to be still. To feel still. He was so far under my skin, for someone I'd spent really very little time with after all. I went and got ready for bed. Did my usual things. As I climbed in, I realized that these same sheets had been on my bed a year ago and more when we'd made love here. I buried my face in them, searching for a scent long washed away, a moment lost. I heard one car, then another go by. A lonesome sound. After that, it was quiet.

16

Control

HERE IS WHAT I remember: It was dark by the time we arrived back at Chelsea after our visit to New York. My eyes felt filled with sand. I had never been so tired. Jana chatted manically with the boys all the way home, but I could not muster a word. I found myself looking over at her a great deal, however, noting the quick, light movements of her hands, the smooth, buttery sound of her voice. She never returned or acknowledged my gaze. I wanted to lay my head down on the steering wheel and weep. But instead I kept my eyes fastened to the road. I felt only relief as we pulled into the parking lot.

The boys seemed tired, too, Rashid especially so. He was the last to disembark. Jana got down out of the van to take his crutches and help him out, and he held on to her shoulder like an old man. She gave him a long hug after he got out and murmured, "You get some rest now. I really enjoyed meeting your parents, Rashid."

"Thanks," he said, wholly unembarrassed by her embrace. To me he said only, "Later, Mr. W." Then he swung away down the path after Sean and Gerald, their figures ghostly in the glow cast by the parking lot's streetlights. Jana watched them go for a few moments as well, then turned to me. Her eyes were blazing. I was still sitting in the van but had moved to the passenger seat to come out her side. She was standing outside of it.

"What the hell are you playing at?" she said.

The vagueness and fatigue I had felt all day suddenly vanished. I matched her furious tone. "I simply said what I believe. I am not going to lie to the boy's parents."

"Lie? Lie! You were vicious. I cannot even *believe* you. You could have offered those people one kind word. You were like . . . I don't know, like some kind of zombie."

"I see nothing so vicious about speaking the truth."

"My God, Jerome. You . . . I don't even know what to say."

I climbed out of the driver's seat so that I stood near enough to touch her. I reached for her, wanting to rest my hand on her shoulder, but she backed away. "No. No. Not anymore," she said. "I have to go." She turned and walked away.

And here is what I remember: When I kissed her in the doorway of her apartment that night we were together, her hair fell over my hands like so much gossamer. She made a soft, slightly despairing moan as my mouth met hers. I could feel the edge of a bra strap cutting into her back, the silk smoothness of her dress, a little damp from sweat against her skin, and under it a vague smell of honey; the slightly chapped texture of her lips. "Man does not want to have desires . . . Whether we like it or not, we have them; whether we like it or not they tickle us, caress us, excite us . . . they press upon us until they are extinguished." St. Augustine said that. Until they are extinguished. When does that happen? When?

And here is what I cannot remember: My hand arcing

through the air toward that boy's face. I remember the hateful words he used. I remember my immediate, overwhelming remorse in the moments afterward. I remember the way he looked at me, with such sorrow and, what's worse, pity. But I cannot remember the moment I hit him. You would think I would. A blow like that. Something so shameful. But perhaps that is why I've forgotten.

Jon was beside us in a moment. He stood next to the boy, solicitous, shocked, and speechless. "Jerome . . . I . . . You better come with us to Fox's office." He barked a few terse instructions to the rest of the team, who dispersed quickly. They too were stunned, of course. I couldn't seem to stop the tears from running down my face. I kept thinking, *I've got to get myself in hand here,* but I couldn't. We must have been quite a sight, going into Fox's office. Fodder, I'm sure, for weeks of gossip.

It was all over rather quickly after that. Jon had no choice but to tell Fox what he had seen. And then the boy asked if Ms. Hansen could come in, and together they showed Fox his Latin midterm and we went over it point by point—Fox is an old Latin scholar himself—well, there wasn't much to say after that. She never looked at me. She never once looked at me. At the end of these recitations, Fox's face was flushed. He sent the boy, Jon, and Jana out of the room; sat back in his chair; looked at me wordlessly.

"I guess all I can do at this point is offer my resignation. And my deepest apologies," I said. "I honestly don't know what happened. Please believe me when I say that, Ted."

"I do. But you must see the position I'm in. For God's sake, Jerome, you hit a student. After nearly flunking him for no good reason. For God's sake."

I said nothing. Fox sighed deeply. "I'll be as fair as I can with you. But I think it best that you clear out your office today. You have until the end of the month to move." His voice went ragged, and he said nothing else. I left the office without looking back. The Bryson boy and Jana and Jon were still standing there as I left. They did not speak. I said nothing to them.

Did I think Fox would defend my actions? They cannot be defended. I saw that even then. As we sat in that room, going over the test, it was as if scales fell away from my eyes. He had, in fact, passed the test by a reasonable margin. I didn't even realize I had graded him so unfairly. I just wanted him to see that life would not always hand him what he wanted. That it wasn't so easy to throw away people's good efforts, my good efforts.

But I would be lying if I said that I didn't still hope for a few wild moments that Fox would laugh and clap me on the back and refuse my offer. That he would say, "I don't know what came over you, Jerry, but I know I can count on you not to behave like this again. You are a fair man. I know that, and I want you to stay." He said nothing of the sort. I suppose he no longer believed anything of the sort. I suppose he had no reason to.

When Isaiah was killed, I flew home from Boston, my eyes dry, my throat burning. I took a cab to our old apartment and found my mother there before the sink, cleaning it diligently with Comet, just as she always did. "Mama?" I said, my voice shaky with sorrow.

She turned from the sink, her eyes blazing, and embraced me. "Jerome. My boy. My good boy come home."

"Mama, what happened?"

She sat down heavily at the kitchen table, sighed, looked out the window. "I'll be damned if I know. I tried to do right by you boys, but that Isaiah, he was hardheaded. You know."

"I know."

"I couldn't tell him nothing. Then he started getting in trouble all the time. Wouldn't listen to me for nothing. You were the one,

Jerome." She looked at me slowly, her eyes lost and foggy. "You were the one I could save."

At the funeral, neither of us wept. We stood in dry-eyed silence, holding hands. Everyone complimented us on how strong we were. I think of that often. That moment. I wonder if there was some way I could have saved him, had I been a different man. I wonder if he did the only thing he could do—there was no one willing to save him. And perhaps not everyone can save themselves. I wonder if my mother taught me as well as I always thought she had.

I told her about my retirement from Chelsea on one of my rare visits to her nursing home in Chicago. She was surprised— "You a little young yet, ain't you?"—but she took my explanation of fatigue and a desire to have more time for scholarly pursuits at face value. She has never understood that I am not a major scholar. I did not tell her the disgrace I had brought upon myself. I let her continue to believe that she had raised at least one honorable man.

Reading and running, that's my life here in the assembly-line quaint Connecticut town that is now my home. I chose it because it is not far from Chelsea and it seemed as good as anywhere else. It is a working- to middle-class community with a fairly sizable Negro population. I did not realize how sheltered I had become living for so long on campus. It's quite shocking, really, American life at the end of the century. The ridiculous clothes people wear and the lack of decorum and the music that is like an assault out of every doorway. I think often of the quiet rigor of my former life. I did not even fully appreciate how much it costs to rent an apartment on the open market. I had saved over the years—my needs were few when I was at Chelsea—and Fox arranged for me to receive my full pension, so I manage. For a long time, I did not know what to do with myself. Without the school schedule to structure my days, I found that I spent hours, days, in a ceaseless replay of my tenure at the school, particularly the final events of my career there. For a while, my sorrow made it difficult even to read, though I came back to that. Running is what kept me sane—the smooth motion of my legs and the chance to stop thinking, if only briefly.

But of course, one cannot go on like that indefinitely. I began volunteering at the local library. Mrs. Hamilton, the head librarian, does not ask a great many questions and seems very glad of my help. I find the work restful, the quiet repetitiveness of shelving and shelving again. Perhaps I will work at the desk, answering questions at some point, but I have avoided it thus far. I am not ready to assume the mantle of authority anew. Not yet. I've begun writing for journals about the classical world as well. And I've begun running competitively. I do well in the senior divisions. I relish the brush and bump of bodies, the sounds and sights of sweat and athleticism. The men I run with, the women I work with at the library, they don't know what I've done. They see only my flesh and bone; a body moving through space. I prefer it that way.

Sometimes my running route leads me through the center of town. I usually loop quickly through before returning to the quieter environs of my street and my apartment. But this Saturday, as I prepared to turn and make my way back home, a familiar voice called my name.

"Jerome!" It was Jana. I thought that I would never see her again. I thought that that would be best. For even now, nearly a year after my departure, seeing her cut at me like a knife. For her to see me like this—surprised, sweaty, wearing a T-shirt that is a relic of my trip to the Motown museum and faded sweatpants—my first impulse was simply to keep running and pretend that I had not heard her. But she called again, and I stopped and crossed the street.

Now that I stood before her, she seemed uncertain what to do. We ended up with an awkward half handshake, half hug. "Jerome. I heard you lived over here. Helen Johnston and I are just here to do some shopping. But I didn't expect to see you."

Helen came over and greeted me, her eyes betraying nothing, then turned to Jana and said, "I'm going to go browse in the bookstore for a bit. Come get me when you're ready." She walked off.

"She knows," said Jana.

"She does?"

"We've become quite good friends. And she knows how to keep her mouth shut. It's between us." She looked away, suddenly shy, then back at me. "Here we are again. Another in a series of awkward moments. Jerome, I've thought of you often, but . . . The school's doing well."

"I'm glad of that. You know I loved that school."

"I know you did. That's why I can't understand . . . I can't understand why you did what you did."

What could I say? I was silent.

"Rashid has really blossomed," she said. "His leg healed and he's running again, better than before. He's been working with a tutor, and he seems happier. His grades are quite good. As, Bs— not as good in Latin. I think he has a C average. But he decided to keep taking it. He likes it, really."

"Does he?"

"Yes. Does that surprise you?"

"A little. I thought he might drop Latin . . . after what happened."

"He's tough."

"Yes." My heart twisted in my chest. I wiped my sweaty hands on my shirt. "Jana, if I could tell you . . . I'm sorry. That's all. I'm sorry."

She gave me a long, measuring look. "I know you are. I'm sorry, too." In that moment, her eyes so green, my heart was broken. I could have loved her. I could have kept her, had I only been the man I claimed to be. I know it. She took my hand. "You take care of yourself, Jerome." She smiled a little. "I like that T-shirt." Then she reached up on her toes and kissed my cheek gently, like a mother, like my mother never did. She crossed the street to her friend. I turned to go my own way and was seized by the sudden unreasonable fear that I would never get home, that I would somehow disappear forever in the suburban maze of look-alike streets. I know what it is to be lost. It is the bitterest thing there is.

ACKNOWLEDGMENTS

As these kinds of pages always note, a book is written in solitude but it's not written alone. A few people and places I'd like to thank (in no particular order):

The MacDowell Colony, the Virginia Center for the Creative Arts and the Writers Room in New York City, for being places of peace where I was free to write.

The Dalton Gang, Cliff Thompson and Jane Kelley, for encouragement and good advice in the early stages of this work.

David Petersen, for telling me I could do it (and that novels are worth it) at times when I wasn't so sure.

My loving and thoughtful readers and friends, Anne Rumsey, Rosemarie Robotham, and Sarah Jacobus, for their enthusiasm and advice (and thanks for that title, Rosie!).

My friends Amy Peck and Simone Leigh for their support in this project and in the project of raising our various children.

Jan Clausen for being the superb writing teacher and editor that she is.

Bryan Goluboff and Nell Mermin for good advice at crunch time.

Danielle Claro for stepping up to the plate when I hardly knew her.

My agent, Geri Thoma, for always treating me like a million bucks.

My editor, Jane Rosenman, for her skilled eye and for taking a chance on a relative novice.

Ethan Friedman for being a bastion of calm for an antsy new author.

Jake Morrissey for handling the closing act with uncommon grace.

Bill Gunlocke for being in my corner for more years than I care to mention.

Martin Moore of Brooklyn Friends School for lending me Latin textbooks when I really needed them.

Kavita Torres, my daughter's caregiver, and the staff and faculty of Brooklyn Friends, my son's school, for taking good care of my kids.

My mother and father, Joan and Robert Southgate, for inspiration; my sister, Teci Baldwin, for being the best salesperson a girl ever had; and my brothers, Robert and Daniel Southgate, for their love.

My husband, Jeff Phillips, and my children, Nate and Ruby Phillips, for filling my life with joy, laughter, and the occasional Pokémon.

And last, but not least, my friend Joe Wood, Jr., to whom this book is dedicated. Joe, a gifted writer and editor, disappeared while birding on Mt. Rainier in 1999. The mysteriousness of his passing makes it difficult to admit that he's truly gone. He was my son's godfather, he helped me in the early stages of this book, and he was like a brother to me for fourteen years. I miss him still and always.

The following books were extremely helpful in shaping this novel: *Boys Themselves* by Michael Ruhlman; *A Hope in the Unseen* by Ron Suskind (the scene in which Rashid insists on wearing flip-flops in the shower was inspired by an incident in this book); *Finding their Stride* by Sally Pont; and *The Future of the Race* by Henry Louis Gates, Jr., and Cornel West. The Latin translations were taken primarily from *The Anchor Book of Latin Quotations,* compiled by Norbert Guterman.

ABOUT THE AUTHOR

Martha Southgate was born and raised in Cleveland, Ohio. She is the author of the award-winning novel *Another Way to Dance* and has written for many publications, among them *The New York Times Magazine, Essence, Premiere, Redbook,* and *The Village Voice*. She is a graduate of Smith College and the MFA program at Goddard College. She lives in Brooklyn, New York, with her husband and two children.

A SCRIBNER
READING GROUP GUIDE

The Fall of Rome

Discussion Points

1. Why does the author choose to switch points of view? How does seeing the story play out through three distinctly different vantages help in your understanding of the underlying themes and tensions therein?

2. What is the significance of the quotes at the beginning of the novel? How do they help inform your reading?

3. Nothing affects the choices, thoughts, and actions of these characters more than the lens through which they perceive the world. At times it seems as if Jerome, Rashid, and Jana often view those surrounding them not as unique, individual beings, but as hybrids of people and places that they have encountered before. Do you agree or disagree that this is true?

4. Similarly, how much of one's connection with another person has to do with a shared past? Mr. Washington quotes Cicero early in the novel, saying, "Our character is not so much the product of race and heredity as of those circumstances by which nature forms our habits, by which we are nourished and live." Do you agree with this? Is this viewpoint inherently limiting in terms of human relationships, or just harshly realistic? What do you think the novel suggests?

5. At one point Jerome Washington ruminates on what he calls "great kindness and openness," stating, "well, those are not the only virtues. And they are, after all, the ones that cost us the most." What do you think he means by this? Are these virtues more dangerous to someone like Rashid than to the other boys at Chelsea? How so? Does the author agree with Washington's opinion?

6. The idea of control is a central theme in this story, and we watch as different characters teeter on the edge of chaos in terms of their bodies, minds, and their surroundings. In the end, what kind of statement do you think the author may be making about

the Roman concept of a "controlled life," keeping in mind the disastrous consequences of Washington's rigidity.

7. How is running a metaphor for Rashid's life? For Mr. Washington's? What did you make of the scene in which Rashid beats Mr. Washington?

8. Discuss setting in this novel, paying particular attention to how the pristine Chelsea campus elicits seemingly disparate feelings for many of the main characters. How does the setting tie into larger themes of order and control and experience vs. heredity?

9. *The Fall of Rome* is a story about growing up, survival, and the coping mechanisms that young black men need to succeed. What are the different strategies that Rashid and Jerome Washington use to make themselves seen in a world that would prefer that they were invisible? Does the author make any judgments regarding whose way is more successful? What was your reaction when Mr. Washington said, referring to Rashid, "He didn't know that the only way to win them over was to concede"?

10. As one of the few black boys in the white, upper-class environment of Chelsea, Rashid bears the burden of being a kind of representative for his race. Look at the different ways that he reacts to this pressure and think about why his reactions might be different than those of a character like Gerald.

11. Discuss the parallels between the characters of Rashid and Mr. Washington, focusing on the traits that their families share—especially their mothers. Think about how they both come to the Chelsea school to escape their history, but find it staring them in the face when they look upon each other. To what extent do you think the anger between them stems from a desire to reject their upbringings? Which character seems better able to handle this combination of past and future?

12. After his trip back to his family's home in Brooklyn, Rashid has an epiphany of sorts when he realizes "He was hated, but it wasn't his problem." What do you think he means by this, exactly? In what ways does this realization ultimately lead to the confrontation on the cross-country field?

13. Where do you envision Rashid in ten years? Do you think he will be a success story? Do you think his opinion of Mr. Washington may change over time?

The rolling hills and fields described in the opening pages of this novel are an accurate description of the campus of the northeastern Ohio prep school that I attended for four years (though it was not a boarding school). Everything else in *The Fall of Rome,* however, is fiction, my favorite way to write. I love making things up. The characters are not modeled on anyone I knew either then or now. My attendance at that school was a formative experience of my life and this book is an attempt to examine, through imagined characters and lives, some aspects of what that experience meant to me and what it might mean for others.

I'm in my forties. I think that people of my age and younger, the post–Civil Rights generation, face a world that is full of choices about what race means that someone of Jerome's age could not possibly imagine. I wanted, in this novel, to examine some of the ways such characters might clash as well as the ways they might come together around race and around values. These issues continue to interest me, and I imagine I'll always keep exploring them in my work.

For more information about the author, visit
www.marthasouthgate.com.

Look for more Simon & Schuster reading group guides online and
download them for free at www.bookclubreader.com.

15994755R00119

Made in the USA
Lexington, KY
29 June 2012